DEATH OF THE

"That woman," said Meg, after Quill had given a clipped, angry account of Helena's demands, "absolutely boggles the mind. So she insists we go through with this cocktail party—even though one of the guests of honor has just been killed?"

"It's just awful to have Dot's death pass totally . . ."

"Unremarked?" suggested John. "Why don't we do something for Dot's family? A donation from the Inn for the funeral?"

"You think we should go ahead with this, too?" Quill asked.

"Short of throwing Helena out—and the revenue for the rest of the year with her—I don't see what else we can do."

"I do," said Meg. "We'll go ahead with this party, but we'll sabotage the food. A little cayenne in the *crème brûlée* . . ."

"No!" shouted John, Quill, and Doreen together . . .

MORE MYSTERIES FROM THE
BERKLEY PUBLISHING GROUP...

DOG LOVERS' MYSTERIES STARRING HOLLY WINTER: With her Alaskan malamute Rowdy, Holly dogs the trails of dangerous criminals. "A gifted and original writer." —Carolyn G. Hart

by Susan Conant

A NEW LEASH ON DEATH	A BITE OF DEATH
DEAD AND DOGGONE	PAWS BEFORE DYING

DOG LOVERS' MYSTERIES STARRING JACKIE WALSH: She's starting a new life with her son and an ex-police dog named Jake...teaching film classes and solving crimes!

by Melissa Cleary

A TAIL OF TWO MURDERS	HOUNDED TO DEATH	FIRST PEDIGREE MURDER
DOG COLLAR CRIME	SKULL AND DOG BONES	DEAD AND BURIED

CHARLOTTE GRAHAM MYSTERIES: She's an actress with a flair for dramatics—and an eye for detection. "You'll get hooked on Charlotte Graham!"
—*Rave Reviews*

by Stefanie Matteson

MURDER AT THE SPA	MURDER ON THE SILK ROAD
MURDER AT TEATIME	MURDER AT THE FALLS
MURDER ON THE CLIFF	MURDER ON HIGH

DEWEY JAMES MYSTERIES: America's favorite small-town sleuth! "Highly entertaining!" —*Booklist*

by Kate Morgan

DAYS OF CRIME AND ROSES	WANTED: DUDE OR ALIVE

BILL HAWLEY UNDERTAKINGS: Meet funeral director Bill Hawley—dead bodies are his business, and sleuthing is his passion...

by Leo Axler

FINAL VIEWING	DOUBLE PLOT
GRAVE MATTERS	

PEACHES DANN MYSTERIES: Peaches has never had a very good memory. But she's learned to cope with it over the years.... Fortunately, though, when it comes to murder, this absentminded amateur sleuth doesn't forgive and forget!

by Elizabeth Daniels Squire

WHO KILLED WHAT'S-HER-NAME?	REMEMBER THE ALIBI

HEMLOCK FALLS MYSTERIES: The Quilliam sisters combine their culinary and business skills to run an inn in upstate New York. But when it comes to murder, their talent for detection takes over...

by Claudia Bishop

A TASTE FOR MURDER	A DASH OF DEATH

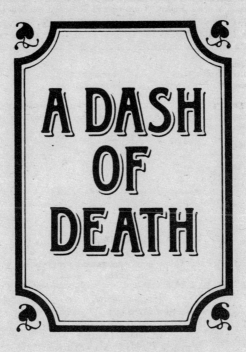

A DASH OF DEATH

Claudia Bishop

BERKLEY PRIME CRIME, NEW YORK

A DASH OF DEATH

A Berkley Prime Crime Book / published by arrangement with
the author

PRINTING HISTORY
Berkley Prime Crime edition / March 1995

ISBN: 0-425-14638-3

Berkley Prime Crime Books are published by
The Berkley Publishing Group,
200 Madison Avenue, New York, NY 10016.
The name BERKLEY PRIME CRIME and the BERKLEY PRIME CRIME
design are trademarks belonging to Berkley Publishing
Corporation.

PRINTED IN THE UNITED STATES OF AMERICA

10 9 8 7 6 5 4 3 2 1

To my sisters,
Cynthia and Whit

ACKNOWLEDGMENTS

For their support in the technical areas of this book, I would like to thank Beth Martin, M.D., of the Hematology Department at Strong Memorial Hospital in Rochester, New York; Tom Flood of the Finger Lakes Paint Factory; Chad Sheckler of Refractron Technologies; and Ann Logo, O.T. Any errors in their fields of expertise are due to my inability to understand.

For their personal support, I'd like to thank Miriam and Rachel Monfredo, and Nancy Kress.

The Cast of Characters

The Inn at Hemlock Falls
Sarah Quilliam—the owner-manager
Margaret Quilliam—her sister, the gourmet chef
John Raintree—the business manager
Doreen Muxworthy—the head housekeeper
Dina Muir—the receptionist
Kathleen Kiddermeister—a waitress
Helena Houndswood—a guest and famous TV personality
Dwight Nelson—Helena's dresser and makeup artist
Tabby Fisher—Dwight's girlfriend, Helena's hairstylist
Makepeace Whitman—a guest and director of the Friends of
    Fresh Air
Mrs. Whitman—his wife

Members of the Chamber of Commerce
Elmer Henry—the mayor
Harvey Bozzel—president, Bozzel Advertising
Howie Murchison—town attorney and justice of the peace
Freddie Bellini—director, Bellini's Funeral Home
Miriam Doncaster—the public librarian
Marge Schmidt—owner, the Hemlock Hometown Diner
Betty Hall—her partner
Esther West—owner, West's Best dress shop
Dookie Shuttleworth—minister, the Hemlock Falls Church of
    the Word of God
Mark Anthony Jefferson—banker, Hemlock Falls Savings
    and Loan
Harland Peterson—president, Agway Farmer's Co-op

Norm Pasquale—principal, Hemlock High School
. . . among others

The Sheriff's Department
Myles McHale—sheriff of Tompkins County
Dave Kiddermeister—a deputy

Employees of Paramount Paint
Dawn Pennifarm—a bookkeeper and supervisor
Rickie Pennifarm—her husband
Sandy Willis—a supervisor
Roy Willis—her husband
Connie Weyerhauser—a supervisor
Kay Gondowski—a supervisor
Dot Vandermolen—a supervisor
Hudson Zabriskie—the plant manager

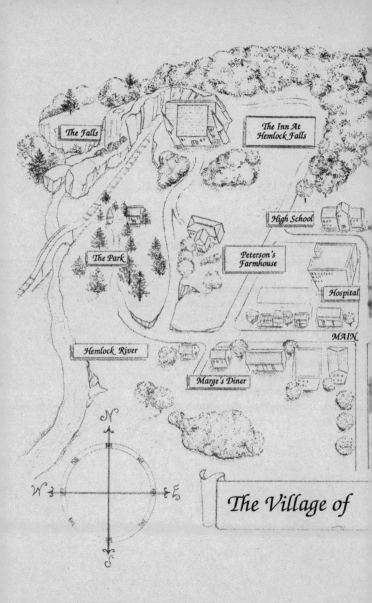

The Village of

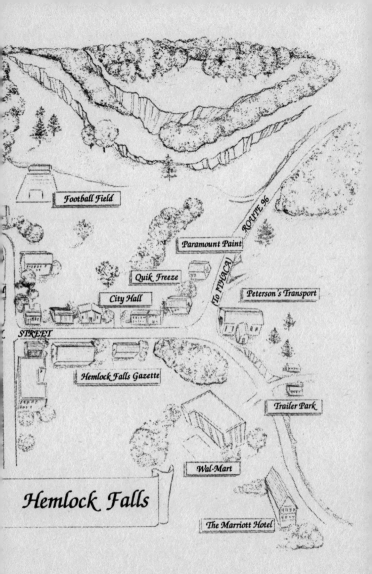

Football Field

ROUTE 96

Paramount Paint

(To Ithaca)

Quik Freeze

Peterson's Transport

City Hall

STREET

Hemlock Falls Gazette

Trailer Park

Wal-Mart

Hemlock Falls

The Marriott Hotel

CHAPTER 1

"If it is Helena Houndswood, you gotta bite the bullet, blow her cover, and nail her to the wall." Harvey Bozzel, Hemlock Falls's premier (and only) advertising executive, passed a careful hand through his thinning blond hair. "Anything else is suicide, business-wise. It's a war, Quill, and the profits go to the general who takes the hill. You get me?"

Quill, bemused, wasn't sure she got it at all. Confronted with what she hoped was a temporary lull in July and August bookings at the Inn she owned with her sister, Meg, Quill called Harvey for help. Harvey demanded an immediate "strategic planning session with all managers of customer-contact personnel." Quill dutifully rounded up Meg (the Inn's gourmet chef), John Raintree (the Inn's business manager), and Doreen Muxworthy (their head housekeeper). All four of them now squeezed together on the couch in Quill's office, facing Harvey like ducks on a shooting range.

In preference to an immediate response, Quill glanced sideways and reflected on the four pairs of feet planted on her Oriental rug. The fiftyish Doreen opted for comfort; a brand new pair of Nikes poked out from beneath her faded print dress. These were in definite contrast to Meg's battered and much smaller pair. Quill's own sandaled feet were tucked next to John's long legs. John looked the same summer and winter: tasseled loafers, sport coat, tie, dress shirt, and chinos; only his coppery skin and coal-tar hair saved him from looking like a clone of every other MBA from down-state schools.

1

"So we get a grenade in there," said Harvey into the silence.

"Do you really think Helena Houndswood will feature the Inn on her TV show?" Quill asked doubtfully.

"T'uh!" said Harvey, rolling his eyes to the ceiling. "Do I not!"

Not sure whether this was a "yes" or a "no," Quill opted for the appearance of comprehension and gave Harvey a decisive nod.

Meg shot Quill an amused look and locked her steely gaze onto Harvey's moist brown one. "Bullshit, Harvey. The woman's hiding out. She registered as Helen Fairweather, private citizen, not Helena Houndswood, TV star. Hasn't shown up in the dining room. Sits in the bar in a dark corner. Walks in the rose garden in a big veiled hat. Makes mysterious calls on that cellular phone. If Quill asks her to do a show on location here, she's going to throw a major hissy fit. The woman has immured herself for a reason." Meg crossed one leg over the other and rotated her dangling foot. As slender as Quill, she was a full head shorter. She was wearing her usual chef's gear: black leggings, sweatshirt, and brightly colored socks. Meg's sock color varied according to her mood. These were yellow. Quill wasn't certain what yellow signaled; it was a new pair.

"What's *immured* mean?" said Doreen.

"Entombed," said Meg.

Doreen sucked in her cheeks and widened her beady eyes. This maneuver—enhanced by gray hair frizzed around an exceptionally high forehead—increased her resemblance to a cockatoo. "Whoa! I shoulda guessed! Her face is all swole. They had a show about celebrity terminal diseases on *Geraldo*."

"She's not sick, Doreen," said Meg. "She's recovering from a face-lift. Or liposuction. Or collagen injections. Whatever it is that celebrities do to keep on looking twenty-eight."

Quill rubbed her temple with one forefinger, pushed the skin up, and turned inquiringly to her sister.

"No," said Meg.

"No?"

"Well, you are the older sister. But you're not that much older. And don't tell me carrot-colored hair is aging because I've heard that one before."

"It's auburn," said Quill, greeting this familiar family argument as a splendid diversion.

"Well, strawberry-colored hair," Meg conceded. "Does fruit-colored hair sound better than vegetable-colored hair? I think not. Anyhow, thirty-three-year-old women don't need face lifts. We can't afford it anyway."

"We could afford the Caribbean, couldn't we? It's cheaper."

"We can't even afford a twenty-year-old lifeguard. And they come *really* cheap. Doreen'll throw sea salt in your bathwater."

"I wouldn't have to pay a lifeguard. Central New York is full of muscled volunteers that'd love to join me in the tub. Harvey can run an ad. In the personals column. That's cheap."

Harvey cleared his throat uneasily.

"Speaking of affordability," said John Raintree, "Harvey's on the clock. We need to settle this. We've got a cash-flow problem, and we've got to decide how to solve it." Tall, quiet, with a chiseled nose and textured skin that reflected his three-quarters Onondaga blood, John kept the Inn from widening into a wholly unstable orbit. Without John, Quill thought, not only would things fall apart and the center fail to hold, the General Ledger would be a total mess. After four years in the business she wasn't entirely sure about the differences (if any) between accounts receivable and accounts payable.

Contrite, she made an effort to stick to the business at hand. "Do you think I should ask Helena Houndswood to film her TV show—"

"Tape her show," said Harvey fussily.

"*Tape* her show here? I just thought Harvey could place a few ads in the travel magazines. Maybe do a mailing to travel agents. Things are bound to pick up."

John rubbed his forehead, for him a rare and extravagant gesture of worry. Although she knew what was coming—she'd heard it all before, which was why she'd called Harvey in the first place—Quill's stomach sank. "It's June," he said. "And we need cash. Spring bookings were lean. The only receivable due is the forty-five-hundred-dollar check from the

Paramount Paint people, for the Bosses Club lunch meetings and the employee banquet last quarter. Payroll's six thousand dollars a month, Quill—and you know as well as I do that New York State will shut you down if you don't pay the help. Bookings are down forty-five percent from last year. For the rest of the summer, all we have is the monthly Chamber of Commerce meetings, and two weeks of reservations for the Friends of Fresh Air."

"Nobody told me about them," said Meg. "Friends of what?"

"It's an environmental group," said Quill. "The director and his wife are coming in today. The rest of the group will be in tomorrow. Fifteen rooms, twenty-eight people. It's on the bulletin board, Meg."

"I seen it," said Doreen, "it's the note marked FOFA twenty-eight."

"Fish on Friday," said Meg. "I thought we were having twenty-eight dinners of fish on Friday."

"That'd be FOF28D," said Quill, who was experimenting with a new shorthand system. "And it'd be in the meals column, not the rooms column. I explained that at our last meeting."

"What the heck am I supposed to do with my order for two crates of cohoe salmon?"

"Mousse?" Quill suggested.

"Paté," said Meg.

"Terrine."

"Aspic."

"Ugh. I hate aspic." Quill made a face.

"Aspic it is," said Meg firmly. " 'Cause honeychile, aspic the meals around here."

Quill groaned. Meg burst into laughter.

"Them two'd cavort if the devil himself called at the front door," said Doreen to nobody in particular. "I like this-here idea Harvey has about war."

"You would," said Meg.

Doreen had a propensity for whacking those who infringed on her value system, which, like those of the very best dog trainers, was direct and unambiguous. She'd developed a bucket-to-the-knees, broom-handle-to-the-midsection technique that owed a lot to old Bruce Lee movies. She was, Quill thought fondly, pretty agile for a fiftyish widow with a tough life behind her.

John cleared his throat. "The Friends of Fresh Air represent a nice piece of business for June. We could use a lot more just like it for July and August."

"What's coming in for July and August?" said Meg.

"Nothing."

"Nothing?"

"No guests and no cash," said John firmly. "Just the check from the Paramount Paint people. Income from the Friends of Fresh Air won't be in for another sixty days since they've all paid by credit card. We'll have to go into our line of credit. And unless I can show the bank significant business third quarter, they're going to be difficult about it."

"Nothing," said Meg. "Oh, god. It's my fault, isn't it. It's all my fault."

"Meg, it's not your fault," said Quill.

"Your business is off forty-five percent?" said Harvey. "Was I right or was I right? I told this whole town that canceling History Days last year was going to be a public relations disaster. And just look at what's happened. The Inn at Hemlock Falls is the third largest employer . . ."

"We are?" said Quill.

"Well, sure," said Harvey.

"But the Qwik Freeze plant and the Paramount Paint people . . ."

"Oh, them," said Harvey, "they've got hundreds. But who is there between them and you?" He addressed the ceiling again. "I told you. I told you Meg's losing that three-star *L'Aperitif* rating was bad news. Bad news. It's a good thing you called me in. You shouldn't have waited. It's probably already too late."

Meg raked her hands through her short dark hair, turned deep red, and started to sputter like a teapot on the boil. Harvey blinked simplemindedly at her. Although the events of the prior year had descended on them like a brakeless tractor-trailer on a downhill slope, everybody in the room (except, apparently, Harvey) knew that Meg was convinced the poor review from *L'Aperitif* was her fault.

Watching Meg eye Harvey, Quill held her breath. On her good days Meg had a full quota of the passionate irrationality common to genius; barely controlled, but tolerable. On red sock days her wrath was volcanic and limited to verbal eruptions. On black sock days she dented things: walls, pots, although up until now, never people. Quill wondered if yellow socks meant that Harvey was going to catch one up the side of the head.

"Shut up, Harvey," said Doreen. "The magazine sent a letter of ab-ject apology, and the critic went to jail. They gave the rating back. Says so on the plaque in reception."

Meg settled back against the couch and said merely, "So there, Harvey, you jerk."

"Let's get back to the point," said John. "You're pretty sure that Helen Fairweather is Helena Houndswood, Quill?"

They followed his gaze to the window. Quill's office was on the ground floor and overlooked the rose garden. Scented Cloud, Quill's favorite hybrid tea, sent tendrils of perfume through the open window. A slim figure in a straw hat dripping with chiffon strolled down the graveled path that wound among the thickly flowered bushes.

"Them fancy trousers she's wearing'll turn green with grass stains," said Doreen in her foghorn voice. "I thought this Helena Whosis was a high muckety-muck about gardens. She don't look like no gardener that I ever seen. You know, she could be one of them celebrity copycats. They had a show about that on *Geraldo,* too."

Quill got up and closed the window. Sound drifted well on the humid June air.

"Not only does she *look* like Helena Houndswood . . ." Meg began.

"Could be a celebrity look-alike," Harvey interrupted with authority. "There's a lot of that sort of thing around."

"Din't I just say that?" demanded Doreen.

" . . . but Dina Muir in reception told me her gold card is imprinted 'Helena Houndswood.' "

"Oh," said Harvey. Having temporarily lost the upper hand, he frowned at Doreen in a minatory way. "She's *the* authority on beautiful living," he instructed the uninterested housekeeper. "She's from a very exclusive background, but she's as down to earth as you or me. Her closest friends call her Hank, not Helena. She publishes those coffee table books. Big expensive ones with four-color plates. And she's written about gardens, table settings, interior design, cooking, and weddings. Her television show has a forty share." He leaned forward and jabbed his thumb in Doreen's direction. "That's eighty million households. She tells America how to live the beautiful life. And when America listens, eighty million households *buy*. If Quill talks her into sponsoring the Inn on her show, you'll have thousands of people beating down the doors."

"We only got twenty-seven rooms," Doreen pointed out.

"Think of the campaign I could write for you guys. Think of the money I'd make." He leaned back and shut his eyes. "Wait. Wait. It's coming to me. I've got an idea. . . ."

They waited expectantly.

"Houndswood . . . or wouldn't she?"

"Wouldn't she what?" said Meg.

"Live the Beautiful Life at the Inn at Hemlock Falls."

Quill sighed. "It seems kind of tacky to me."

"Well!" said Harvey with a huffy air. "This is a preliminary stab at the creative, of course. Naturally I'd need time to come up with something a little more focused."

"I didn't mean your campaign idea, Harvey. I meant asking her to use the Inn in her show. She's here under an assumed name, which means she wants her privacy."

"That one," sniffed Doreen, "is in a snit 'cause no one knows who she is, if you ast me."

John stirred a little on the couch. "Why do you say that?"

"No reason." Doreen shrugged. "Just a hunch is all."

Quill and John exchanged a significant glance.

"You didn't try and sell her stationery?" asked Quill. "Doreen, we've talked a lot about *not* pushing your businesses on the guests." Doreen's enthusiasms, ranging from Christian evangelicalism to marketing Nu-Skin, were short-lived but fervent. Her latest assault on the bastions of the entrepreneurial was peddling expensive stationery. Quill had six variations in size, color, and rag content in the lower drawer of her desk. She'd made these purchases with a sense of relief. Doreen had been flirting with selling nursing home insurance, and stationery seemed a safe—even useful—alternative. At the time she'd reasoned that there'd be no unpleasant consequences to, for example, one's long-term debt load (Nu-Skin) or one's physical person (Church of the Rolling Moses). Now, Quill wasn't so sure. "Doreen?"

"Thought she might use some of that-there Creamy Ivory Geranium-Scented Notepaper." Doreen stuck her lower lip out belligerently. "With the Embossed Bookman sheriff type."

"Serif," said Harvey, "not sheriff, serif."

"Whatever," said Doreen.

"So did she order some?" asked Meg.

"Wanted *me* to pay *her*. Ast if I could afford her, with this smirky kinda look on her swole-up puss. 'You kiddin' me?' I says to her. 'Why'n the heck would I pay you for?' 'Well!' she says in this hoity-toity way. 'You obviously know who I am. Do I have to spell it out for you?' 'Guess so,' I says back. 'Beat it,' she says. 'Stuff it,' I says back."

Incredulity made Harvey pink. "You told Helena Houndswood to stuff it?" He turned to Quill. "She's torpedoed the whole thing. Ruined it. Absolutely. Right down the tubes."

"Not necessarily," said John. "Ms. Houndswood's obviously practiced at the endorsement process. I think a lot depends on the *quid pro quo*."

"Cheek," said Doreen darkly, reliving the moment, "that's what I call it." A cheerful smile split her angular face. " 'Course, if she's lookin' to be em-murred soon, it sorta explains the cheek. Dee-pressed, most likely."

"Aagh," said Meg, "she's not sick, Doreen."

"There's not much to offer her," said Quill. "I mean, we can't afford the kind of prices she commands."

Meg spread her arms wide in an all-encompassing gesture. "Look at this place. It's possible that I'm the greatest cook in the known universe without a four-star rating, but it's definite that you're the greatest decorator of Inns. It's gorgeous, Quill. The woman'd be nuts not to want it as background for her TV show."

Quill twiddled her thumbs. The Inn dripped with charm, from the Tavern bar with its polished mahogany floor and

wainscoting to the reception foyer with the original cobblestone fireplace and flower-filled Chinese urns. Each of the
guest rooms was uniquely decorated from the blue and yellow
Provence suite with its wrought-iron balcony and Adams-style
fireplace to the spare and lovely Shaker suite. The singles
and doubles were draped in hard-to-find patterned muslins,
chintzes, and linens. All the rooms were dominated either
by expansive views of the perennial garden or the hemlock
groves and the waterfall. The building itself sat on a granite ledge overlooking the sweep of Hemlock Falls, flanked
on two sides by flower and herb gardens and backed by a
grove of hemlock trees. No matter what her mood, Quill
could always find part of the huge old place that gave her
pleasure.

"She drinks sherry in the bar every afternoon, doesn't she?"
asked Meg. "So she must have seen your paintings. Ten-to-one
the woman already knows who you are."

"Was," said Quill. "I haven't picked up a brush in a long
time."

"A mere hiatus," said Meg airily. "Once a celebrity, always
a celebrity."

"Meg! I was mentioned in *Art Review* once, and that was
when I quit the business. That hardly qualifies me as a celebrity."

"It might," said John. "Even I knew who you were when
you hired me, Quill. It's likely she might. And there's Meg,
of course. The two of you are well-known in your own way.
I think you ought to feel her out."

"Ugh," said Quill. "Ugh, ugh, *ugh!* I hate stuff like this."

"Then you girls just leave it to me," Harvey said. "Hank
and I both talk the talk, if you get my drift. I'll give her
just a smidgen of some pretty powerful ways I can boost
her image. Maybe even see if she wants to go national with
a 'Houndswood or Wouldn't She' blitz. Plus, and here's a real
important thing, gals, I can reassure her Meg's not on the skids,
foodwise."

There was a short silence.

"Not a bad idea, Harve," said Meg, through her teeth. "Not
a bad idea at all. Of course, Quill might stand a better chance.

Just because she's a woman—sorry, Harvey—'girl.' If Ms. Houndswood—sorry again, Harvey—'Hank'—has just had a face-lift, she might not want to talk to a man. Just yet. It's kind of a girl thing, Harve. If you get my drift."

"Um," said Harvey uncertainly.

"Now, *foodwise*, Harve," Meg continued, her voice rising, "let me tell you something *foodwise*."

"Stop," said Quill. "I'll do it. I'll talk to her."

"Fine," said Meg, suddenly cheerful. "When?"

"Well." Quill thrashed a bit, feeling like a fish which had successfully avoided the bait until the third cast. "When's she checking out?"

"She booked for three weeks," said John.

"But there's no time like the present, Sis."

"Don't call me Sis. I hate it when you call me Sis." Quill sighed. "I don't have the time. I have to collect that forty-five hundred dollars from the Bosses Club. I dropped Dawn Pennifarm a note asking her to bring it with her."

"We're that cash short?" said Meg, startled. "Since when have we started harassing customers for payment?" She jiggled one foot nervously. "Does this mean you're going to hassle me about kitchen supplies again? Are you insisting I cancel the salmon?" She raked her hands through her hair. "You know I can't cook if I have to worry about budgets. I hate worrying about budgets."

Quill glanced at John. "Over to you," his look said. "Well, we do need the money, Meg. We're not hassling the Bosses Club exactly, but John and I talked it over, and we decided to be firmer with slow payers, the Paramount people in particular."

"They're very slow pay," John repeated, deftly picking up his cue. "Hudson Zabriskie claims the company's having a slow quarter and wants to discuss a lower-cost lunch menu."

Meg scowled. "But the same quality, I suppose."

"Of course," said Quill, "they appreciate great food. We can serve soups and stews instead of meat entrées. They *love* your cooking, Meg. It's why they come. If they didn't care, they'd be down to Marge Schmidt's diner like a shot. Anyway, I need to pick up that check and talk to Hudson about revising the lunch budget. That's a little more urgent than this TV thing."

"Talking to Hudson shouldn't take more than three or four hours," said Meg with cheerful sarcasm. "They don't call him the Bloater for nothing. And what's more important, Quill? Losing ten percent on their lunch costs or, as Harvey says, angling to have eighty million American households beat down our door? Talk to Helena Houndswood first, then tackle Zabriskie and pick up that check from Dawn."

"And I have to tour the west end of town issuing tickets for people who haven't fixed up their businesses for Clean It Up! Week." Quill brightened with an idea. "Tell you what, Meg. You take on Clean It Up! Week and I'll talk to Helena Houndswood."

"Clean It Up! Week is a crock. The Chamber of Commerce has no business telling perfectly respectable citizens how their storefronts should look. They're a bunch of fascists anyhow."

"From the way you're talking, anyone would think Mayor Henry's Mussolini. All it is—all it's *ever* been—is a polite reminder to people to keep their buildings neat."

"Who's on the list?" asked Meg suspiciously. "West end of town? That's Nickerson's Drug . . ."

"And you like Nicole Nickerson."

" . . . and the post office. Aaah! Vern Mittermeyer! That lizard! Last time I went to the post office, he kept me waiting thirty minutes to buy stamps. I'd love to whack him one over a Clean It Up! Week violation. What's the Chamber want him to do?"

"Repaint the trim."

"Good luck," said Meg scornfully. "I'll bet he said it wasn't in the budget. . . ."

"Ah, Quill," said John.

"It doesn't have to be in the budget. Connie Weyerhauser arranged for Paramount to donate three gallons of Crimson Blaze."

"Quill," said John. "In the interests of civic tranquillity . . ."

Quill caught his eye. "Never mind, Meg. I'll take care of it. I'll take care of all of it."

"The Bosses Club meets until five. It's eleven o'clock right now. Talk to Helena immediately. Get it over with. You'll feel better."

Crossly deciding that Meg had the tenacity of a shorter-than-average pit bull, Quill gave up. "All right. Okay. I'm going." She put her hand on the office doorknob, then turned around and looked at her staff. Meg, John, and Doreen nodded encouragement. Harvey, eyes closed, was murmuring "Hounds*wood* . . . could, should, would, hood," his habit when searching for rhyming words.

"Excelsior!" Meg gestured toward the rose garden.

"I'm going, dammit."

Quill's office was located behind the reservations desk in the front foyer. As she closed the office door behind her, she automatically surveyed the area, checking to see that fresh flowers had been placed in the large Chinese urns that flanked the cobblestone fireplace (they had), that no stray luggage had been left on the polished oak floor (it hadn't), and that no guests had been cast forlornly adrift, waiting for service. The foyer was depressingly empty, except for Dina Muir, the Cornell student who worked as a receptionist part-time.

"Any messages?" asked Quill with hope.

"Just Sheriff McHale. Wants you to call him back to confirm your dinner date tonight at ten-thirty." Dina's hair was cut short and framed wide, innocent brown eyes. They widened even further at the change in Quill's expression. "Is anything wrong?"

Myles. Quill closed her eyes. She thought of her studio in Manhattan, now a Chinese delicatessen. "Do you know if Helen Fairweather is still in the rose garden?"

"You mean Helena Houndswood? Oh, God." Dina slapped a hand over her mouth, removed it, and said, "She swore me to secrecy. Nobody's supposed to know she's here. I found out because of the credit card. Isn't she gorgeous? The TV show is *fab*-ulous. She just knows everything about how to live right. She was in the rose garden, but she just this minute went into the bar. You won't tell her I told you who she is? I mean, I gave my blood oath that I'd keep it a secret. I only told Nate and Meg, of course. And now you. Rats. Stars like she is just get hounded to death, she said. Now you look even worse. Are you sure nothing's wrong?"

"If you absolutely had to sit down, would you choose a rock or a hard place?"

Dina grinned. "Which is Sheriff McHale?"

"My mother would say a rock. A positive brick. A safe harbor in the storms of life." Quill picked up the desk phone and punched in Myles's number. "Hey," she said, when he answered.

"Quill"—Quill was a sucker for deep, manly voices, and there was no question that the six-foot-three, broad-chested Myles McHale had one—"about dinner tonight."

"Yes, Myles. I'm not sure . . ."

"I'm making a run to Syracuse on a missing persons. I don't know when I'll be back. I'll need a rain check."

There was a silence. Quill knew he wouldn't ask about the other. He'd asked once, and he'd wait until she made up her mind. She wondered how long he'd wait. Lots of people waited until they were drawing Social Security to get married. "So," she said brightly, "who's missing?"

If he was impatient with her, she didn't hear it in his voice. "It's not who as much as what. Hudson Zabriskie claims there's a cash shortage at the plant. And the bookkeeper didn't show up for work this morning. Hudson's always been able to put two and two together to make five, so the two events may not be related. But we'll see."

"The Bloater? The guy from Paramount Paints?"

"Yeah."

"It's not Dawn Pennifarm, is it? The bookkeeper?"

Another silence, that of a sheriff being circumspect. Quill rolled her eyes at Dina then gave him a verbal nudge, "Myles?"

"Might be," he agreed cautiously.

"Hell." Dina's eyesbrows rose. Quill gave her love to Myles and hung up the phone.

"There *is* something wrong," Dina said sapiently.

"A rock, a hard place, and the deep blue sea," Quill murmured. "Helena Houndswood's in the rose garden you said?"

"She's not in the rose garden," Dina said. "The lounge, I think."

It was not cowardly, Quill decided as she headed out the front door, to take a few minutes in the rose garden. Dina might have mistaken the TV star's destination. Besides, she needed time to plan the attack.

The rose garden was only a quarter of an acre, and it took Quill less than five minutes to determine that Helena Houndswood wasn't there.

The air was moist and cool from the nearby waterfall. Quill inhaled with delight. Water roared over the lip of the granite gorge with a muscular rush that sent spray as far as the koi pond in the center of the garden. Quill strolled down the path to the pond and pulled a few wild chamomile from the lavender beds surrounding the basin. Sunlight sparkled on the water, reflecting tiny shards of light from the scarlet-silver carp. Quill snapped the stem of a blousy tulip and poked gently at the fish. One of the seven turned and nibbled at the stem, its open mouth like a baby bird's. Quill chased the fish with the tulip stem until the vigorous rapping of knuckles on glass roused her. She glanced toward the sound. Meg, John, Doreen, and Harvey stared accusingly through her office window. She sighed, waved the dripping tulip at them in a gesture of surrender, and went to the Tavern Bar. She'd ask Helena Houndswood if she'd feature the Inn on her show, get turned down, march into the Bosses Club meeting and demand forty-five hundred dollars from Hudson Zabriskie and get turned down, call up Myles McHale on his car phone and turn *him* down, and then go live in Detroit and sell real estate.

Maybe, thought Quill, Helena Houndswood would be surrounded by adoring fans, or her agent, or on the phone, so clearly occupied with something else, it'd be rude to interrupt. Maybe she wasn't even there.

At first the Tavern Bar looked empty, except for Nate the bartender. Quill liked the room, which was situated on the northwest corner of the building, separated from the dining room by thick plaster and lathe walls. Her eye traveled around the bar appreciatively, moving from the teal walls to the brass and mahogany bar, to the floor-to-ceiling windows at the west end.

Helena Houndswood, arbiter of the Beautiful Life, role model to millions, was sitting in one of the easy chairs drawn up to the windows overlooking the hemlock grove, sipping a glass of sherry, her cellular phone at her ear. She was alone. She looked cross. Quill sighed and proceeded across the mahogany floor with an air of confidence she was far from feeling.

CHAPTER 2

Dina was right, Helena was blond-haired, blue-eyed gorgeous, although much smaller than she appeared on television. Her thinness was that of the dieter for whom denial was a religion. Her straw hat lay next to the chair. The swelling around her eyes and chin had ebbed, leaving no bruises. From Quill's limited knowledge (one blind date with a plastic surgeon) she guessed that Meg had been right about the collagen injections and wrong about the face-lift.

Helena, ignoring Quill's approach, folded the cellular phone with a snap and began examining one of Quill's acrylics, the heart of a Kordes Perfecta hybrid tea. There was a slight frown on her face. Quill cleared her throat. She raised her exquisite eyebrows and said coldly, "Did you want something?"

Her voice was soft and low, which may have been an excellent thing in a woman, Quill thought, if it hadn't been so repelling. "Ms., um, Fairweather, I'm Sarah Quilliam, one of the owners here. Do you have a moment?"

One eyebrow went a little higher. The expertly glossed lips turned down in a charming, rueful pout. "You know who I am, don't you? Or if you don't know, you're determined to find out." She extended a slim hand. The nails were perfect. "I would have thought celebrities were rare in this backwater. But then, I'm constantly amazed at the reach of my books and my show. How do you do?"

Quill shook her hand. "We get very few celebrities here,

Ms. Houndswood, but we're all great fans. May I sit down for a minute?"

"Call me Helena. Not Hank, please. Since that article in *People* came out, every pretentious little bastard in the country calls me Hank. I hate it when people call me Hank." She waved a hand in the direction of the chair on the opposite side of the table.

Quill sat down and folded her hands in her lap. "Are you enjoying your stay? Is there anything you need to be more comfortable?"

Helena ran one hand through her moussed hair. "The food is close to terrific. The interiors are tasteful. The grounds are absolutely B plus. I am amazed. Amazed and charmed."

Quill worked this through and decided if you discarded the "amazed" part, it amounted to a compliment. She took heart. "It's really my sister's cooking that's made our reputation. Meg has a three-star rating from *L'Aperitif*." She took a deep breath. "We think we have a broad appeal. To . . . to . . . the same kind of people that watch your show, for instance."

The clear blue eyes narrowed. The frown deepened. "Let me guess. You think it might be a nice backdrop for the show. *Quelle surprise*, as we say in the Big City." Helena returned to her indifferent contemplation of Quill's acrylic, tilting her head to one side, an art gallery mannerism Quill had never figured out. What did a painting offer better sideways than it didn't straight on?

"If you like the Inn . . ." Quill began.

"Oh, it's not bad. This, of course"—she waved her hand at the painting—"is rather nice. It's the largest collection of hers I've seen. Even the galleries don't have as many. Of course, her output wasn't what you'd call prodigious to begin with. . . ." She smiled at Quill's expression of surprise. "You know, I don't believe you realize what you have here. No, you don't. How charming!" She leaned forward and patted Quill's knee. "That, my dear, is a Quilli . . ." Her eyes narrowed. The fluty vowels dropped into a flat midwestern twang. "A Quilliam," she finished, "and you're Sarah Quilliam. Of course. How delightful." She withdrew her hand. "I should have known. I'm sure I did know, actually. I mean, the place reeks of your taste." She measured Quill with a long look.

"So. This is where artists of talent end up when they quit the rat race? Why'd you do it? I mean, you were getting terrific press. And the price on your work's gone up. A lot. Rising fame scare you or something?"

Quill couldn't think of anything to say. Helena answered the question herself. "The stress got to you. God, I can relate to that. The pace. The writing. The cameras. Even the goddam lights." Absently she smoothed her upper lip, which didn't help the puffiness at all. "Worried all the time about the fucking media. The fucking ratings. And of course, now there's the fucking china contest."

Fucking, thought Quill, must be a part of the famous down-to-earth charm. "The china contest?"

"It's a beautiful life," said Helena obscurely.

Quill, wondering if this referred to a Capra remake she knew nothing about, said "a-*hum*" with a great deal of authority.

"The winner is going to be featured on the show in three weeks. Actually"—she cast a swift appraising eye over the bar—"I was already thinking of doing it live from here. Great background. You wouldn't mind, sweetie, would you? That's what you were after, wasn't it?"

"Yes," said Quill, dizzy. She swallowed, pinched her own knee hard, and looked wildly around for some support. She signaled Nate the bartender with a "thumbs-up," and mouthed "wine" at him. He looked at his watch in surprise, pointed to Helena with a raised eyebrow, and at Quill's nod, poured two glasses of sherry and brought them over.

" . . . and of course it's utterly, utterly confidential, dear, but the winner's from Hemlock Falls."

"I'm sorry," said Quill, "what?"

"Do listen, sweetie." She looked up as Nate set the second sherry next to her empty glass. "I didn't order that."

"On the house, Miss Houndswood."

"Good. Another when this is gone, then."

Quill, engaged in mental gymnastics, finally recalled that Helena's TV show was called *It's a Beautiful Life*. Not only that, an old issue of *Architectural Digest* had something about an *It's a Beautiful Life* design competition for tableware. She choked on the sherry. She remembered, now. The prize was a million dollars. The contest had banned professionals. No members of the Artist's Guild. No architects. Nobody who'd been paid for professional design work. "The winner's from *here*? From Hemlock Falls?"

"Yep. It's not you, is it, sweetie? We'd have to work something out, you know. No pros. At least, not that my fucking public could find out about."

"No," said Quill evenly, "it's not me. The rules were pretty clear, weren't they?" Immediately regretting her flash of annoyance, she said politely, "Can you tell me who it is? Or will the winner be announced on the show?"

"No. No. No. The winner has to be notified. The contract's got to be signed. A sample table setting is being manufactured by little gnomes somewhere even as we speak. There's a hell of a lot to do, frankly, which is why I came up so early." She passed her hand over her upper lip. "I've just been . . . gathering my resources before buckling down to it. So, yeah, I can tell you who the winner is. I'm sure you know her." She dug into her purse and withdrew a Filofax. "You know, it's quite exciting really. *It's a Beautiful Life* is by, for, and about the crème de la crème." Quill, hearing the sudden passion in her voice, was careful to maintain a neutral expression. "You wouldn't believe some of the Names who submitted drawings. Right from the Old Hundred."

"You mean the Four Hundred?" corrected Quill absently, and at once realized her mistake.

Helena paused a beat, looked pointedly at Quill, and resumed evenly, "Four Hundred. As I said." She dropped to a confiding tone. "The selection was agonizing. Of course, I did it myself. Who, I asked myself, is the right sort to be the winner? Not only must the design be tasteful, elegant, *and* discreet, but it must be beautiful. And the winner must be beautiful in the Houndswood tradition." She grasped Quill's wrist. Her fingers were cold and slightly sweaty. "I spent bloody *weeks* at it. And do you know what was the best tip-off? Of course you do. I mean, I spent an entire show on it just last year."

"What?" asked Quill.

"Stationery."

"Stationery?"

"Stationery. The Beautiful Life is Beautiful in all details. The well-bred woman is a woman of elegance of dress, manner, and mind. And what is the first line of defense against an intrusive world? Elegant stationery."

Quill looked at Helena's empty sherry glasses. "Sure," she said warily.

"Anyhow. Here's our winner. I'll show you the design first." She produced a large manila envelope from her purse and handed it over.

Quill opened it with care. Inside were watercolor drawings of a china setting. The design was lovely; a delicate tracery of perennial herbs twined around an exquisitely rendered rose-breasted grosbeak, its chest a cloudlike drift of violet suffused with pink.

"These are wonderful," said Quill.

"You'd know, wouldn't you?" There was a peculiar desperation in her voice. "I mean, *you* can tell crap from genuine talent. If anyone's got an eye it's you. It's genuine, isn't it?"

"Genuine?" said Quill, bewildered. "If you're asking if there's real talent here, yes. There is. It's an amateur talent, that's clear. It's not . . . I'm not sure just how to express it. It's not a *unified* work. My guess is that it's a student's effort. Not a young artist, necessarily, but someone who's learning from somebody. You can see that there's another mind at work besides the artist's. I don't teach, but if I did, I would take whomever did this on as a student. It's marvelous."

"And you could tell if, say, the person who won really did the drawing. Or if it was taken from somewhere else."

"I suppose if I looked at the artist's other work, I could make an educated guess. Do you suspect fraud?"

"Oh, no, no, no, no. I just have to be careful."

"These are just terrific," said Quill. "The design's incredible. It looks like a million dollars."

"I hope it's worth a hell of a lot more than that. I share in the royalties." She gave Quill a candid grin. "We figure a first-year gross of half a million in sales, with growth somewhere in the region of one, one point five million, maxing out around two. If we're lucky, it'll be a backlisted design, and the royalties will roll in for a good long time."

"Backlisted?"

"Like Royal Crown Derby, or Wedgwood, or any of the biggies. Classic china's big business."

"And someone from Hemlock Falls won? This is wonderful."

Helena handed Quill the contest entry. "Here's the name. Don't forget, sweetie, you're one of the first of the locals to know. You owe me one."

The entry letter was written on stationery with a high rag content. The color looked like Creamy Ivory. Quill held it to her nose. It smelled like Scented Geranium. She looked at the embossed name and address: Bookman serif type, Doreen's best-selling stationery. No! thought Quill to herself, and grinned. A momentary vision of Doreen with a million dollars and a star turn on *It's a Beautiful Life* made her toes curl with pleasure. Too bad Doreen couldn't draw.

"Elegant, isn't it?" said Helena anxiously. "The stationery? As I said, the Beautiful Woman's first line of defense against decaying standards. You know the winner, of course."

Quill unfolded the letter and read:

Constance G. Weyerhauser

The Hall

Hemlock Falls, New York

She gave an involuntary expression of delight. "This is fantastic. Helena, this is terrific. I can't think of anyone more deserving."

"Too much to hope it's the lumber people, I suppose."

"No," said Quill, "it's not the lumber people."

"And you must know Constance."

"Yes," said Quill, "I know Constance. She may not be quite what you—"

"Where the hell's the Hall?" Helena interrupted. "Somebody's got to notify her so we can get the damn contracts signed. My people want to tape it. Get the first reaction on tape so we could run it on the show. Can you imagine anything tackier? I mean, what woman of taste and discretion would stand for it?"

Quill knew several. Among them Constance Weyerhauser. "Somebody? You aren't going to do it?"

"Look, sweetie. Since you know her, what about arranging an introduction? Let her know about the win . . ."

"You're sure you don't want to tell her?" said Quill. "You've put so much work into this."

Helena's eyelids flickered. "No," she said. "I'm sure she'll want to have some time to reflect on this privately. She may not even want to be on the show. Which is *fine*. Just *fine*. All we are contracted to do is feature the china. We don't have to feature the person." She hesitated, then said, "Frankly, emotion's so *sticky*, don't you think? I mean, control and discipline are important parts of the Beautiful Life."

Quill, who'd thought until now that emotion was as much a part of a beautiful life as food and sex, opted for a non-committal "mm," then wondered if she ought to consider the advantages of asceticism. Except that she couldn't see any advantages to asceticism if she had to give up Myles McHale or her sister's cooking. On the other hand, maybe she would paint more. Painting well required concentration. Focus. The paring away of what Helena Houndswood would undoubtedly call nonessentials. Like Meg. And the Inn.

"Sarah?"

"Yes. Sorry. I was thinking." A second thought occurred to her; Helena had arrived at the Inn Sunday evening. This was Wednesday. What if she'd already asked about Constance Weyerhauser, which would have been only natural. And if she already knew about Constance and her daughter . . . somehow, Quill didn't place much stock in Helena Houndswood's compassion. On the other hand, if she wanted Quill to prepare Connie a little bit . . . "Shall I see if Connie can be here about seven o'clock?"

"We'll have cocktails. I've got my lawyer and producer joining me at eight-thirty for dinner. Look, it's what . . . lunchtime? I'm desperate for a bit of a nap and then some fresh air. I'd love to see your village. It's delightful. I'm going to take a walk to your post office to deliver a package to my publisher this afternoon." She made a *moue* of mock distress. "Galleys, I'm afraid. The deadlines in this business are lethal. Why don't you come with me? You can show me all the most adorable peeps."

"Peeps?"

"Views. Sights. Pretty places. I'll go up to my room and change. There's a good chance I'll be recognized, so you can protect me from the ravening hordes."

"We'd be happy to get the package to the post office for you. There's no need to . . ." Quill hesitated, " . . . expose yourself if you don't want to."

"The price of fame." Helena laughed dismissively. Clearly, her enforced seclusion was beginning to wear.

"I've got quite a bit to do," Quill apologized. "There's a customer group I have to check on about a rate reduction, and a few other things"—like, she thought, that bloody forty-five-hundred-dollar check—"and I'd love to have a little time to spend with Connie Weyerhauser. It's going to mean so much to her. Are you sure you don't want to tell her yourself?"

Helena shrugged.

"You know, this is just like those old TV shows with the happy endings." Quill looked directly at her. "Connie's black. She has a young daughter who's been in and out of the hospital. Cerebral palsy. This is going to be just the best thing that's ever happened to Connie and her daughter. They're wonderful people."

"Sick kid on the show?" Helena wrinkled her nose attractively. "As the kids say, 'not.' You see? a really sensitive woman wouldn't want the publicity. You sound her out. See if she's the sort of person who prefers anonymity. You tell her we'll be *glad* to offer it. Delighted."

"I really don't think it's appropriate for me to talk with her about that," said Quill, by now convinced Helena had known about Connie and Barbara. "It isn't her race that bothers you, is it?"

"Who, me? Absolutely not. And I resent the insinuation. Call her. Just make sure she's here at seven or so. And I'll meet you in the lobby at three o'clock. That should give you plenty of time to run all your little errands."

"Helena, I really have to pass on this. I think you should tell her, and I don't have the time today to walk to the post office."

She raised an eyebrow in inquiry. "Really? Then maybe you

can give me some idea of where we should tape the show. Maybe the Inn isn't the best place to shoot after all."

Quill counted to ten and swallowed hard. At least she could check Vern's progress on repainting the post office building, which would cross another item off her To Do list. "About three o'clock, then."

"Good girl." Helena patted her arm, then walked briskly out of the room. Nate, coming to the table to clear the empty glasses, said, "So, boss. What's she like?"

"Subtle," said Quill. "Very subtle. Nate, did she ask you anything about Connie Weyerhauser?"

"Black gal works at the paint factory? Nope. She going to give us some PR?"

"She's going to shoot her show here."

"No kiddin'?"

"I've got to tell everybody. And Nate. You know Connie Weyerhauser fairly well, right?"

"Sure. I bowl same night as she does down to the Hall. Good gal." He thought a minute. "Hell of a bowler."

"The Legion Hall, you mean. She's had some wonderful good luck. Meg in the kitchen?"

Nate looked at his watch. "They'll all be there. It's lunchtime."

When Meg and Quill had decided to purchase the Inn five years ago, the kitchen had been in the most urgent need of remodeling. Quill had determined to save the brick floor and the hearth; Meg had taken over from there. A huge Aga dominated the center of the room, flanked on three sides by double-wide butcher-block and stainless-steel counters. Birch shelving ran the length of the north and east walls; the south wall was composed of windows overlooking the vegetable gardens. Quill entered through the swinging doors from the dining room. Doreen, John, and her sister had pulled stools up to the counter and were eating soup. They put their spoons down and stared expectantly at her.

"Lunch," said Quill with a casual air. "I'm starved." She sat next to Doreen. One of Meg's *sous* chefs brought her a large bowl of gazpacho and a small loaf of sourdough bread.

"Well?" demanded Meg after a moment.

"Yes."

"Yes!? She's going to use the Inn?!"

Quill nodded. "That's not all. You guys keep this quiet until I tell her, but you know Connie Weyerhauser?"

"She's a member of the Bosses Club. Line Supervisor, third shift at Paramount," said John. "Heck of a bowler, I understand."

"She's got that sick kid," said Doreen. "I work with her down to the clinic once in a while. You know, they got that volunteer program helpin' 'em exercise."

"What about Connie?" said Meg.

"She's won a million dollars."

"You're kidding!" screamed Meg.

Quill explained the design contest, to general congratulations.

"So she's gonna be on the show, too?" said Doreen. "Cripes!"

"Has Helena met her yet?" asked John cynically.

"Um," said Quill. "She says she hasn't. But she knows she's black. And she knows about Barbara. I told her, but I'll bet she found out before. She wants me to tell Connie about the win. Assure her she doesn't have to actually appear on the show."

"It can't be a problem," said Meg. "Not in this day and age."

"Right," said John. "So you're going to tell Connie now?"

"Have they finished lunch?"

"Ayuh," said Doreen. "Went right back to meetin'. That bookkeeper Dawn Pennifarm ain't there, though. I ast 'em. Said she din't show up for work this morning."

Quill's bright mood clouded. "Damn. That check. It's possible we're going to have some problem with that. Myles said Hudson thinks Dawn's taken off with some company money."

"I don't believe it!" said Meg indignantly.

"Let's not jump the gun," said John. "Quill, would you like me to talk to Hudson?"

"Nope. I can handle it. Who's manager here anyhow? I'll talk to Hudson. Hudson's in the meeting, isn't he?"

"Oh, yeah," said Doreen, "spouting his usual hoo-hah."

"Well, he'll be able to give us the check," said Quill confidently. "Meg, Helena wants to plan a small party for Connie about seven o'clock."

"How many?"

"Let's make it for seven people. She'll want to bring her husband and daughter."

"Seven at seven it is. You're going to stand by, I take it."

Quill looked at John, who smiled sourly. "Yes," she said, "I think I should."

Hudson Zabriskie, general manager of Paramount Paints, was slouched against the wall outside the conference room gazing dolefully at nothing in particular. He was exceptionally tall, a fact usually unnoticed because he slouched. It wasn't the "I'm-going-to-knock-my-head-on-the-ceiling" slouch of, say, a basketball player, it was more of an anxious hunch. Just why Hudson hunched like that nobody knew. He had a very nice wife who ran a tailoring business, a good job, and attended Dookie Shuttleworth's Hemlock Falls Church of God with every appearance of spiritual satisfaction. Doreen thought Hudson's nerves rose from the management skills required by Paramount Paints' female workforce. When Quill, too indignant even to shriek, had taken exception to this theory, Doreen had quoted neurological studies (courtesy of a dogged perusal of an article in *Newsweek*) confirming women were more verbal than men. The Bloater, Doreen said, couldn't make any situation clearer, even if the plant were ablaze and all he had to holler was "Fire." Women, said Doreen with satisfaction, din't put up with that kind of crapola. Especially the tough cookies at Paramount Paints.

Hudson greeted Quill like a balky engine on a cold day: "Hello, hello, hello, Quill. Didn't expect to see you today."

"I'm so glad I caught you," said Quill. "I have just a couple of things. Some *really* good news for Connie, and a small request—John thought that we might be able to pick up that quarterly check."

Hudson jumped like a startled fawn. "That's Dawn Pennifarm's job. She's not available."

"Doreen did mention Dawn had to miss the team meeting today. Is someone taking over from her while she's . . . she's um . . . away?"

Hudson gave her a hunted look. "I am. How much was the check for?"

"Forty-five hundred?" said Quill.

"Forty-five *hundred*? Oh, god. Oh, god. This is terrible news. Just terrible. I'll take care of it. Don't do a thing." His mustache trembled. "There's nothing else, is there?"

"Well, there's some terrific news that's going to cheer everyone up. Do you mind if I pull Connie out of the meeting?"

"Connie Weyerhauser? Right now?"

"Honestly, Hudson, I wouldn't interrupt if it weren't the most marvelous news. Really."

"The team's achieving consensus," said Hudson. "Excellent training, excellent. It's given me a real strategic perspective."

"Is it okay to interrupt the meeting?" Quill repeated patiently. "Should I wait until a coffee break?"

"I'll go in with you. They should be finished just about now. They're in there," he said unnecessarily. "Your new conference room. Great remodeling job. New York's pleased."

"John will be delighted to hear it."

Although it had started as a Tavern more than three hundred years before, at various times in its history, the Inn had been a sanitarium, a Home for Wayward Girls, and, because of its proximity to Seneca Falls, an occasional safehouse for the underground railway run by the abolitionist Glynis Tryon. It was John who'd suggested a new incarnation to attract lucrative corporate accounts: the addition of a conference center. The old ballroom had been successfully converted to accommodate business meetings. Double pocket doors slid open into the hallway. Inside, on the wall opposite the doors, was a large cabinet which concealed a VCR, a white board, a bulletin board, and a cork board. The white board was on display as Quill and Hudson joined the "Bosses Club."

Four women sat around the polished conference table. The board was filled with exhortations in black and red marker:

BOSSES BUST ASS WE'RE A LEAN MACHINE. A series of square boxes connected by arrows was labeled: PARAMOUNT PAINTS PRODUCT DELIVERY PROCESS.

A woman Quill didn't know looked up with a ferocious scowl as they walked in. "We've finally figured out what you meant, Hudson, you asshole." Harshly dyed black hair was pulled uncompromisingly from her face. Years of cigarette smoking had carved deep grooves on either side of her thin-lipped mouth. "Siddown, and we'll tell you how we'll pull it off."

Hudson sat. Quill stood in the doorway.

"Sit with us, Quill." Sandy Willis, lead supervisor for one of the production lines, greeted Quill with a smile. She was thin, with an intense, cheerful demeanor that Quill had always found appealing. "It's good to see you again. I think you know everybody except our newest member, Dot Vandermolen. She's just been promoted. Dot. This is Sarah Quilliam."

"Congratulations!" Quill said as she sat down.

The black-haired woman grunted.

"Just give us a second, Quill, okay?" Sandy turned to her teammates. "Dot, let's not get too insulting. Why don't we take another coffee break and cool off. Then we can fill Hudson in on our decision."

"I just want this son of a bitch to know we can cut the remake stats to below half percent. But that means no layoffs, right, Hudson?" Dot drew furiously on her cigarette, and just as furiously stubbed it out. "I figger it's my responsibility to the guys on the line to go over that whole file, there"—she pointed at a stack of manila folders—"and see they're getting a fair shake."

"We're in synch, we're in synch"—Hudson nodded—"but, ladies, and this is a large *but* . . ."

"Like yours, Hud," said Dot.

The three other women looked shocked for a moment, then there was a chorus of laughter.

Hudson, who did, thought Quill guiltily, have a large squishy sort of rear end, pulled on his pencil-thin mustache with short, agitated jerks.

"We're going to come awfully close to the strike days of

ten years ago if we can't guarantee no layoffs," said Sandy.

"Absolutely," said Hudson. "No question. You've got my word on that, Sandy."

"I hate to say anything, Mr. Zabriskie." Kay Gondowski, round, sweet-faced, and hesitant, cleared her throat a little nervously. Her voice was almost inaudible. "But didn't you say that last year? I mean, I'm not sure, but I know we got that three percent gallonage increase for you, and you let five people go four months later."

"Kay's got a legitimate issue," said Sandy firmly. "It's verifiable, too. Dawn's got those minutes from last year."

"But Dawn's not here," said Hudson swiftly. "I've told you ladies how important New York feels attendance is. Now Dawn's a very good example of what I was about to tell you. She's a regular member of this team, she's in a responsible position, and did she bother to call with an excuse when she missed her shift this morning? Has anyone even heard from her? I think not."

"Connie?" said Sandy. "You're backup for Dawn. You've got those files? It'll show those layoff figures."

Connie was a large woman with a rich, slow voice. Unlike her teammates, who preferred bowling jackets and jeans, Connie wore a calf-length skirt and print blouse. Small gold earrings gleamed against her dark skin. She pulled a computer printout from a large accordion folder. "Here they are. You were right, Kay. Last Year To Date. Production up twelve percent; employment down fourteen percent."

"There!" said Dot vindictively. She jerked her chin at Quill. "What dy'a think of *that*?"

"Quill's not interested in our little battles," said Connie peaceably. "But I'll bet I know what she *is* in here for. That check, right?" Connie thumbed methodically through the file. "Check for four thousand five hundred sixty-three dollars and eighty cents?"

"Yes," said Quill gratefully.

Connie's brow furrowed. "Sorry, honey. Just got the stub for it. No check at all." There was an uneasy silence around the table.

"Oh, dear," said Quill. "Well, it doesn't matter now. Connie, could I talk to you outside a minute?"

Sandy shrieked and bounced in her chair. "Look at her! Look at her! See that big shit-eating grin? We've won! I knew it! We've won a million bucks!"

CHAPTER 3

"You *all* won it?" Quill said.

Connie, smiling so hard Quill thought her face would split, nodded majestically. "The whole Bosses Club!"

"Whoop!" screamed Sandy Willis, leaping onto the conference table. Her tennis shoes beat a firm tattoo on the mahogany surface. She danced her way down to the end and back, pausing midway to wiggle her rear end in Hudson Zabriskie's astonished face. He had turned pale, then red, then pale again at the news.

"I get it, too, don't I?" said Dot. "You said I was part of it, didn't you?"

"Sure," said Sandy, rather shortly. "We all get it."

"Shee-it!" shouted Dot, then muttered fiercely, "I'm going to quit my *job*. I'm going to quit my *job*. I'm going to . . ."

Kay Gondowski burst into tears. Quill searched in her skirt pocket for a Kleenex and handed it over.

"Everybody settle down," said Connie. "C'mon, guys. Sit! Sit! Sit!"

"Woof!" said Sandy, grinning hugely. She heaved herself off the table and settled into a chair.

"We're rich," wept Kay.

"Okay. Quiet," Connie ordered. "Nobody quits anything until we figure this all out."

"Let's buy the factory!" shouted Sandy. "We'll give everyone a raise!"

"And send Hudson to hell, to hell, to hell," Dot chanted,

31

punctuating each *hell* with a blow of her fist.

"A million dollars," sobbed Kay.

"Yes!" shouted Sandy, shooting her fist in the air. "A million dollars!"

"Split five ways," said Connie. "We figured that out, remember? That's two hundred thousand each including Dawn and Dot, here. We haven't got it, yet. We wait until we get it, and *then* we talk about quitting. We can invest it at the bank. I talked to Mark Anthony Jefferson, just asking him, you know, and he said two hundred thousand dollars invested at six percent is twelve thousand dollars a year."

"Twelve thousand dollars a year," sobbed Kay, "for free."

"Taxes," said Hudson suddenly, "you ladies forgot about taxes. There's absolutely no way. No way at all. Nobody can live on twelve thousand dollars a year." He smoothed his mustache.

"The mixers on the line do," said Dot sharply. "We've been telling you all along, Hud, they ain't paid enough."

Quill cleared her throat. "You *all* won?" she said again. "How did you do it? I've seen the design. It's just gorgeous."

"Kay watches *It's a Beautiful Life* every week," Connie explained. "She told us about the contest six months ago. We're all on the bowling team at the Legion Hall Tuesday nights. So every Tuesday night for a month—"

"I bought us a pitcher of beer," said Dot. "Remember that. Every Tuesday night since I joined. You said I could be in on it, too. And we brainstormed on how to win that million bucks." She shot a conciliatory look at Hudson. "Just like you taught us in team training."

"We pooled our money for a sketch pad and watercolors," said Kay so softly Quill could barely hear her. "And we put our heads together and came up with this design. Dawn drew it."

"And drew it and drew it and drew it," said Connie, chuckling. "Whoa, but that girl wanted some plumb ugly stuff on the saucers."

"The teacup shape," said Sandy. "We fought about that for weeks!"

"We used Connie's stationery because it was so classy,"

Kay confided in her near-whisper.

"I've got to call my girl, Barbara," said Connie, "and my Roosevelt. And my grandmother. Whoo!" She shook her head, unbelieving.

"We're supposed to meet her at seven o'clock?" asked Sandy. "Helena Houndswood?"

"In the Tavern Bar," said Quill. "I've asked Meg to make some hors d'oeuvres. On the house."

"Helena Houndswood," breathed Kay. "She's so beautiful!"

"We'd better go and get cleaned up," said Sandy. "We can't meet Helena Houndswood dressed like this." She indicated her bowling jacket, jeans, and baggy T-shirt with a stagily elegant sweep of one hand. There was a general scraping of chairs. Hudson Zabriskie held up his hands. "Ladies, ladies, the shift doesn't end until five-thirty. . . ." A chorus of dismay made his mustache jump. "But this time, I'm making an exception. Just give me another hour, here, and then you can all go home and get ready for tonight. I may even join you, if you'd permit it."

"Sure, Mr. Zabriskie," said Connie briefly, "whatever you like." She gave Quill a hug, then turned to her teammates. "We'll dress up a bit, guys. Like for the bowling banquet."

"Whoop!" shrieked Sandy. "Let's slam through the rest of this stuff."

"I'll see you out, Quill," said Hudson, gnawing a fingernail as the door slid closed behind them. "New York's going to be upset. Very upset. I'm not sure how HR will react to this."

"HR? I don't quite . . ."

"Human Resources. There'll be a lot of publicity. Things were going very, very well at the plant. Extremely well, since I took over. Just two more quarters and New York is going to be pleased. Very pleased. But this!" He flailed both hands in the air.

"Everything is going to be fine," said Quill diplomatically.

"Productivity's bound to be affected. Of course, I've handled situations like this before quite well, but still . . ."

"And I'm sure you'll handle it well, again." Quill drew a deep breath. "I'm really sorry, Hudson, but I've got to ask you for that check."

"Dawn will be back tomorrow," he said. "Next day at the latest. I can't authorize what would be a duplicate payment." He rolled an eye at her, then took a sudden, intent interest in the wainscoting. "She'll be back to collect her winnings. I mean, once word about this gets around . . ."

Quill debated with herself. Myles never got angry, precisely, but he was bound to dry up as a source of information if she told Hudson she knew that Dawn was missing, apparently with the Inn's operating capital for the month. Tiny beads of sweat had appeared at Hudson's temples. He suddenly seemed very . . . short, thought Quill. And she'd bet half that missing check that "New York" didn't treat him any better than his employees did. "Let's not worry about this now. Not when the Bosses Club's had such terrific news. Maybe I can stop by the plant tomorrow and we can straighten this out."

"I'm sure we can work something out," Hudson said uncertainly. He shifted from one foot to the other.

Quill glanced at her watch, then touched his shoulder. "I'll see you this evening, then."

A pleased expression lightened Hudson's face. "I wouldn't shirk that duty, Quill," he said earnestly. "The girls really need me tonight. You realize I've been used to dealing in some large arenas. It's not technically in my job description, but that's never stopped me. So I guess I'll be back for this . . . she's ah, here, is she?"

"Ms. Houndswood, you mean? Yes, I'm supposed to meet her in the lobby at three, which means I *really* have to go, Hudson. I'll see you tonight." She shook his hand and fled.

She reached the lobby as Helena Houndswood drifted down the stairs in a cream-colored walking skirt and cotton gauze blouse. "That's gorgeous," said Quill, without envy.

"You like?" Helena cocked her head and whirled gracefully. She adjusted yet another straw hat—this one covered with ecru silk roses—then drew a thick manila envelope from the oversize handbag she carried. "My galleys. Guard them with your life." She followed Quill out the front door. Outside, she threw her arms wide and inhaled sharply. "Marvelous! Marvelous! And that view! It's idyllic. Relaxed. Unstressed. The Country Life. You know . . . I'm getting the germ of an idea for a book, here." She stopped short, frowning. "Helena Houndswood presents—It's A Beautiful Life on the Farm!"

"Of course," said Quill weakly. "Um, Helena, about Connie Weyerhauser . . ."

Helena gave her a sharp sideways glance. "So. You reached the lucky winner?"

"Yes. They were thrilled."

"What do you mean, 'they'?"

Quill explained.

"Why the hell didn't they put all their names on the contest entry, then? Did you say one's called Gondowski for God's sake? And a—what do you call it now? 'A person of color.' "

"Paramount's very proud of its diverse workforce."

"Jee-sus! Oh, for God's sake, Sarah, get that look off your face. I'm thinking of my audience. I'm no fucking bigot."

Quill bit her lip, hard.

"Five winners. God, that'll be a field day for that fucking studio lawyer. The fees'll be tripled. How the fuck did it happen? Why didn't they put *all* their names on the entry?"

"Well, I asked them that. Apparently Connie'd bought this new stationery from . . . well never mind who . . . and they'd seen your show on how stationery was the first line of defense against a vulgar world—" Quill broke off, aware that this wasn't getting anywhere. "Helena, they're so excited about this. You can't imagine what it means to them."

Helena said enigmatically, "Quite the little Girl Scout, aren't you?"

Quill told herself she wasn't going to lose her temper, suggested they begin their walk, and pointed out what she hoped were interesting features of the gardens surrounding the Inn as they walked down the gentle grade leading to the village. "The roses, of course, you've seen. I'm not really sold on the hybrid teas, as you noticed . . ."

"Nor I," said Helena agreeably. "So tacky, don't you think? Rather *nouveau riche*. Or perhaps I should say sterile, in the face of the vitality and vigor of the Old Roses."

Quill, finding no possible response to this, went on. "Mike, our lawn guy, suggested the plantings here." She indicated the sweep of dwarf dahlias lining the driveway to the Inn. "They turned out well, don't you think?"

Helena bent over a clump of yellow pom-pom dahlias and mused, "Unusually early for daisies, isn't it?"

"Actually they're both dahlias," corrected Quill cheerfully, then immediately regretting the lapse, said, "The British Dahlia Society's registered more than twenty varieties, which is a lot to keep up with, of course. Mike forces them in the greenhouses out back."

"All twenty?" asked Helena sweetly. "How clever of you."

The village lay at the foot of the Inn, curving around a bend in the Hemlock River. They walked through the heavily wooded Park, passing the bandstand and the statue of General C. C. Hemlock, who had founded the village three hundred years before. From the statue it was less than five minutes walk to Main Street.

The Chamber of Commerce, and through them the zoning board, were clearly dedicated to civic pride; most of the buildings on Main were of cobblestone, carefully restored and meticulously maintained. The rest were white clapboard trimmed in black, in keeping with the town's Colonial heritage as interpreted from the village building code. Along Main Street's flank, huge baskets of scarlet geraniums swung from the wrought-iron street lamps. Black painted planters filled with early blooming marigolds and purple pansies flanked wrought-iron benches underneath. There were some advantages, Quill thought, to the chamber's fierce dedication to such civic activities as Clean It Up! Week.

"Marvelous," murmured Helena, frankly peering up and down the street. "I envy you this life, Quill. I can see exactly why you left SoHo. This is so unpeopled."

The current population of Hemlock Falls was three thousand four hundred and twenty-six, and on any given day of the week perhaps ten or twelve citizens were out shopping, gossiping, or running errands. If Helena was out looking for an audience, thought Quill, she'd just have to accept that this was it. She caught sight of Esther West, standing in front of her dress shop in a print dress splashed with scarlet begonias talking animatedly to a customer. Neither of them looked toward Quill and her companion. Quill waved. Helena swept off her hat. The famous mane of golden hair gleamed in the afternoon sun.

"Charming, charming, *charming*," Helena projected. "We've got to get all this on tape for the show. We'll bring in some extras, of course. Preppie couples—awful word!—and a few Golden Retrievers. Darling, we're going to put you on the map." She ran a hand through her hair, gesturing widely. Esther still hadn't noticed them.

Directly across the street from the dress shop, Elmer Henry, Mayor of Hemlock Falls, emerged from Marge Schmidt's Hemlock Hometown Diner, Harvey Bozzel on his heels. The two men stopped in their tracks. Elmer was wearing two BOOST HEMLOCK FALLS buttons on the lapel of his shiny polyester coat. Harvey grabbed Elmer by the arm and whispered in his ear, then started toward them at a dog trot, dragging Elmer behind him like a bashful barge. Esther and her customer turned to watch where Harvey was headed. Esther's jaw dropped. She shrieked.

Helena glanced casually at her watch. "God. Here they come. We'd better get going. Where is this post office of yours? I've got to get my package off."

She matched Quill's brisk pace down the sidewalk, the mayor and his entourage puffing in her wake.

The post office—a defiantly modern building—stood in the middle of the historic district, at the corner of Main and Maple, across from the Hemlock Falls Savings and Loan. One of Vern Mittermeyer's postal workers had sanded the flaking red trim and was in the middle of repainting.

"That looks wonderful, Lloyd," Quill said as they approached the front door.

"Might look good. Don't paint so good." He waved a loaded brush at the window ledge. "Spots something awful, this stuff."

"Excuse me," said Helena. "We'd like to get in?"

Lloyd pursed his lips. "Now, it's a good thing you stopped by, Ms. Quilliam. You're a painter, right? You know what's wrong with this stuff?"

"Excuse me!" Helena edged rancorously past the open can of Paramount Crimson Red, her skirt dangerously near the dripping lip.

"I'm not that kind of a painter," Quill said to Lloyd. "But it does look a little thick."

"It don't stick right. Stinks, too. Guess that's why they give it to the post office. Vern's always said folks don't app—"

"Sarah!" said Helena in a dangerous tone, "I'm *late*."

Quill pushed the door open for her.

The post office hours were listed in large black letters on the glass: HOURS 8:00 to 12:00. 1:00 to 5:00. Below this, in aggressive red marker, was hand-lettered: ACCORDING TO POSTAL CODE 2.134 NO EXCEPTIONS! THIS MEANS YOU.

Helena turned to Quill with a raised eyebrow.

"Vern Mittermeyer's postmaster," said Quill, knowing this was an inadequate explanation. "He's very . . . dedicated."

"Sweet," said Helena. "Look, it's quarter to four, already. I've got to get back and change for that seven o'clock cocktail party." She looked behind her. Harvey, flanked by Esther and a pregnant customer, was less than a block away. Elmer puffed a few steps behind.

"Vern shouldn't keep you too long," said Quill dubiously.

They went into the building, the door swinging shut in Harvey's face. He pressed his face to the glass. A circle of moisture formed beneath his nose.

Quill saw with relief that only one customer stood at the counter. "Eloise!" she said loudly. "How have you been? Helena, this is Eloise Nicholson. Eloise has lived in Hemlock Falls for . . . how long is it?"

"Eighty-nine years!" said Eloise proudly. "I was born here. I haven't seen you for the longest time, Quill." She adjusted the hearing aid under a fluffy white curl and tottered forward on her cane. "How is your dear sister?"

"She's just fine!" shouted Quill. "And how are you?"

Pleased, Eloise planted a foot on either side of her cane and took a breath to respond. Helena looked at the clock on the wall and pressed past Quill to the counter. "I need to send this overnight to Manhattan."

"Gotta get in line," said Vern, nodding to an undefined space behind Eloise.

Helena thrust her famous profile next to his and put the package under his nose. She tapped the return address meaningfully with a buffed fingernail. "I'm on deadline, here," she said.

Vern eased from one skinny hip to the other. "Next!" he shouted at Eloise.

Eloise blinked. "I'll be just a moment, dear Quill." She turned, set her large plastic handbag on the countertop, and rummaged through it.

Helena rapped the counter sharply. "Will you take this while she's finding her mail, please?"

Vern blinked at her slowly, like a particularly malevolent turtle. "What'cha got there, Eloise?"

"My rebates, Mr. Mittermeyer." Eloise emerged from her purse triumphant, a thick sheaf of pink envelopes in her hand. Quill recognized Doreen's Pink Morning sixteen percent rag content stationery from the budget line.

Vern cast a beady eye over the envelopes. "Need the ZIP codes."

"Then you can take this while she gets them," snapped Helena.

"Eastman Kodak Company, Rochester, New York," said Vern, squinting at Eloise's first envelope. "Gotta look that up for ya." He turned, pulled a thick volume from the shelf behind him, thumbed through it, then read, "One-four-six-oh-four."

"One-four-six-oh . . . four?" Eloise wrote as she spoke.

"Ayuh." Vern took the envelope, shuffled to the out-of-town mail bin, dropped it in, and shuffled back to Eloise. He picked up the second envelope. "Procter and Gamble," he read aloud.

In the ensuing minutes Quill discovered that Eloise had coupons for a disproportionately large percentage of the Fortune 500.

" . . . Chicago, Illinois," finished Vern, finally, "oh-oh-two-six-seven. That'll be it, Eloise." He cast a severe look over Helena's head. "Next!"

Helena stepped forward.

"He'p you?"

"This is to go overnight to Manhattan," said Helena between her teeth.

Vern looked at the clock. "You gotta come back tomorrow."

"What?"

"You gotta get overnights to Manhattan in before four o'clock," Vern said. "Otherwise it won't get there until Friday. This is Wednesday, see? You mail it today, it ain't gonna get there until Friday."

"And what if I mail it tomorrow morning?"

"Thursday?" said Vern. His face brightened perceptibly. "Oh, it'll get there Friday, for sure."

Helena's face turned a dangerous shade of pink.

"Take the package, Vern," said Quill.

"If I mail it now," said Helena, "it won't get there until Friday."

"Right."

"And if I mail it tomorrow?"

"Oh, it'll get there Friday, all right," said Vern.

The dangerous shade of pink deepened to emergency mauve.

Quill pulled the manuscript from Helena's unresisting fingers. "Vern," said Quill. "We want this package to get there Friday. How should we do it?"

"Friday?" Vern thought this over. "Couple of ways to do that. Two-Day Priority. Or you could come back tomor—"

"Two-Day Priority," said Quill. "That's exactly what we want. Thank you, Vern. Helena, there's an amazing crowd of fans outside. Why don't you take care of some autographs and I'll get this sent off?"

"Is there a back way out?"

"Well, yes, but I thought—"

"My fans?" Helena didn't laugh, precisely, it was a sound more like the high-pitched squeal of an old Chevy rounding a sharp bend at high speed. "Fuck them." She slung her heavy handbag over her shoulder. "No. I want a place to dump this bastard's *body*. Is there one of those big trash bins out back? That'll do just fucking fine."

"Oh, my," said Eloise, pleasurably offended.

Quill guided Helena to the door and pushed her into the waiting arms of the crowd. Eloise thumped out after her.

Vern snapped his gum and gazed incuriously at Quill, "He'p you?"

"How much is that, Vern? For Two-Day Priority."

"She shoulda sent it Monday."

"What?"

Vern gestured at the large red, blue, and white sign under the clock. "Tells all about it on that sign."

"She was in here Monday?"

"Lookin' for the Hall. What Hall, I says to her. You mean the Legion. Thought it was some mansion. I says to her, I says, you mean the Le—"

"Nine-ninety for a one-pound package," Quill read from the Priority Mail sign. "Here's ten. Keep the change."

"Baltimore don't allow us to keep the change," said Vern doggedly.

Quill grabbed the dime. Then pushed her way out the front door and into the small crowd on the sidewalk. Eloise, balancing on her cane, was clearly in the middle of a story involving the "F" word, famous actresses, and overnight Express Mail. From the look on everyone's face, it was a hit. The actress in question was nowhere in sight.

"Up the hill and through the woods," said Elmer Henry, in response to Quill's question. He stuck out his chest and lowered his head to form a third chin. "Quill, could you approach the young lady to appear at the Chamber meeting tomorrow? It'd guarantee us a pret' good turnout, and you know how the members have been missing meetings lately." He leaned forward and whispered, "Course, if what Eloise says here is true . . ."

A backfire from somewhere near the park obscured his whisper, and Quill said, "Pardon, Mayor?"

" . . . 'fuck'!" shouted Elmer, to his constituents' consternation and his own alarm. "This bidness of the language . . ." he trailed off uneasily.

The ensuing discussion seemed endless. Quill waited patiently for a tactful opening; at the first opportunity she promised to do her best, then said, "Could you guys excuse me? I've got . . ." Quill stopped, not sure what she'd got. "My hands full," she finished.

She walked down Main to the park road intersection, trying to arrange pieces of the puzzle. Why would Helena have lied about meeting the Bosses Club? *Had* she met the Bosses Club? She stepped off the curb into the street and jumped back as a large red pickup truck turned the corner with a shriek of its overinflated tires and a second backfire. Quill had seen the driver before: Rickie Pennifarm, Dawn's husband.

"Hey!" yelled Quill, waving her hand. "Rickie. Stop!"

He shot a bloodshot gaze over his shoulder and gunned the motor.

What she should do, thought Quill, was go back to the Inn and follow Rickie to his trailer and see if he knew anything about the forty-five hundred dollars John needed to make payroll. Quill walked back through the park wondering if Helena Houndswood's lies mattered and guiltily acknowledging that she'd far rather untangle Helena's odd behavior than go bill collecting. The Bosses Club's preference for polyester and home perms didn't fit Helena's notion of the Beautiful Person living the Beautiful Life. But so what? She couldn't change the facts: the women had won the contest, and even Helena couldn't take the money away from them. What she could do was make life pretty unpleasant for everyone in the next three weeks with snide comments, outrageous behavior, and obnoxious demands.

Quill passed the statue of General C. C. Hemlock and stopped at the entrance to the footpath through the birch woods. The sky's blue was past celestial, she thought, green scents spiraled through the sunny air, and she was heartily sick of Helena Houndswood. A walk through the birch trees would put things in better proportion.

The woods were silent, except for the cracking of twigs beneath her feet. It was cool without the direct rays of the sun, and Quill rubbed her arms, suddenly oppressed by the quiet. A black fly snarled past her ear, then another. Gradually the tide of silence was overcome by insect whine. Quill stopped to look for the source. She'd walked into black flies once before, and they had a sting to rival hornets. A thick cloud clustered at the base of a bodelia bush. She stepped back onto a discarded pile of plastic. The color was familiar. She picked it up and shook it out. A bowling jacket, soggy with moisture; the embroidered name on the pocket read *Dot*.

Quill frowned at the blood on her hand. Then froze. And for a long, icy moment refused to look at the mass of flies and what they fed on.

CHAPTER 4

"Are you sure you're all right?" John sat next to Quill on the couch in her office, an arm companionably around her shoulders. Meg was curled in the chair behind Quill's desk. Doreen leaned against the closed door, arms folded. "Do you want a little more brandy?"

Quill shook her head and set the snifter on the coffee table. "No, I shouldn't have had that bit. I was just so cold."

"Horrible," murmured Meg.

"Sher'f comin'?" asked Doreen.

"Myles is still in Ithaca. Dave Kiddermeister's in charge," Quill said. "He said he had everything under control." She ran her hands through her hair. "Dave thinks it looks like a hunting accident."

"A hunting accident? In June?" Meg slung her feet on the desktop. "Bullshit."

"Folks after woodchucks this time of year?" observed Doreen. "Hard to mistake a person for a woodchuck. On t'other hand I din't know her. This Dot."

"Not a lot of people did," said Quill. "She lives—lived—in a trailer out near the paint factory. A husband, Dave said. The boys are grown and have left home. One of the other deputies knew the family. Not very popular, I guess."

"Well, it's too bad," Meg said briskly, "but I don't know what we can do about it. And you look a little less ghastly than when you came in, so I'm getting back to the kitchen."

Quill frowned. "Just like that?"

"Sorry. But I didn't know Dot Vandermolen from Adam. I'm concerned about you, of course. It must have been awful, seeing the body."

"Well, it was. But that's not the most awful part."

"What could have been more awful than finding a corpse with its head blown off?" said Meg.

"I don't think it was an accident."

"You mean murder?" Meg's eyebrows lifted. John groaned. "Who would want to kill Dot what's-her-name? Vandermolen."

"I don't know anything about Dot Vandermolen personally," said Quill. "But the woman just won two hundred thousand dollars. And she was very aggressive. And besides . . ." Quill trailed off. Helena Houndswood had passed through the park not ten minutes before Quill found Dot's body. The "backfire" Quill'd heard when she was in front of the post office had obviously been the shots that had killed her. But if Dave Kiddermeister thought it was a hunting accident—were the backfire noises she heard rifle shots? Where would Helena get a rifle? She'd been carrying an overlarge handbag. Did they make rifles that collapsed like umbrellas? Quill frowned and pulled at her lower lip.

"Besides what?" asked John.

"I did see Rickie Pennifarm driving away from the park," Quill admitted. "In that brand-new Bubba truck he owns with the lifts and the giant tires . . ."

"And the gun rack," finished Meg. "There you are, then. Did you tell Deputy Dave?"

"Yes. But why would Rickie Pennifarm want to shoot Dot?"

"More for him and Dawn," said Doreen. "Don't have to split that million five ways."

"I don't think so," Quill said. "I mean, the money would go to the heirs, right? Not the rest of the group."

"Not necessarily." John tapped his pencil against his lip with a thoughtful expression. "Sometimes those contests aren't assignable. We could check that out. Why don't you ask Helena, Quill?"

Quill got to her feet. "I'll leave that to Myles," she said virtuously. "In the meantime, I'd better make sure Helena understands it'd be inappropriate to have the party now. John, do you know if they make rifles that collapse like umbrellas?"

"That what?" A suspicion of a grin lightened his face. "That *was* a large bag she was carrying," he agreed.

"You think Helena had somethin' to do with this?" Meg ran one hand through her hair. "Jeepers, Quill."

"I'm just going to talk to her about the party—and maybe a few other things. Under the circumstances, I'm sure Helena will want to wait a few days for the Bosses Club celebration."

"Bet she won't," said Meg.

"Of course she will. Even Helena Houndswood can't ignore this."

"Wanna bet?" Meg followed her sister to the door. "You just let me know *instantly* if we've got a party tonight."

"There won't be a party tonight," said Quill. "Where is she?"

"Outside," said Doreen briefly. "Went down to the wood to talk to Deputy Dave. Pokin' her nose in, I call it."

Quill overtook Helena at the dahlia border. Her complexion was its usual porcelain perfection. She was observing the dwarf pom-poms with critical respect. "Do you know," she said as Quill came up, "I had a fan call in to one of my flower specials last year and absolutely insist that these adorable little things were part of the daisy family?" She slipped her arm confidingly through Quill's. "Doom, death, and disaster, I understand."

"It's horrible," said Quill shortly.

"Hunting accident, according to that bovine deputy. I went down there of course—can't keep the reporter out of this little girl—and he found the bullet casing. It's a what? A two-seventy caliber. Deputy thought someone was hunting out of season."

"It was a rifle wound?"

"Apparently. Now. About the party for these tacky little winners . . ."

Quill stared at her. Helena wasn't carrying her handbag. It hadn't been large enough to conceal a rifle. She was still wearing the long, full skirt and loose overblouse. Could she have tucked the rifle inside her clothing, somehow? Swiped it from Rickie's truck and replaced it? Would Rickie let her borrow the rifle to murder Dot?

"These little fits happen often, sweetie?"

Quill blinked. Helena snapped off a dahlia and stuck it in the brim of her hat. "It's almost twenty to six. Your little party is set up for seven, *n'est-ce pas*? I'm going to need the time to recharge myself to meet these—how many women did you say? Just three, now, right? Can you be a doll and take care of them for me, if I'm just the teensiest bit late? I need a good long soak in that marvelous whirlpool tub of yours. I feel quite—not fresh."

"You're not thinking of going ahead with the party?"

"Let me remind you, sweetie, I've got exactly three weeks until air time. I didn't know this Dot. I'm dreadfully sorry for the accident, of course, but time and TV wait for no man. And I've got a lot to do to shape those women up. No? You think I'm wrong to go ahead? Tell you what. You call those girls and offer them a choice; party tonight to celebrate their win, or a suitable time for mourning somebody they didn't seem to like very much anyway from what the deputy tells me. The less notice that's taken of this the better."

"Perhaps I can find another location for the party," said Quill, a little stiffly.

"You're serious!" Helena laughed. "Get real, sweetie. Where else is there in this burg?"

"There's a Marriot on route fifteen. I'm sure they'll be glad—"

"Come on. Both of us have stepped over worse on the streets of Manhattan. And you really want to send all this money to a competitor? Look. We'll go top flight. Okay? I'm always looking for delicious new ideas for the show. Tell what's her name, Meg, that I'll think about a cooking segment on the shoot. Maybe. Just maybe."

Rage made Quill dizzy. She turned abruptly and left to find Meg. She, John, and Doreen had abandoned the office for the dining room and some hot tea.

"That woman," said Meg, after Quill had given a clipped, angry account of Helena's demands, "absolutely boggles the mind. So we've got a cocktail party for how many? Kay, Sandy, and Connie? I'd better check the supplies."

"Do you think they'll show up?" said Quill. "Sandy and Connie and Kay. And what about Dawn?"

Doreen gave a cynical snort.

"It's just awful to have Dot's death pass totally . . ."

"Unremarked?" suggested John. "Why don't we do something for Dot's family? A donation from the Inn for the funeral?"

"You think we should go ahead with this, too?" Quill said.

"Short of throwing her out—and the revenue for the rest of the year with her—I don't see what else we can do."

"I do," said Meg. "We'll go ahead with this party, but we'll sabotage the food. A little cayenne in the *crème brûlée* . . ."

"No!" shouted John, Quill, and Doreen together.

"Let's go ahead," said Quill reluctantly. "At least she wants you to go all out, Meggie."

"All out? In less than two hours? Damn it, I knew I shouldn't have canceled that salmon. How am I supposed to go all out without any salmon?"

"All of it?" said Quill. "What are the environmentalists going to eat? The Friends of Fresh Air?"

"What about them?" Meg began to rake her hands through her hair, an ominous sign.

"Environmentalists don't eat meat, Meg. At least, I would expect that they'd eat more fish than meat. They suck fish up like vacuum cleaners. Everyone knows that. Why did you cancel all the salmon?"

"Because you made me!" Meg shrieked untruthfully. "I've got shrimp and haddock. That's it." She pulled a pen from John's breast pocket and began to scribble on the tablecloth. "Quennelles of scampi and haddock?" she muttered. "Are you kidding? When are they coming?"

"Two of the FOFA people have already checked in," said John calmly. "Makepeace and Abigail Whitman. He's the director. Ten more couples are arriving this evening."

"You'll just have to send them down to Marge Schmidt's,"

said Meg. "I can't do environmentalists and Helena Hounds-wood, too."

"They did ask for nonsmoking rooms," said Quill. "Doreen, you made sure . . ."

Doreen set her teacup down with a smack. "I'd just like to know how come everyone's in a state of the jimjams. I know my job, don't I? I don't suit, I can always get a job down to the Marriot on route fifteen. They got a better health plan, anyways." She scowled. "And no fancy actress throwing her weight around."

"Let's not let her get to us," said Quill. "It's going to be much worse if we start whacking each other. Doreen, if you could find out from Mr. and Mrs. Whitman if any of the group is vegetarian, I'll call the supplier and reorder the salmon."

"You stay out of my kitchen!" Meg jumped up, slammed through the dining room doors to her stove, only to reappear seconds later. "They won't deliver without a check. Did you get that money? Is there any money in this place? Or do I have to screw the delivery boy to get fresh fish!" The double doors banged shut.

Quill put her head in her hands.

"Them yellow socks," Doreen observed. Then, "Time that one had a date, if you ast me."

Quill peered at her through her fingers and refrained from saying that nobody had. "Maybe we should close up for a week?"

"I'd rather not," said John. "That's disaster plan B. In the 'How did you like the play, Mrs. Lincoln' vein—did you get that check from Hudson?"

"No," said Quill. "Dawn Pennifarm didn't show up for the Bosses Club meeting. There was a check stub in her bookkeeping files, but no check. Hudson said he couldn't reissue a check without knowing what happened to the first one. I think we've got trouble. Do either of you know Dawn Pennifarm very well?"

"That husband Rickie of hers is a no-good," said Doreen. "Seen him at the Croh Bar much more'n I should." She chewed on a lump of sugar, reflectively. "Mean son of a gun."

"Do you suppose she just left town with as much money as she could scrape together?" said Quill. "I didn't know her very well, but she was a pretty angry person. A lot like Dot Vandermolen, as a matter of fact. Little younger."

"Word is Dawn's been at the battered women's shelter more than once," John observed.

Quill hesitated. John was a member of AA, and loath to betray any of its members. "Has Rickie been part of your group?"

John moved the sugar bowl to the exact center of the table. "I don't think the homelife is too good."

Quill, who knew John better than anybody else, decided this was as far as he'd go with a yes.

"And Dawn sure don't have much of a job at that there factory," said Doreen. "I worked there once, you know. Back some ten years ago. Awful, the fumes and all. OSHA come in twice time I was there to shut the joint down."

"It's gotten a lot better since Hudson's taken over," said John. "Paint manufacturing's tough. A lot of the solvents they used to use in oil-base have been banned."

"Not exactly a desirable career," said Quill. "Dawn sounds like a woman with lots of reasons to leave town."

"But she won that million bucks," said Doreen. "She'd stick around for that."

Meg poked her head through the swinging doors. "They're bringing the salmon right up. They'll wait for the cash for a week or two. And guess what? They've got crab!" She disappeared, Quill hoped, for the last time. Once Meg got down to cooking, her temper became serene, if not sunny.

"I won a million bucks, I'd belt that Rickie good and stick around to pick it up." Doreen crunched a second lump of sugar.

"They didn't know about the win until today," said John.

Quill shoved the sugar bowl left of center. "It's possible," she said, "that Dawn knew two days ago."

"But the only one who knew about the win before this afternoon was Helena Houndswood," said John.

"Exactly." Quill sat back in her chair and folded her arms. "There's more. Helena took the same path I did back to the

Inn this afternoon, John. She wasn't more than ten minutes ahead. Let's say that Dawn isn't missing. Let's say she's . . . well, permanently out of the way. Let's say that . . ."

"No," said John. "No. No. No! Put it *out* of your mind, Quill. We've got problems enough without this. Helena didn't even know Dot Vandermolen by sight. If anyone's responsible for anything, it's Rickie Pennifarm."

"But why would Rickie shoot Dot?"

"That's not our problem, Quill. We've got a host of others. Let's not borrow any more. And speaking of borrowing—I'm going to have to do something about cash flow pretty soon. I need a decision from you about whether to get personal loans from the bank, or delay payment to suppliers, or close the Inn for a week or two."

"Problems with the bank. Bodies in the bushes. Witchy actresses. Decisions. Yuck! I'm moving to Alaska." Quill tugged furiously at a strand of her hair and bit it. "You're right. Involving Helena in this doesn't make sense. I must be losing my mind."

John covered her hand with his. "I don't mean to be intrusive, Quill, but maybe this marriage business with Myles is getting to you a little. Have you talked to Meg?"

"No."

"Time to stop takin' care of her," said Doreen gruffly. "She should be takin' care of herself. Does all right on her own if you ast me."

Quill shook her head. "She's still mourning Colin. I can tell. Sometimes I think if he'd had an illness, she would have coped with it better. She would have had more time to think what life would be like without him. But the car accident was so sudden. And they were so happy. It was awful."

"She'll marry again," said John.

"Both of you should," said Doreen. "Fix all this up."

"How would marriage fix all this up?" Quill demanded indignantly.

"Reg'lar sex life," said Doreen. "Good for ya."

"I've *got* a regular sex life!" She moved restlessly in her chair. "It's not just Meg that's keeping me from a decision about Myles. My own marriage wasn't a perfect romance

ending in sudden death, John. It was grisly, day-to-day awful.
And he wasn't a bad guy. I'm not certain I want to jump into
that kind of contract again. We're doing well, here, aren't we?
I mean, it's taken a pile of work for all of us to make the Inn
successful. I'm proud of it. We've done it together. We're
happy the way we are. Why change it?"

"I suppose we'll pull out of this slump—assuming the bank
gives us the line of credit," said John.

"That's the accountant in you," said Quill. "I made sure
you were properly gloomy about business forecasts when we
hired you. Who wants a cheerful business manager? You're
in charge of doom, death, and disaster, and I'm in charge of
keeping the guests happy and the staff comfortable. . . ."

"Quill?" Dina Muir, her hair ruffled, approached the table
at a run. "There's about fifty people in tuxes and stuff milling
around the lobby. What am I supposed to do with them?"

"Fifty people?" Quill looked at her watch. "Good grief, it's
almost seven o'clock. It's not the Bosses Club, is it?"

"And their husbands, kids, mothers-in-law, cousins, plus
half the Chamber of Commerce. You'd better come quick."

The lobby was as jammed as Bloomingdale's the day after
Thanksgiving. Quill surveyed the crowd in astonishment. The
front door opened. Helena Houndswood, still in her rose-
covered hat and floating skirt, drifted into the room. She
stiffened. The crowd surged forward. She jammed the hat
over her head and ran upstairs.

"That was her!" breathed Sandy Willis. "See, Roy, I told
you! It's really true!"

"You're early," said Quill. She looked around the room.
"All of you."

"Not all of us," Sandy said. "We keep calling Dawnie, but
she hasn't shown up. And Kay's not here yet." She glanced
at Quill, then quickly away. "You heard about Dot?"

It seemed to Quill that the massive crowd quieted a little.
"Yes. I'm sorry. I know that Helena insisted on the party, and
you must feel just awful about it."

"Yeah. Well, to be perfectly honest, that's not real true, you
know what I mean? Thing is, none of us knew her all that well.
And she kind of horned in the china contest, once she joined

the bowling team and the Bosses Club. Dave Kiddermeister said it was a hunter or something?"

"Myles hasn't done an investigation yet," said Quill carefully. "He's in Ithaca."

"Dave's good at his job. Looks like a hunting accident, probably is a hunting accident. That's what everybody else thinks. And Quill. Nobody wants this to drive Helena Houndswood away. You know what I mean. I mean, it's not like it was on purpose or anything. Just an accident."

There was a murmur of agreement among the crowd, like the threat of tidal wave on a sunny afternoon at the beach. Quill thought of Elmer and Harvey and Esther West chasing Helena Houndswood down the street that afternoon. Single-handedly, the actress had transformed the nice neighborly citizens of Hemlock Falls into raging opportunists.

Sandy tugged at the skirt of her evening dress. "Anyway, it's okay that we're early, isn't it? And we look okay, don't we? We weren't sure that she wouldn't have the TV cameras right here, and everything, so I called the girls and told them to really put on the dog."

"You look fine," said Quill.

Sandy's advice to dress up had been interpreted in varying ways. Connie herself was in pale blue chiffon, with a lace top, capped sleeves, and a full skirt that came just below her knees. Her satin shoes were dyed pale blue to match. Sandy had opted for basic black, with a scoop neck that revealed the sharp lines between a deep gardening tan, the pale tops of her freckled breasts, and more than a hint of her underwire bra.

Several perfumes fought the air: Evening in Paris, which Quill hadn't smelled since she was eight years old; Obsession; the room-deodorant smell of Liz Claiborne. The Bosses Club was augmented by husbands and boyfriends (mostly sport coats and string ties) and the Chamber of Commerce, Elmer Henry a self-important bulge in their center. A number of ruddy-looking people in hiking shorts and T-shirts lettered FOFA: WE'RE THE FRIENDS OF FRESH AIR! added to the general confusion.

Feeling somewhat like a border collie ordered to "herd them ducks!" Quill set about the task of sorting the Bosses

Club into the conference room and the interlopers from the village into the dining room. She turned the FOFA members over to Doreen to show to their various rooms. John took the husbands, boyfriends, excited relatives, and Hudson Zabriskie into the Tavern Bar, "just," Quill explained to Sandy's husband Roy, "until Ms. Houndswood can meet the winners. She's only expecting the Bosses Club, you know."

"They all split the cash, equal," said Roy anxiously. "She knows that, don't she?"

"Quill'll take care of it," said Sandy, pressing close to his side. "She and Helena are practically best friends."

"Tell Nate to run a house tab, Roy. Sandy, I'll see your team in the conference room in about ten minutes. We'll serve you dinner there. I'm going to check with Meg to see everything's all right."

Quill walked into the kitchen, slapped her hand on the counter, and said, "Whiskey for me. Fresh horses for my men."

"How's by you, Colonel?" asked Meg cheerfully. She twitched pieces of mint leaves gracefully into place on a plate of cucumber-caviar toast rounds.

"Fine. Just fine. Nobody seems to miss Dot, much. I mean, there's a few comments of the 'shame about the body in the woods, but where's Helena!' variety, but no one's crying in their beer, that's for sure. They're all too worried Helena's going to leave town. Harvey even asked me if he thought the Chamber should write an official letter of apology for the disturbance. Can you believe it?"

"You look like a game hen confronting the ax. Have a glass of sherry. It'll settle you."

Quill sank into the rocking chair near the cobblestone hearth and accepted a glass of the Spanish Pale Dry Meg kept in a cupboard. "Let's put a lock on the kitchen door."

"A large German shepherd would do just as well."

"The way the day's going, it'd bite all the guests and we'd get sued and have to give up the Inn and move to Detroit."

Meg set the cold food aside and started filling delicate shells of pastry with a mixture from her pastry cone. She began to sing, words she'd made up to the melody of Chopin's Polonaise: "Vic-tor-ri-ous! (you bet) and the food it will be glorious (I'm set) . . ."

Quill, rubbing the back of her neck, felt some of the accumulated agitation of the day slip away. "You're not having a hissy fit over all the guests?"

Meg gestured backward with her wooden spoon. "I called in the *sous* chefs. First time all summer. And the salmon's here. And the crab."

"So everything's hinky."

"And I've got a new dish. What do you think?" Meg handed her a plate of plumply browned pastries. "Spinach and *herbes varieux*."

"*Herbes varieux*? Old herbs?"

"Various herbs. We are getting on in years, aren't we, that we've forgotten all our French. Time for a face-lift. Just ask Helena for the name of her doctor."

"They're terrific." Quill bit a second one in half. "She'll love them."

"La Helena's in the bag. That fourth star is just around the corner." She switched to "When You Wish Upon a Star," stopped, and said suddenly, "You don't think she might feature some of the cooking in the show?"

"*Et tu*, Margaret?"

"If you mean by that am I going to suck up to Helena Houndswood just because she's an arrogant, unfeeling celebrity show host . . . you bet your butt. I need my reputation back, Quill."

"You never lost your reputation," said Quill. "You've always been terrific. And some bitchy TV person who doesn't know a dahlia from a daisy has nothing to do with who you are or what you can do."

"Thank you, Doctor. You know where that kind of attitude got me in the past. Maybe it's time I sort of soft-pedal things a bit. Think about you for a change, instead of me."

"Has John been talking to you?" demanded Quill. "He couldn't have, he hasn't had the time." Her sister in a penitent mood was unsettling. "I mean, come on, Meg. You're a great chef. I expect volcanic temper tantrums from you. I expect red sock days and béchamel flying through the air at regular intervals."

"Well." Meg fiddled a bit with the pastry cone, then turned and slid the tray into the broiler. "Is somebody going to tell me how many reservations we've got? These hors d'oeuvres are going to be ready in about six seconds, and I've got to do a quick estimate of the specials."

"John'll come in with the count." Quill got to her feet. "I'll carry some of that stuff in to the Bosses Club, if it's ready. Or do you think we should wait for the Star to descend? She went up to change clothes again."

"How many times is that today?" said Meg, clearly fascinated.

"I counted once this morning, once this afternoon, and a third time for cocktails. She's booked the dining room at eight-thirty for dinner. For four. I wonder if she'll change a fourth time for that?"

"Bet you she does," said Meg.

"Nobody can take that many showers in a day."

"A dollar fifty says she does."

"Done." They shook hands. A timer rang, and Meg slid the cheese puffs out of the oven. "I'll take these in to the Bosses Club, Quill. I want to congratulate them in person. Why don't you slip into something more . . . you know . . ."

"You don't like this?" She glanced down at her challis skirt.

"It's a little . . . small town."

Quill stamped up the stairs to her suite of rooms defiantly determined to look small town.

She decided on a calf-length black skirt, a lavish white silk blouse, and high strappy sandals which looked so sophisticated that she got cross and had another glass of sherry. She drained it with a flourish. Everyone, she decided grandly, if a little vaguely, deserved what they were going to get.

"This is wonderful," said Helena with apparent sincerity to the gratified winners some thirty minutes later. "You all are marvelous. I'm just so sorry I can't stay for the dinner Sarah's arranged for you and learn all about you right now! You all worked together to win the prize? I am just so impressed, I can't even begin to tell you. This is *fab*-ulous."

"All of us," said Sandy Willis. "Dot, too, of course." There was a short—very short—moment of silence between the women, whose starstruck gazes hadn't left Helena's face from the moment the actress had arrived at the conference room in a Diane Freis cocktail dress. "And don't forget Dawn and Kay. They're part of it, too. I'm sure Kay is going to be along any minute. She was that excited to be here."

Quill poured herself a glass of sherry and brooded. Where *was* Kay?

"Nobody answered at her house," said Connie. "Roosevelt and I drove by on our way here and her trailer was dark. Her car was gone."

Quill, startled, hadn't realized she'd spoken aloud. "She's a widow, isn't she?"

"Cancer," said Connie, nodding grimly. "Got him last year. He was only forty-six. Smoked like a chimney. Sons are grown and out of the house."

"Kay and Dawn were that close," said Sandy. She swallowed the last of a grapefruit and vodka drink Nate called a Fuzzy Navel. "Maybe Kay took out after Dawn, and that's why she's not here. Say—what happens if Dawn or Kay don't show up at all?"

Nobody answered this question. Helena had a brightly interested, concerned look that Quill thought as phony as a two-dollar bill. Except the Federal Mint had issued a two-dollar bill, hadn't it?

She set the sherry bottle down with a determined thump and brooded darkly. Myles would know about the two-dollar bill. And about what had happened to their forty-five hundred dollars. And whether Rickie Pennifarm had murdered poor Dot. Except Myles was in Ithaca. Or Syracuse. On the other hand, it looked very much like Myles McHale standing, no, looming in the doorway to the conference room. "Hey," said Quill. He looked terrific. She walked unsteadily out to the hall.

"Hey, yourself," said Myles. "I hear you discovered a body."

"That was no body. That was Dot Vandermolen." She blinked

at him. "Or Dawn Pennifarm. Or Kay Gondowski. They're all gone. Are you back to investigate?"

"The investigation can wait a bit. Dave did a credible job. And you were a good witness. You saw Rickie's pickup truck leaving the area near the shooting a few minutes before?"

Quill nodded and kept on nodding. "Heard the rifle shots, too, I think. But then, so did the mayor and Harvey and Esther. I don't know about Eloise Nicholson. She's pretty deaf. But you're back." She stopped nodding, not entirely certain why she'd started. "You don't think Rickie did it?"

"Dave's already got most of the force looking for him. He'll pick Rickie up eventually. We'll see when Dave brings him in. I'm back here to investigate Dawn Pennifarm. She's now been officially missing for more than seventy-two hours."

"She's run off with our money," Quill mourned. "And that's not all. The Bosses Club won a million dollars. The Inn's going to be on TV. Kay Gondowski's missing. And I don't like . . . certain people."

"Not me, I hope."

"Nope. Not you. Not good ol' gorgeous you. Certn'ly not you." Quill hiccuped.

Myles leaned forward, brushed her cheek with his lips, and inhaled. "Bad day?"

"Certn'ly not!" said Quill indignantly. "Well, moderately bad."

"Why don't I get you some coffee, and we'll talk about it."

"There's a whole fresh pot in the conference room." Quill leaned against the wall and closed her eyes. Time passed. Myles wrapped an arm around her and gave her a warm mug of coffee. She sipped at it, leaning into him. "That sherry must have hit me," she admitted. "It was just three little glasses. I think."

"That's quite a collection in there." Myles nodded toward the conference room. "Who's the blonde?"

"For the fourth—and last—time today," said Quill. "It's Helena Houndswood. Murderess." She explained. It took two more cups of coffee. By the third cup, her head had cleared. "So what I'm worried about is Kay. Honestly, Myles, you don't know Helena. She should have gone ballistic over these winners. And you went in there twice. And what was she doing?"

"She was quite pleasant," said Myles. "But then, some murderesses are."

"Quite pleasant. You see? I thought so," said Quill. "And if you don't call that suspicious, I don't know what you call suspicious." She squinted at him. "What do you think happened to Dawn Pennifarm? Do you think she took off with a bunch of payroll receipts from Paramount, and our forty-five hundred dollars? Or do you think Helena Houndswood paid her a tidy little sum on the side to disappear. And where's Kay? Tell me that!"

"One thing at a time, Quill. I haven't had time to look into Dot's death. As far as Dawn Pennifarm is concerned, we don't have charges on her. Hudson doesn't know if any money's missing or not."

"He doesn't know?"

"He claims that Dawn Pennifarm was 'empowered' to handle the bookkeeping, and his orders from New York are to let the employees make decisions pertinent to their job descriptions. He saw monthly numbers and didn't get involved in the day-to-day accounting. He won't know if there's a shortage until Dawn's backup gives him a report."

"That's Connie," said Quill. "She's Dawn's backup."

"As far as Dawn herself is concerned, I checked with the women's shelter. Bebe Cardoza said she came to some kind of crisis point last week during one of the group therapy sessions. My guess is that she headed for Detroit to her sister's. With or without your money."

"Dawn wouldn't have left now," said Quill instantly. "Not without her two hundred thousand dollars."

"You're assuming she knew about winning the two hundred thousand dollars, Quill. From what you've just told me, no one knew until today."

The look on Myles's face was all too familiar: wariness that she was sticking her nose into his investigations; slight amount of exasperation; amusement. Quill's frown turned into a scowl. "Dot's dead. Dawn's gone. And Kay is missing. None of this has anything to do with Rickie Pennifarm. If it does it's because of Helena Houndswood and that million dollars. Don't look at me like that."

Myles raised an eyebrow.

"That 'what does the little woman have in her pretty little head now,' look. Miss Kitty," she added obscurely.

"You're too young to remember *Gunsmoke*. What do you mean, Kay is missing, too? She's an hour overdue for a cocktail party."

"One of the most important things in her life! You should start thinking about the possibilities here, Myles."

"I don't think anything until I have some facts. And you don't think about this at all, Quill. You're licensed to run an Inn, not the Tompkins County sheriff's department. Connie Weyerhauser's here, isn't she? I need to talk to her. Bebe Cardoza said if Dawn had talked to anyone about where she was going, it'd be Connie."

"It's what, seven forty-five? We're serving dinner at eight o'clock for the Bosses Club. Helena's got a party coming in at eight-thirty, so they should be breaking up pretty soon. This was a sort of combination celebration and introduction. I'll take you in now, if you don't mind dealing with Helena. She's"—Quill hesitated—"a little difficult."

Helena was not difficult at all, which irritated Quill profoundly. "God, he's *gorgeous*," she whispered to Quill, after Myles had skillfully extracted Connie from the group. "Lucky old you . . . unless it's not what you'd call an exclusive relationship? Don't answer that. I'll be crushed if it is. Be a doll, make my excuses to these girls, will you? I've got to run up and change for dinner. My producer's due in for a meeting, and the poor lamb will be frantic if I'm late. You might see if he's checked in, by the way, and let me know. The lawyer, too, the schmuck. And tell that good-looking sheriff to stop by the table around nine-thirty or so, will you? My nose tells me something's going on with this Dawn person. We'll want a teensy bit of brandy in that nice dark Tavern Bar of yours. You'll arrange that? Girls!" She clapped her hands suddenly. Sandy and Connie fell worshipfully silent. "Tomorrow morning. Ten A.M. sharp. Makeup session. Eleven-thirty we'll have a chat with the lawyer people and get all that icky business stuff out of the way."

"Tomorrow morning?" said Sandy.

"Yes, darling. We don't want the grass to grow under our feet."

"We gotta work," said Sandy. "Line's changing over to latex."

"Well, of course, but the . . . what is it . . . paint people can do without you for a few hours. I'm sure there's other workers who can handle whatever."

"Line's changing over to latex," said Sandy desperately. "And with three of us gone . . ."

"What she means is that we've been running oil base for the last two weeks and we have to shut down, clean the ball mills and the mixers and get them ready to make latex paint," Connie said. "It's a complicated job, and you can't do it without the supervisors. We're the supervisors. You know, the Bosses Club."

"We'll quit," said Sandy.

"We're not doing anything until we get the money settled," Connie said. "Here's what we do, Sandy. We tell Hudson to schedule the changeover third shift."

"He won't pay overtime," warned Sandy.

"Who cares?" said Connie. "We're rich!"

"I do," said Quill. "You guys will be exhausted. You won't get any sleep."

"We wouldn't anyhow," said Sandy, grinning. "Makeovers? New clothes? Two hundred thousand bucks? Whoop!"

"Whoop!" added Connie, with her rich laugh.

"We're going to sit with the guys in the bar until dinner's ready," said Sandy. "You want to join us, Quill? The drinks are on us!"

"Bring them back here for dinner in about twenty minutes," said Quill. "That will give Kathleen time to set up. I'll join you as soon as I can."

"You'll have to excuse Sarah, girls," said Helena, "she's got to do some things for me. Check on those other arrangements for me, will you, Quill? And don't forget the hunk."

"Don't forget the hunk," Quill repeated gloomily in the

kitchen some minutes later. A walk through the herb gardens
at the back of the Inn had cleared her head of sherry fumes.
She'd come into the kitchen by the back door to a scene
of cheerful activity. The *sous* chefs simmered sauces and
grilled fish. Meg herself chopped meat at the long butcher's
block, whacking the bits in time to Figaro's aria from *Il
Barbiere*. The only Italian she remembered from the solo was
"bravissima Figaro," which made it repetitive as well as tune-
less. She abandoned the aria for nursery rhymes. "Ooooh . . ."
Meg sang, in response to Quill's summary of Helena's interest in Myles. "I went to the Animal Fair. The birds and
the beasts were there . . . And what became of the hunk, the
hunk, the hunk . . . No. Wait! I've got it!" She stopped short
and gesticulated wildly, the meat cleaver in her left hand.
This precipitated obvious anxiety on the part of the youngest
sous chef, a Russian exchange student at the Cornell School
of Hotel Management. Meg crouched double, raised her left
shoulder, dangled her left hand, and shuffled sideways across
the slate floor. "Hunk, Dr. Frankenstein? What hunk!" She
straightened up. The Cornell student eyed the meat cleaver in
alarm. "Remember? *Young Frankenstein*? Mel Brooks? Quill!
Snap out of it! We're going to be on TV! The world will
see our marvelousness. And the bookings will come rolling
in. . . ." Her face brightened as she was reminded of yet a
third song. Andrew Lloyd Webber·suffered next: "And the
boo—o-okings kept rolling in from every side. Evita's pretty
hands stretched far and they stretched wide. . . ."

"In one of her fits, is she?" said Doreen, stomping through
the swinging doors that led from the dining room. Simulta-
neously she and Quill bent over to look at Meg's socks.

"Argyle," said Quill.

"Figures," said Doreen. They straightened up. "She needs
to go on those there friendly fresh-air hikes. Best thing for
her. Clear her head. Get right up near to God and Nature."

"So they're all settled in?"

"Ayuh. They like it fine. Anyhow, they need a bunch more
rooms for next week. Said it's one of the best places they bin.
They ast me to join 'em." Doreen smoothed her apron with a
pleased expression.

"Uh-oh," said Meg.

Quill, foreseeing the end of the stationery, which had been so uneventful, commented that the FOFA people had seemed very nice in a tone wistful with hope.

"Don't know about nice," said Doreen in a considering way. "Don't know that folks been persecuted like them are nice. Brave, more like."

"Persecuted? Hikers?" shrieked Meg. "Pooh!"

Doreen gave it as her opinion that them Quakers weren't as peaceful as they made out.

"You mean they're the 'Friends of Fresh Air' as in the Quakers are called the Friends?" said Quill.

"Ay-uh."

"But the Quakers are pacifists," said Meg. "And I thought the FOFA people were environmentalists or something."

"Yes, ma'am," said Doreen, "and you know about farmers. Them farmer Quakers just persecuted them Friends of the Fresh Air right out of the Church." There was a familiar, fanatical gleam in Doreen's beady eyes.

Meg and Quill exchanged a look. Meg's said, "Don't ask."

"What's this about farmers and environmentalists?" asked Quill.

"Horse shit," said Doreen.

"I beg your pardon?"

"Manure," said Meg. "I heard part of this while you were occupied with the Bosses Club. Manure disposal, to be precise. I was at the Heavenly Hogg's Farm today to order sausage, and you wouldn't believe the hassle over proper manure disposal. Mickey Dooley was telling me all about it."

Quill's sherry intake had left her with a monster headache. She remembered Doreen's entrepreneurial track record. She briefly mourned the demise of the stationery business. "Doreen."

"Yes'm?"

"Are the FOFA people here to stage a protest over Hemlock Falls' farmers' manure disposal practices?"

"No'm."

"They aren't going to march down Main Street waving signs about slurry control?"

"No, ma'am."

"All that's happening is that they absolutely love this place and want to book more rooms for the next week?"

"Yes, ma'am. If there's room. Thing is, they like that the TV people are gonna be here. On account of they're celebrities."

Quill eyed her, frustrated.

"Star magic," said Meg. "See? It's working already, I told you, didn't I?"

"Yes," said Quill, "it's great."

John came into the kitchen.

"My god," said Meg, "he's smiling."

"What is it?" said Quill. "Dawn Pennifarm showed up with the check?"

"Almost better than that." John swung a long leg over a stool and sat down. "We're totally booked for the next six weeks. Between the Houndswood TV people and FOFA, we're full. No Vacancy. Full House."

Meg performed a drumroll with her wooden spoons. "So soon, John?"

"I got a call from the Golden Pillar people . . ."

"That huge travel agency?" said Meg.

"They've heard she's staying here, and reserved half the rooms for the fall season. Once word gets out, they said, their clients are going to come down in droves. And"—he paused impressively—"*L'Aperitif* called. They want to review us for that fourth star." Meg screamed. "But not until early next year. Come with me and just take a look at the dining room, Quill. All of you."

They followed John to the double doors. Doreen pushed them open a crack. The room was jammed. Helena Houndswood sat at the table in the center of the room, directly under the crystal chandelier. The light gleamed on her golden hair. There were three men with her; the lawyer and the director, Quill guessed, and the third, broad shoulders straining his old tweed sport coat, was Myles "Hunk" McHale.

"Will you look at that," marveled Doreen, "sitting jawing at the table just like she was anybody ordinary and not a stuck-up actress with a swole upper lip. Wonder what the sheriff thinks?"

Helena leaned forward and spoke into Myles's ear.

Myles threw back his head and laughed.

"Stop that," ordered Doreen, "bad for ya."

"Stop what?" said Quill.

"Grinding your teeth," said Meg.

CHAPTER 5

◆

With John right behind her, Quill pushed through the swinging doors. Meg's manic mood should have tipped her off; the dining room was full to overflowing and a riot of noise assaulted her. Extra tables had been tucked into the corners of the room. She had chosen mauve, cream, rose, and pale yellow to complement the view of the falls and enhance the enjoyment of Meg's food, but the room's usual quiet serenity was gone, swallowed up by bodies, food, and chatter.

Their waiters swirled around the room like skaters on a pond, trays held high over the diners' heads. Peter Hairston, one of the Cornell graduate students without whom Quill couldn't have staffed the Inn, gave her a high sign and pointed at Helena's table, miming "wine." John, whose knowledge of wines precluded the need for an official *sommelier*, threaded his way deftly toward Helena Houndswood's table and struck up a properly serious conversation with a slender, harried-looking man with a bald head. The producer, thought Quill. And she owed Meg a dollar and a half; Helena had changed for the fourth time into a little black dress that was very black, very little, and exposed a lot of gorgeous bosom. At Helena's left, a man with gray hair and a square, florid face was eating his way through what looked like Meg's latest experiment in starters, crab profiteroles. The lawyer. The fourth person at the table was, of course, Myles McHale, with the slight smile that always jolted Quill's heart. They were seated at table seven, the one with the most sweeping view of the gorge and the

66

waterfall. Helena's teeth gleamed wolfishly white under the chandelier.

Most of the prominent citizens of Hemlock Falls were crowded at the surrounding tables, at a respectful distance. Their faces, thought Quill crossly, resembled the carp in the pond outside: bulging eyes, mouths open, rubbery lips. Elmer Henry sat with his wife, Adela, and Esther West. Howie Murchison, the town attorney and justice of the peace, shared a table with Harvey Bozzel and a blond cashier from the SuperSaver. It was hard to tell whether the blonde was with Harvey or Howie. Quill wondered briefly at Claire Murchison's absence. Even the Reverend Dookie Shuttleworth sat at a table for six with two of his deacons and their wives, Dookie conspicuous for his completely bewildered expression. Quill spied Marge Schmidt and Betty Hall, partners at the Hemlock Hometown Diner, at a table for two against the north wall. Marge waved a beefy fist. Quill waved back and threaded her way through the crowd, murmuring greetings. People were excited in a repressed, self-conscious way: elaborately casual attitudes (knees carelessly crossed, elbows on the table); overly careful speech ("Please pardon us, Ms. Quilliam, can we move this chair out of your way a little bit?"); and a great deal of attention to hair and clothing ("This old thing? I've had it in the closet for years, Elmer. Of course you've seen it before. Comb your hair, dear. Not at the table! Go to the men's room.").

"Good grief," said Quill when she reached Marge and Betty's table.

"Hook a chair for Quill from Norm's table, Betty, willya?" At Norm Pasquale's protest, Marge's heavy jaw thrust forward in instant belligerence. "Stuff it, Norm, you ain't using it." Quelled, Norm sank into silence. Marge extended a pudgy hand, and Quill shook it warmly. "How's it goin'?"

"Okay, I guess," Quill said. Aware of the dubiety in her tone, she grinned suddenly at Marge, who grinned back.

"Looks a bitch, from here," said Marge. She shot a penetrating look at Helena Houndswood from under a beetling brow. Her massive cheeks rotated slowly, and she swallowed the last of Meg's country pâté with a small burp. "Good business, though."

"Very good," Quill agreed. "For the whole town, I should think. She's going to feature the village on the TV show, you know."

"No kiddin'."

"John says that these production crews usually have the crew meals catered. We thought you two might be interested. You won't mind if we mention you to them?"

"Hell, no." Marge chuckled. Even Betty smiled faintly, drawing delicately on her cigarette, then carefully stubbing it out. "Things pickin' up for you, then."

"I hope so."

"Good. We could use a few more a them brochures of yours near the cash register. Running a little low."

"Thanks." Quill straightened the crystal salt and pepper shakers. Marge and Betty's Hemlock Hometown Diner was *locum* for any and all town gossip. Most of the men and women from the surrounding farms had breakfast there at least one day a week—and all the businesspeople in town lunched there. "So what have you heard?"

"Heard about Dot."

"Did you know her, Marge?"

"Nope. Came into the diner once, maybe twice. No more'n that. Piece of work, though, wouldn't you say, Betty?"

Betty, who was as thin as Marge was fat, examined her lipstick in the bowl of her soup spoon. "Not as much of a troublemaker as that Dawn Pennifarm. But I wouldn't call her a good old girl. Not by a long shot. Does anyone know who did it, that's what I want to know. Didn't think Dot was neighborly enough to make enemies."

Quill thought this through for a moment and decided it made sense. "Kept to herself, then. So the town thinks . . . what?"

"Accident," said Marge laconically. "Now, about this million bucks." Marge was clearly unimpressed with the sum involved; as one of the richest residents of Tompkins County, she didn't need to be.

"Yes," said Quill, with the distinct feeling that Marge wasn't changing the subject.

"Kinda oiled her way into that china contest," said Marge. "From what I hear."

"Sandy told you?" said Quill. "Was she upset about it?"

Marge nodded, her chins folding and unfolding like a fan.

"Million split four ways, now. Very nice for 'em," Betty agreed.

Marge dusted her hands briskly together. "You heard Dawnie's gone missing?"

"Myles just put out an APB this evening."

"And for Rickie, too, I hear." Marge regarded her with a sapient eye.

Quill took the bull by the horns. "Do you think something funny is going on?"

"Where's that no-good son-of-a-bitch husband of hers? That'd be my guess."

"Buffalo," said Betty.

"Buffalo?" said Quill.

"Been there a week. Got back today I guess, in time to shoot Dot. He was in for breakfast last Sunday just before he left. Got fired from the Qwik Freeze for mouthing off. Looking to find work in Buffalo, he said." She picked a flake of tobacco off her tongue. Marge grunted. "All that ol' boy's looking for is trouble. Thanks, honey."

Kathleen Kiddermeister, one of the Inn's more reliable waitresses, placed a steamed artichoke in front of Marge and a plate of cold asparagus in front of Betty. Marge daintily stripped an artichoke leaf and tasted it. "Tell Meg this is good, but she's a little heavy with the comfrey."

"I will, thanks." Quill knew that Marge was a good cook, and had an even better palate. Meg had said once that if Marge ever went into gourmet, instead of what the diner owner referred to as "Four Square American," she'd hang up her wooden spoon. "So you think Rickie's behind this."

Betty breathed on her soup spoon and polished it with her sleeve. Marge ate another artichoke leaf. "Tell you what I think," Marge said flatly. "It might look like that ol' Rickie done away with Dawn and shot Dot in the woods this after-noon. Might look like that. But Rickie can't hit the broad side of a barn on a cold day in Juneau. So, I'd say if he done Dot, it was an accident. Ain't nobody proved he done Dawn, neither."

"I'll tell you what," said Quill, her gaze drifting to Helena, who had one scarlet-nailed hand on Myles's knee, "I don't think Rickie's involved, either." Quill rose and replaced the chair at Norm Pasquale's table with a word of thanks. The high school bandleader and his wife didn't respond. They were gaping at Helena Houndswood, along with the rest of the diners. Everybody had been seduced, except, Quill thought, for good old pragmatic Marge.

"Be seein' you at the chamber meeting tomorrow?" said Marge.

"Yes. Lunchtime."

"Elmer didn't tell you? We thought we'd come around ten. Conference room's available, ain't it?"

"Sure," said Quill. "Have we got that much business to discuss?"

"TV people'll be here," Betty explained. "Whole town's going to want to see what they do with the girls."

"Makeover," sighed Marge. She belched, patted her ample stomach, and fixed her little turret eyes on Helena Houndswood. "I hear she can make the plainest old girl look just like her. I hear that she ain't even all that cute when they take the makeup off, and all." She sighed, a little wistfully. "She's sure got that Myles goin', though, don't she?"

"Does she? I'm afraid I didn't notice," said Quill with an assumption of carelessness and decided that she really needed an aspirin from the reception desk. She walked by Helena's table with a gracious, rather queenly air, and nodded casually to Myles. He waved one hand in her direction without taking his eyes from Helena's face.

The aspirin was in its usual place at the reception desk, which was without its usual receptionist. Quill, aware of irascability, found Dina lurking in the kitchen, one eye between the crack in the swinging doors. "Can you believe Ms. Houndswood's dress?!" she said as Quill ushered her back to the lobby. "I mean, have you ever seen anything more fabulous in your life? It's just—"

"Fabulous," agreed Quill. "Dina, I know you want to look at Helena Houndswood, but you really shouldn't have left your post. You know our rule about the phones."

"But I was looking for you!" said Dina indignantly. "There's been these weird phone calls."

"Weird? You mean obscene calls? You're okay, aren't you?"

"Oh, mouth-breathers." Dina dismissed this with an airy hand. "No. I mean weird. Some guy who sounds drunk out of his mind asking if Dawn Pennifarm's here. That's the bookkeeper that's run off with all our money, isn't it? I said no the first time, and then he called back, and called back, and I finally decided I should talk to you or John about it, and that's why I was in the kitchen, it wasn't because I'm, like, some starstruck kid who hangs around backstage."

"If it's Dawn's husband we'd better get some help. Is Myles still slobbering . . . where's Sheriff McHale?"

"Right in there with Her," breathed Dina. "Didn't you see?"

"Oh! Yes. Come to think of it, I did see him at her table." Dina's cynical expression, Quill felt, was unbecoming to her tender years. "I'll go see now. In the meantime, would you check with Mr. Whitman for me? He told Doreen he wanted more rooms for next week. Make sure you cross-check with John about how many TV people are going to be here, so we don't overbook."

"Yes, ma'am," said Dina. "Can you believe all the business She's brought in? It's simply *fab*—"

"Dina!"

"Yes, ma'am."

Quill looked at Dina's fresh and innocent face. She thought of Meg in the kitchen, ebulliently cooking her way toward fame and fortune. She thought of Myles "Hunk" McHale flirting like any starstruck fool. She was, she thought, jealous.

"Dina," she said, "I am such a jerk."

"No, you aren't."

Quill squinted at her.

Dina patted her arm. "Myles thinks you're the absolute nuts. *I* think you're the absolute nuts. She's just . . . famous. Everybody gets a little wonky around somebody famous. She'll leave, and it'll be all over. You'll see."

Quill drew a deep breath.

The phone rang.

"Don't answer that!" said Dina.

"Don't answer the phone?" said Quill. "You think it might be the guy after Dawn?"

"Let me get on the extension first. I'll go into your office. Then Myles'll have corroborating evidence."

"No. *You* get Myles and I'll try to keep him on the phone. Then he can hear for himself."

Dina raced out of the foyer. Quill picked up the phone.

"Quill?" A lost voice. Thick, foggy. Slow. A woman's voice. "Quill? Can you help? I need help."

"Kay?" shouted Quill. "Kay, where are you?"

Tires squealed out front. A shotgun blast splintered the front door. A hornet bit her temple. The phone flew out of Quill's hand. She shouted, surprised. Blood ran down her cheek and drenched the white silk of her shirt.

There was an eclipse of light; an interval with time suspended. The first and only time she'd had an anesthetic was at fourteen, when she'd had her wisdom teeth extracted. She felt like that now, a little buzzy, remote, aware of the room and the people in it at a distance.

She felt as though she'd slipped into a parallel dimension.

"No hot soup," said Quill.

"She's dee-lirious," said a familiar voice. "Get a ice pack." Doreen.

Quill's cheek was crushed against a hard fabric-covered surface that moved up and down. She had a warm hat on her head. She blinked. The surface was Myles's chest; the hat his hand cupping her head.

It started to rain.

"Doreen, put that ice down," said her sister. "She's not delirious, she's been shot."

Angry voices shouted beyond the shattered front foyer. Myles's chest was replaced by her sister's. The floor shook with pounding feet.

Quill sat up. Her head was clearing. Her stomach lurched. "May I have some Alka-Seltzer?" she said.

"The ambulance is coming. Can you just lie back and take a couple of deep breaths?" Meg's voice held a note Quill had only heard once before, the night the highway patrol called to tell her Colin had been in the accident that had killed him.

"Meg, I'm fine." She peered at her upper arm. Her silk blouse was stained red. Her head hurt. She looked up at Meg. "What the heck *happened*?"

Meg's face was pale. Her hair stuck up in spikes. She smiled anxiously. "Somebody blasted the front door with a shotgun. It looks like you got in the way."

"Dissatisfied guest?" Quill sat up.

"Very funny. Just sit there, Quill. Andy Bishop's coming and so's the ambulance. Myles said don't move."

Quill frowned. Her head hurt like the dickens. "There's something I have to remember. Just before this happened?"

"Shock," said Doreen in gloomy satisfaction.

"This is so embarrassing," said Quill. "I'm fine."

She got unsteadily to her feet, Meg holding her firmly. The foyer was as jammed as it had been earlier when everyone had shown up at once to see Helena Houndswood. Doreen, John, and Meg surrounded her; beyond them seemed to be everyone who'd been within hollering distance of the Inn: Elmer and the rest of the Chamber of Commerce members; the FOFA people; Helena and her lawyer and producer.

"Nuts," said Quill. She looked helplessly at John, who promptly and tactfully began to move people back to the dining room.

"I don't care what the sheriff said, you go upstairs and lay down," said Doreen fiercely. Then, to Meg, "You take your sister up to her room, Missy. I'll go get the first-aid kit and be right on up." She peered at Quill's temple. "Guess I'll bring the sewing kit."

"I guess you won't!" said Meg, startled. "Why don't you stay here and tell Myles where we are?" She walked behind Quill up the stairs, arms extended protectively, until Quill told her crossly not to be an ass.

"So what happened?" asked Meg, once they'd reached the privacy of Quill's rooms.

Quill explored her forehead with tentative fingers. Her hand came away sticky with blood. "I thought you could tell me."

"Let me see that." Meg grabbed her arm. "Ugh. Looks a

mess." She went into the bathroom. Quill heard the sound of running water. Meg re-emerged with a damp towel and began to sponge off Quill's temple. The color was back in her cheeks.

"Ow!" said Quill. "That stings."

"Just shut up. Andy'll be here in a minute. If you were a Rock Cornish game hen, I'd put a few stitches into you myself, but since you're not, I'll wait for him."

"Meg, there's something I have to remember. It's important. What happened exactly?"

"Well, it's no use asking me. *I* don't have the foggiest idea of what happened. I heard this 'boom!'—then Dina started to scream and I ran into the foyer along with half the population of the village and there you were sitting on the floor with this confused look on your face and blood all over your head and neck."

"I thought I'd been stung by a wasp."

"There was blood all over the wall behind you. We'll have to repaint. Anyhow, I went over and tried to make you lie down. Myles thundered in behind me along with a bunch of guys from the lounge." Meg began to wave her arms dramatically, the towel a pink-stained flag. "He pulled his six-shooter—"

"It's a thirty-eight," said Quill dampingly.

"Whatever, and raced to the front door, yelling, 'Get down!' It was thrilling. He looked out the front door, holding the gun up just like in the movies. He looked back at you— simply *haggard* with despair, as Esther West might say—and I said, 'She's alive!' " Meg snapped the towel with relish. Quill ducked out of the way. "He was back in a few minutes, minus the handcuffs in his belt, I should add, and came and picked you up like a baby. Then you came to and said you wanted soup. What kind of soup? I'll get you some."

"I wasn't unconscious," said Quill indignantly, "and I didn't want soup. I said 'no hot soup.' I remember everything except what happened right before and after I was shot."

A sharp knock sounded at the door, and it opened almost immediately.

"Doc Bishop," said Meg, "and his handy little black bag."

They grinned at each other. Andy was fair, with the tight-knit slender build of a tennis player. He'd opened a family practice in Hemlock Falls soon after the sisters opened the Inn. He was single, and for a few years there'd been a succession of pretty office nurses until he hired the stolid wife of an auto mechanic who'd settled in with a firm hand and a gimlet eye. Quill, noticing Andy and Meg notice each other, had a flicker of hope.

"Wow," said Andy, examining her temple with light sensitive fingers. "You were lucky. I came through that front door and wondered if I'd brought enough catgut." He set his bag on the floor and pushed Quill gently into an arm chair. "I'm going to clean that up and give you a shot of Novocain. This is going to take a stitch or two."

"Is there a bullet in there?" Meg asked with what Quill felt to be ghoulish interest.

"Nope. She's lucky," said Andy. "It was a rifle, with 270 caliber bullets. Rickie Pennifarm hunts deer, I guess, when he isn't hunting his wife. And no, there are no bullets in there."

"Dawn Pennifarm's husband shot me?" said Quill. "Did he shoot Dot, too? Is he crazy?"

Andy drew on a pair of plastic gloves and selected a syringe. Quill winced at the sting of the anesthetic. "Do you know what happened?"

Andy broke open a packet of catgut and threaded a needle. "Count backward from ten." The *snick* of the needle made a sound like a small bite into an apple. Quill made a face at her sister. "Myles had Rickie handcuffed in the patrol car, and the weapon in custody. He's waiting for Deputy Dave to take Rickie off to the slammer, then he'll be up. My guess is Rickie thought Dawn was here, although everyone downstairs is saying he wanted to get rid of you because you were a witness to his getaway from Dot's murder this afternoon. Maybe he thought Dawn was Dot in the woods today. I heard Dawn was missing, and that Rickie was slamming all over town looking for her. What do you remember about tonight, Quill?"

"Nothing," said Quill. "And it's driving me crazy. I know there's something important, but all I can recall is dragging

Dina back from the kitchen to her post at reception. It's the oddest thing, Andy; after that, the next thing I remember is my wisdom teeth."

"No hot soup!" said Meg in triumph.

"Retrograde amnesia," said Andy. "Often happens after an accident. Your memory will come back in a couple of days. And besides, Dina should remember. She was there." He knotted the catgut, snipped it off with a pair of surgical scissors, and swabbed the wound with a piece of cotton. "Not too bad, if I do say so myself."

"There was a phone call," said Quill with an effort. She yawned suddenly.

Andy snapped on a penlight, looked into her eyes and suggested a good night's sleep. "I've got some Demerol, if you need a painkiller."

Quill shook her head. She felt fine. "I don't think I need anything." She yawned again, convulsively. "I'm just so sleepy all of a sudden."

"Shock," said Andy briefly, "no biggie. Get a good night's sleep and don't get that wet until I take the stitches out. Anything else I can do for you? Cissie Axminister's dilated four centimeters, and I should get back to the hospital. Labor," he added unnecessarily. Outside, the ambulance wail rose to a shriek and died abruptly. "I'll head those guys off, Quill. Meg, are you coming downstairs with me?"

"I'd better wait until Myles gets here."

He left, with a swift, intimate smile for Meg.

"Oh, ho," said Quill, "blows the wind in that quarter?"

"He's asked me out a couple of times for coffee," said Meg with a shrug. "I told you that."

"You told me you gave him a 'heck, no.' He looked like he'd gotten a 'well, maybe.' "

"Well, maybe," said Meg.

Andy had left the door slightly ajar. Myles pushed it aside and walked in. There were lines in his face Quill hadn't seen there before. Quill got to her feet and, to her astonishment, began to cry.

"Shock," said Meg wisely, patting her back. "Maybe I should pour you a glass of sherry."

Myles held her, carefully. "She just needs some sleep."

"Did you lock Rickie up?" asked Meg. "Did you find out what happened from Dina?"

"Dina's had a fit of hysterics. Says she can't remember a thing. I collared Andy downstairs to give her a sedative. And Rickie's on his way to jail."

Quill blew her nose into Myles's handkerchief, cleared her throat, and said in a rather foggy way that she couldn't remember anything, either, but she'd be damned if she had hysterics.

"Did he shoot Dot, too?" asked Meg.

"It's possible." Myles touched Quill's bandaged temple. "Dina did say that there's been a series of phone calls to the desk from a man who sounded like Pennifarm." He set Quill back in her chair, took her bathrobe from the back of the bathroom door, and wrapped it around her shoulders. "Did you take any of the calls?"

Quill shook her head. "I don't remember."

"Andy said her memory would be back in a couple of days," offered Meg. "Any leads on Dawn at all? I think you should borrow my meat mallet and pound the truth out of that little creep. I'll bet he shot both Dawn and Dot and tried to get Quill."

"I think we should hang on a bit until we've collected all the facts. Connie Weyerhauser said the whole Bosses Club knew that this was the week the win would be announced. Dawn was sure they were going to win. Connie said she was planning to use the money to move out of Hemlock Falls and away from Rickie. She doesn't think that Dawn would have gone anywhere far, just yet. If Rickie scared her off, Connie's convinced she's hiding somewhere near here. Who knows? Now that Rickie's in custody, she may come out of hiding."

"She's not at the battered women's shelter?" asked Quill.

"No. And her sister in Detroit hasn't heard from her. Connie did suggest checking with Kay Gondowski. Kay still hasn't shown up for the celebration, and it's what . . . nine o'clock . . . but Kay lives alone, and Connie thinks she would have helped hide Dawn from Rickie."

"If that's what happened," said Quill. "Myles, don't you think it's very odd that two of the winners of this contest have disappeared in as many days and a third one's been shot!?"

"Yes," said Myles.

"What about Sandy and Connie?" demanded Quill. "Are you putting guards on them, or something? I mean, what if I'm right and Helena Houndswood is approaching each one of them in turn to pay them off so they won't embarrass her. And if they won't accept a payoff . . ."

"You might be right," said Myles equably. "It's just as likely that we're dealing with separate instances. We have a reasonable explanation for all the events except Dot's murder. Rickie says he didn't do it. Said his pickup ran out of gas near the park. He left it there and walked to the gas station. When he came back he claims someone had fired his rifle and replaced it in the gun rack."

"And you believe that?" Meg demanded.

"That gives Helena Houndswood means, motive, and opportunity," said Quill. "She was in the woods exactly at the time Dot was murdered."

"So were the rest of the Bosses Club," said Myles. "Hudson finally let them go at four-thirty."

Quill stared at him. "You've got to put a tail on Helena, Myles, before the whole Bosses Club ends up in the ravine."

"Oh, come on," said Meg. "The woman's a TV star, Quill, and you don't climb to the top of her profession by letting a little setback like the Bosses Club throw you for a loop."

"You don't know her," said Quill sleepily, "she's bananas on the subject of the crème de la crème and the New York Four Hundred and all kinds of things." This time when she yawned, her jaw almost broke.

"What happens to the million dollars if there's only, say, one member of the Bosses Club left?" asked Meg.

"I checked with Helena's lawyer at dinner," said Myles. "The money's not assignable."

"And that means . . . ?" asked Meg.

"And that means it's like a tontine; the survivor takes all."

Quill put her head in her hands. "Then that might mean . . . Connie?! Or Sandy?! I don't believe it."

"You need to follow Andy's advice and get some sleep." He picked her up out of the chair easily.

"I'll get back to the kitchen," said Meg. "Is there anything I can do, Quill? Do you want some soup? No? Then I'll see you in the morning." She left, closing the door quietly behind her.

Quill submitted to being put to bed by Myles with reasonable grace. He stood looking down at her, his face shadowed behind the circle of light cast by the nightstand lamp.

"You don't think Sandy or Connie has anything to do with this, do you?"

"Go to sleep, dear heart."

"You never call me dear heart," said Quill sleepily.

"Not since the last time you were shot."

"You're the least sentimental man I know."

"Would it help, Quill, if I were more sentimental?"

"No," said Quill, "it'd help if you'd appreciate how good I am at detecting and let me help you solve your cases."

He snapped off the light. "I'm going back to headquarters. Andrew thought I should sleep at my place tonight. I can sleep on the couch, here, if you need me, Quill."

"No," said Quill, "I'll be fine."

She woke in the middle of the night, and said into the empty darkness, "Kay?" as though she had been called, and getting no answer, went back to sleep.

CHAPTER 6

Quill woke suddenly just before the morning alarm, urgency and a sharp headache both propelling her out of bed. For an entire year after she and Meg had purchased the Inn, she'd had dreams of missing the opening of a new show, nightmares of searching the crowded streets of New York for a gallery address she could no longer remember. The same feeling nagged at her through a hasty bath and a close inspection of her head wound. It felt inches deep and a mile wide. She peeled the bandage back and saw a neatly stitched incision about the size of a tarragon leaf. She searched irritably through her closet for a loose-fitting blouse that would be comfortable and cool enough for what promised to be an unusually warm June day, then hurried downstairs to the reception desk. Maybe Dina was in, her hysteria gone. Maybe she remembered what Quill had forgotten. Dina wasn't at her post, but the director of the Friends of Fresh Air was. Makepeace Whitman and his wife were flushed and sweaty from an early morning hike. Quill introduced herself and apologized for failing to greet them when they'd arrived. "But I see you've already made yourself familiar with the grounds. Did you have a good hike?"

All the Friends of Fresh Air had the indefinable air of Renaissance saints, Makepeace and his wife in particular. They were both blond and slender. Their skins glowed with a well-scrubbed pink Quill associated with babies. They smelled of mint and rosemary.

"We saw the sun come up over the gorge," said Mrs. Whitman in her soft voice. "The light was purely of the Lord's making."

They linked hands.

"The air's magnificent here," said her husband. "Very little taint of the city."

"We saw a rose-breasted grosbeak," said Mrs. Whitman. "Exquisite!"

Quill thought of the china. "They're rare," she said, "but they're beautiful birds."

"Disappearing before the advance of man and the gasoline engine," said Makepeace with disapproval, "as are many of God's creatures of the air and earth."

"Yes," said Quill, "I'm so sorry."

"We simply bathed in the sunshine," said Mrs. Whitman, "and we feel so refreshed."

"You must be hungry, then. Would you like me to make arrangements for breakfast? If you don't want to eat here, there's a very nice diner in town."

"Bacon"—Makepeace shook his head—"and sausage, no doubt. These small-town diners. It's a constant wonder to me that places as close to nature as Hemlock Falls should have diners. Do you have a full range of yogurts?"

"If we don't have what you like, just ask, Mr. Whitman. We'll be happy to get it for you. Are the arrangements all right? Is there anything we can do to make you more comfortable?"

They exchanged a limpid blue gaze.

"This actress disrupts things," Makepeace complained.

"That disturbance last night . . ." said Mrs. Whitman, "and the hunting accident."

"Disruptions in the natural flow," her husband concluded. "Very distressing."

"Miss Houndswood is here for her television show," said Quill. "The disruption will be for a while, I'm afraid. As for last night . . ."

"Gunshots!" said Mrs. Whitman. She shuddered. "*Not* what we expected."

"I'm so sorry," said Quill. "But our sheriff's very capable, and the man is in custody. It's possible he was responsible for both incidents. It must have been very upsetting. Are you from a farming community yourselves?" She thought of the Amish. "Pennsylvania?"

"Queens," said Mrs. Whitman.

"Queens, New York?" said Quill.

"Last night," said Makepeace reprovingly, "was not at all conducive to the healthful contemplation of nature's glories."

"No. I suppose not. If there's anything at all I can do for you . . ."

"Perhaps maps?" suggested Makepeace. "Of hiking areas well away from the polluting areas?"

"Maps? We would be glad to provide maps."

"And if my wife and I could alert the rest of our group as to where these television cameras might be—"

"Oh, that won't be for weeks yet," Quill assured him.

"We would like to know, just in case," said Mrs. Whitman. Her blue eyes drifted to the ceiling, and she repeated dreamily, "Just in case. One never knows about these people."

"I'll see what I can do. If you'll excuse me. Our receptionist's just come in, and I need to speak with her. About those maps." Quill gave Dina a small wave of recognition and stepped aside as the Whitmans went up the stairs.

"That's the cleanest couple I've ever seen," Dina observed as she watched them leave. "How are you doing? You sleep okay? Does you head hurt? Jeez . . ." She examined it with frank curiosity. "It looks *awful*."

"I'm fine," said Quill. "It was just a scratch. Dina, what do you—"

"Just a scratch? You get half-killed by a maniac with a shotgun and you call it just a scratch? Did you see the wall! Gross!" She pointed at the speckles of blood on the cream paint.

"There's more blood on the wall than there was on me," Quill said. "It'll need repainting, though. Maybe you could mention it to Mike when you see him. He's mowing today, but tell him the lawn can wait. Dina, what do you remember of last night?"

"It was horrible. Horrible!" She settled behind the reception desk with a thump. "I had nightmares all night. Like one of those tapes on an endless loop, you know? I kept seeing it over and over again in my mind. Like when I saw that Freddy Kreuger movie a few years ago and just could not get that scene with the cheerleader out of my mi—"

"So you remember what happened?"

"Sure! Freddy's got these steel knife fingernails—"

"I mean about the shooting."

"Remember! I'm going to replay this for the rest of my—"

"Tell me exactly what happened."

"You don't remember? Did you hit your head when the blast knocked you over? You mean you have amnesia?"

"It's kind of amnesia, but Andy Bishop said it will go away after a few days. I can't recall a thing except finding you in the kitchen. And I have the most awful feeling that something important happened after that."

"You got shot," said Dina with a kindly, let-me-help-you expression.

"I know I was shot. What happened before I was shot?"

"Well, we came back here. And you were saying how you hated Helena Houndswood and everything . . ."

"I was?" Quill flushed guiltily. "Did I say anything really awful?"

"Not in so many words. But you were kinda—jealous like— you know? Specially since she was sucking up to Myles, and I guess he wasn't feeling too bad about that himself. . . ."

"We came back here." Quill placed herself in front of the desk. "And you sat down . . ."

"And I sat down, and I told you not to answer the phone."

"Not to answer the phone?"

"Yeah. And that's what you said. 'You don't want me to answer the phone?' And I said, 'Rickie Pennifarm keeps calling and making the most gruesome threats, and then hanging up,' and you said, 'Get Myles.'"

"What kind of threats?"

"Oh, you know. Like, 'Is Dawn Pennifarm there? You better find her. I have to talk to her.' Drunk," said Dina with relish, "drunk and crazy, and then he tried to kill her and ended up almost killing you."

"So he called . . . how many times?"

"Oh, I don't know. Five. Six maybe. And then he called one last time and you picked up the phone and I went to find Myles. What did he say? More threats, probably."

"I can't remember any of this." Quill ran her hands through her hair. "Not a bloody thing. You say I picked up the phone . . ."

"And then I heard this gigantic roar, of his pickup truck, you know, and then like a wheelie, you know, the tires squealed, and then 'Blam!' this gigundous blast shook the door."

Quill walked over to the front door and pulled it open. The edge of the frame was splintered with buckshot. The door itself was intact. "Was the door open?"

Dina frowned. "Yeah. It must have been. I leave it open summer nights because it gets so warm in here. So the gunshot blasts through the foyer and you scream 'I've been shot! My god, I've been shot!' "

"I did?"

"Well, maybe not those exact words. I would have, that's for sure. And I came running back and you were passed out on the floor. That must have been when you hit your head," said Dina kindly.

"I didn't hit my head. And I'm pretty sure I just sat down. I didn't fall." She frowned with the effort of recollection. "I had the phone in my hand, you say?"

Dina nodded vigorously. "Talking to that crazy Rickie Pennifarm."

"How could I be talking to Rickie Pennifarm? He was outside blasting the doorframe with his deer rifle."

"Jeez. That's right." Dina looked genuinely puzzled.

"So if I wasn't talking to Rickie Pennifarm because he was outside in his pickup truck, who was I talking to?"

"Beats me."

"Who put the phone back on the hook?"

"Gosh, Quill. I have no idea. Somebody must have, though. I mean the lobby was full of all these people in about sixty seconds, and Sheriff McHale was holding on to you looking like he was going to *kill* who'd ever done it, and Meg was practically fainting . . . and everybody was screaming and everything. It was," she said with satisfaction, "a real mess."

"This doesn't sound right," said Quill.

"I'm not saying my memory's perfect," said Dina indignantly, "but I saw what I saw."

Quill pulled at her lower lip. "I hope Andy's right. I hope this comes back to me." She shook her head. "I'll go nuts if I try to force it, or start to remember things that didn't happen at all."

"I have to give a deposition, you know," said Dina. "You have to give two. One about finding that Dot Vandermolen, and the other about getting shot. Myles said I was too upset to take a statement right then and there, so both of us have to go down to the sheriff's office this afternoon and tell Deputy Dave what happened. Do you think you'll remember who it was on the phone by then?"

"What time are we supposed to be there?"

"Myles said the sooner the better. He said as soon as I felt calm enough to go down, I should. He said to let you sleep. But here you are—up and around and everything. I'd feel calmer if you went with me. But I've got to do my shift this morning, so I was thinking maybe this afternoon. But we can go together, Quill, can't we?"

"Of course we can. I've just got to get through the Chamber of Commerce meeting."

Quill ate a quick breakfast and methodically went to all the staff present to ask who'd hung the phone up the night before. She was met with blank incomprehension, earnest efforts to remember—and no answers. By ten o'clock, when the chamber members began to arrive for the ad hoc meeting, the sense of unease was a steady presence in the back of her mind.

She was, for once, prompt for a Chamber of Commerce meeting, in the hope that since everyone at the meeting had been gawking in the foyer the night before, at least one of the more civic-minded citizens might have a clear recollection. "Nope," said Elmer Henry, when he met her outside the conference room. "Don't recollect at all."

"Hear Myles has got Rickie Pennifarm in the lockup," Elmer continued as they walked into the conference room. "Can't believe he had the gonads to shoot the sheriff's girlfriend. Always was a bozo, that boy."

Quill wondered if Rickie Pennifarm would have been less of a bozo in Elmer's eyes if he'd shot, say, a passing tourist. She settled into her accustomed place between Miriam Doncaster, the town librarian, and Esther West.

"He really wasn't aiming at you or anybody else, you know," Elmer said reassuringly. "He just wanted to get Dawn's attention."

"I heard that three men had to hold Myles back from thrashing Rickie within an inch of his life," Esther said with suppressed excitement. She adjusted one of her mother-of-pearl earrings and hitched the buckle of her white patent leather belt one notch tighter. "I heard Myles was simply *wild*."

"You've been checking out too many bodice rippers," said Miriam. She cocked a wise blue eye in Esther's direction. "Mysteries are a lot less heated. The new Monfredo came in yesterday. I'll put you on the waiting list." She winked at Quill. "How are you feeling, Quill? Andy Bishop said it was only a flesh wound."

"It's fine," lied Quill, whose head hurt like the devil. "Miriam, do you remember seeing the phone off the hook last night?"

Miriam squinted with the effort of recollection. "Yes."

"Did you see anyone put it back on the hook?"

"Yes. Mrs. Whitman. She said she was Mrs. Whitman. I asked her about her T-shirt. You know, it had the FOFA logo."

"Mrs. Whitman? The Friends of Fresh Air Mrs. Whitman?"

"That's right. She tried to recruit me. Quill—about these FOFA people . . ."

"Did she say anything into the receiver?"

"I don't remember."

Quill, making a mental note to ask Mrs. Whitman who'd been on the line, relaxed a little. Now she was getting somewhere.

Harvey Bozzel swept in, wearing his best suit and carrying a new leather briefcase. He smiled whitely in the general direction of the assembled chamber members, then dropped a confiding hand on Quill's shoulder and whispered, "Is she coming?"

"Who? You mean Helena?"

"I thought you were going to ask her to attend the meeting this morning. Remember? We took a meeting on the street yesterday. Near the post office."

"Took a . . . ? Oh. No, Harvey, I didn't get a chance to ask her. Besides, she's upstairs with the Bosses Club. They're having their first makeover."

"Dawn didn't show up, did she?" said Esther. "I hear she hasn't turned up yet. There's talk of dragging the river."

"Who's talking about dragging the river?" demanded Elmer.

"Why, down to Marge's this morning," said Esther. "Everybody is. Marge, wasn't everyone talking about looking for Dawn Pennifarm in the river?"

"No funds to drag the river," said Elmer, "lessen we get some volunteers. And what do they want to drag the river for?"

"Dawn Pennifarm," Esther said. "And I hear Kay Gondowski's gone missing, too. They already found Dot, of course."

"Talk was Rickie mighta put the body in one of them refrigerators down to the dump," said Marge. "Nobody said nuthin' about the river. For Dawn or for Kay. Kay's not in the river anyhow. She's just so shy she run off to her son's in Cohocton. Bet you even money she'll be back this morning."

"Bodies in the river?" said Harvey Bozzel. "There's a story here, folks. This has got Hemlock History Days beat six ways from Sunday."

Elmer rapped his official gavel and stood up: "This meeting of the Hemlock Falls Chamber of Commerce is now in session."

"Mayor?" said Harvey, getting to his feet. "May I say something?"

"We got the old order of bidness, the minutes, and then new bidness," said Elmer. "You wait a bit, boy."

Harvey nodded wisely, then turned to the members with an expansive gesture. "First, I'd like to say that the turnout for today's meeting augurs well for community spirit and public relations!"

Elmer whacked the gavel. Harvey ignored him.

Quill glanced around the conference table. Chamber members she hadn't seen for years had come to Elmer's ad hoc meeting: Harold Pearson from Qwik Freeze; Cornwallis Nugent from Nugent's All-Ways Insurance; Chris Croh from the Croh Bar. She hastily wrote: Harvey talks: ASK???, then listed "Attendees: THE USUAL, plus," and began to transcribe names.

" . . . minutes, Quill?" said Elmer.

"What?" Quill looked up; thirty members of the Hemlock Falls Chamber of Commerce were studiously ignoring a red-faced Harvey and staring at her.

"Elmer asked Harvey who died and left him king?" Miriam summed up in a rapid whisper. "Then he slammed his gavel again, told Harvey to shut up, said the Helena Houndswood show was new business, and it wasn't even on the agenda, and asked for last week's minutes."

Quill flipped hastily through the notebook, cleared her throat, and peered at her undecipherable notes.

"Just the agenda, Ms. Secretary," said Elmer formally.

" 'Tabled for June discussion,' " Quill read aloud, " 'paint and pound.' " She blinked. "I'm sorry, Elmer, that must be a note to myself. I can't remember what 'paint and pound' is for."

"Town cleanup," said Elmer, who had long ago adapted to Quill's self-admitted peculiarities in matters of shorthand. "Clean It Up! Week. Matter of civic pride. The town's gotta look good. Specially since we may be on TV pretty soon. Matter of civic importance."

There was an expectant silence. Elmer had finally brought up what was on everyone's mind.

"Timely, very timely," agreed Freddie Bellini, the funeral director, cautiously.

"This is a progressive village," Elmer reminded Freddie sternly. "Now, we got the Dump Day to schedule, and the report from the Assessment Committee. We'll get to more important things in the proper way. Procedure, you see. Rev'rund Shuttleworth, you're the chairman of the Assessment Committee. What's your assessment?"

Everyone relaxed slightly with the assurance that the Helena

Houndswood TV show would be addressed in due course.

Dookie, with his gently fuddled air of hearing only celestial voices, had been elected to the position of Assessment Committee chairman by popular acclaim. "Since nobody," Marge Schmidt had opined, "was about to kick a man of God in the butt for telling them to clean up their crap." The acceptability of the Assessment Committee chairman was vital to the success of the Hemlock Falls Clean It Up! Week, such well-known cantankerous and thrifty souls as Vern Mittermeyer being in favor of the patched and paintless school of building maintenance.

Dookie got to his feet. "Brethren?" he said, with a large-minded, if tentative, assurance that there were no goats among his sheep. "Let us pray."

There was an abrupt ducking of heads.

"Lord, give us strength to accept the human challenge presented by Clean It Up! Week. Amen."

"Amen," the members echoed.

"You may sit," said Dookie, although nobody was kneeling. "Lord, these are the souls who have heard your call to clean up . . ."

"It was my call, Rev'rund," said Elmer, "just to set the record straight."

"First to clean it up, Lord, is your servant the mayor, at the town hall, to keep the grass trimmed, the Dumpster repainted, and the parking lot free of coupons, flyers, and other detritus. How's that going, Mayor?"

Elmer flushed to his third chin.

"Next, Lord, your servant Esther West, to keep more seemly dresses in her shop window. Ladies' underthings, Lord, were meant to be concealed and not revealed. Have you changed your display, Esther?"

Esther adjusted the shoulder pads of her cotton pique jumpsuit with a "tsk!" of annoyance and a muttered, "Heck, no."

Quill listed the malefactors with absentminded determination, finishing with Dookie's request to ask the Lord's servant Vern Mittermeyer to complete the repainting of the post office trim with dispatch. "Hopefully, a dispatch greater than his record of attending to the mail," hissed Esther in Quill's direction.

"About this repainting of the post office," said Vern Mittermeyer heatedly. "The damn paint's no good. Splotches awful. The budget's been cut all to hell, this year. The town wants a contractor to repaint, they gotta see to it themselves. Might not be in the regulations, anyhow."

"Nothing in the municipal budget for federal buildings," said Elmer promptly. "I know what you earn as postmaster, Vern Mittermeyer, and you can afford to buy a couple of gallons and paint it yourself, easy."

Vern, with all the outrage of a Shakespearean asked to do a bump and grind, said it was against Federal regulations.

In the ensuing acrimony (a familiar feature of chamber meetings, and for which Quill had a special written "time out" symbol in the minutes), she reflected on the whereabouts of Dawn Pennifarm and Kay Gondowski.

Quill furiously doodled a rose-breasted grosbeak, entwined with rosemary and thyme, a check for $4500, and an extremely unflattering caricature of Helena Houndswood, with the mayor and Harvey kissing her feet.

A ripple of applause broke her concentration.

"You got that, Quill?" said Elmer. "Make a note to send a formal thank-you."

"Um. Yes." Quill raised her eyebrows frantically at Miriam, who obliged her with a smile.

"Paramount Paint donated four gallons of Cardinal Crimson Latex Exterior Paint for the use of the post office. Everyone voted to thank Hudson without letting him know Vern doesn't like it. They don't want to be rude."

Quill scribbled, then said in a low tone, "Miriam, you'd be so much better as secretary than I would."

"Uh-huh," said Miriam promptly. "No way."

Quill wrote: Bribe Miriam to take this lousy job! Then she drew a picture of Meg piling desserts in front of Miriam at lunch.

Elmer expanded his considerable chest with a deep breath. Everyone came to attention. It was clear they were going to finally come to the point. "We got a lot of bidness to cover, folks, so do I hear a motion to table the rest of the reading of the minutes from last week?"

"I so move," said Howie Murchison. The town attorney was looking a little strained, and more rumpled than usual. Miriam leaned over and said *sotto voce*, "Claire left him last week. For an insurance salesman." Quill raised both eyebrows. That explained the blond cashier last night at dinner. Miriam raised her hand and said loudly, "I second," and sent Howie a sympathetic smile.

Quill wrote: Howie DATE Miriam? and scribbled a pleased looking Miriam at the altar, with an equally happy looking Howie.

"Order of new bidness," said Elmer. Harvey raised his hand, waited for Elmer's reluctant, but acknowledging nod, then leaped to his feet.

Quill sighed, flipped her notepad open to a new page and scrawled the date and time.

Harvey cleared his throat. "Folks, the first order of new business should concern us all. One of our leading citizens was attacked at her place of business last night. We all know who"—he gestured largely in Quill's direction—"and we all know *what* happened. I'm issuing a call to action. A call to the men of Hemlock Falls to form a coalition for the protection of our women. I move to create a Victim's Fund, the first proceeds of which should go to pay the medical bills of our hostess."

Quill doodled a smiley face on her official minutes pad, then added a pair of horns and a pitchfork. She scribbled a little Harvey figure on top of the pitchfork.

"No need to suck up to Quill so's she'll get Helena Houndswood to this meetin'," Marge said with deadly, if elephantine, accuracy, "from what I seen in the dining room last night, the sheriff's got more influence with that there Helena than her. And what medical bills are you talkin' about, anyways? Andy Bishop said it was only a flesh wound. She's right here, healthy as a horse."

Quill drew a little Marge figure in flames under the pitchfork.

"Golly," said Miriam into her ear. "Those sketches are good."

Quill gave a guilty start.

"Important thing is," Marge boomed on, "how are we going to get in on this Helena Houndswood thing?"

There was a chorus of "yeahs" and one "right on," this last from Harvey, nothing if not firm in the belief that majority rule made the world safe for profitability.

Elmer rapped his gavel. "The floor is now open for discussion on more new business."

Harvey's hand shot up. "This remarkable turnout of the membership of the Hemlock Falls Chamber of Commerce," he said solemnly, "is here, I am sure, partly in tribute to the bravery of Miss Sarah Quilliam." He began to clap. The chamber joined him, mostly, Quill knew, because it was a conditioned reflex. Quill turned pink.

"Although a newcomer to our ranks"—(Harvey had moved to Hemlock Falls two years after Meg and Quill bought the Inn, which made Harvey a flatland foreigner if anybody was)— "she has dedicated herself to the interests of our town without hesitation. So I know she will heartily support our next endeavor to make Hemlock Falls as well known as Rochester, New York, in this great land of ours."

Elmer looked impressed. Miriam, who clearly had doubts whether anyone cared about Rochester except for George Eastman—and he was dead—dropped Quill a wink.

"What endeavor you got in mind, Harve?" asked Elmer with interest.

"A show," said Harvey simply. "A show to replace our late—and much lamented—Hemlock History Days. A show which will demonstrate to people of all kinds the dignity and commercial viability of our community. A show which will demonstrate the desirability of living and working in Hemlock Falls to those not fortunate enough to live and work here. A show, ladies and gentlemen, which will bring new blood to Hemlock Falls."

Esther, who'd written and directed the annual pageant for Hemlock History Week, gave an excited squeak. Dave Shoemaker, who sold real estate part time, exchanged an interested look with Matt Crawely, general manager of the Wal-Mart.

Harvey reached under his chair and set an A-Frame on the table with a great flourish. "Citizens, I bring you one of the most important ideas—conceptually speaking—that Bozzel Advertising has had in the past decade." He flipped the first frame of the pad up:

THE LITTLE MISS HEMLOCK FALLS
IT'S A BEAUTIFUL LIFE
TALENT AND BEAUTY PAGEANT

and underneath:

YOU'LL FALL FOR US

"This is it, guys," said Harvey enthusiastically. "We have a beauty pageant for all female residents of Hemlock Falls under ten. And we get the coverage for it on Helena Houndswood's show!"

There was a buzz of excited comment.

"We get our finest citizens to act as judge—like you, Mayor, and maybe some others—and the little ones, dance, sing, whatever, and dress up in their best. And we get the kid who wins to show all the folks out there in TV land what a great place this is to live and work. Norm—we'll take the viewers to the school to show 'em how weapon free the schools are and what not. She'll shop at the Wal-Mart. Maybe get a couple of dresses at Esther's shop, West's Best, right, Esther? Go to Bellini's Funeral Home to show folks where grandma and grandpa are buried—we can fake that a little bit, Freddie. Go down to Marge and Betty's diner for Saturday breakfast. I *mean*"— Harvey leaned forward and thumped the table dramatically— "we can hit every high spot in this town!"

"Little Miss Hemlock Falls." Elmer, the father of three girls, eight, ten, and twelve, nodded thoughtfully. "I like this, Harve. I like this."

Esther was almost blue with excitement. "Only I think ten is a little young. Maybe we could get a teenage contest going." (Esther's daughter was sixteen.) "They have," Esther explained earnestly to a frowning Harland Peterson (one six-year-old granddaughter), "a little more poise at that age."

"Harvey," protested Quill, "I don't think this is—"

"We can work up something very tasteful in white satin," said Freddie Bellini.

"The children's book room at the library?" asked Miriam, Quill's second-to-last hope.

"Miriam!" said Quill. "Harvey! Mayor!"

"And of course, since Ms. Houndswood is already planning to shoot the winners of the china contest right here at the Inn," said Harvey rapidly, avoiding Quill's outraged gaze, "Quill's the one with the inside track. I move that Quill form a one-woman delegation to approach Ms. Houndswood about having the pageant featured on the shoot."

"Shoot?" said Elmer. "You want to include Rickie blastin' Quill's front door?"

"No, no, no," said Esther, who owned the complete Guide to Television Production in videotape, "he means the camera shoot."

Elmer rapped the gavel once again. "Quill? You want to say something."

"Guys," said Quill, "a little girl's beauty pageant is just an awful idea. I mean . . ." She faltered to a stop. "Reverend Shuttleworth," she said. "Don't you find the idea of a beauty pageant for little girls exploitative? I mean . . ."

An expression of mild surprise crossed Dookie's face, which may have been occasioned by the fact that he had been addressed at all. He opened his mouth.

Noreen DeVolder, owner-operator of the Hemlock Hall of Beauty, snapped her gum with authority and interrupted to volunteer free hair and makeup for the girls. They'd look, she said, like little angels when she and the gals got through with them.

Harvey gazed from Quill to Dookie and back again with a thoughtful expression. Suddenly he snapped his fingers and sat forward in his chair. "We'll have to get the whole choir in the background as the winner shows the folks at home where she goes to church. The Reverend here needs to let the folks at home know that this is a godly town."

Dookie closed his mouth.

"A prize, perhaps, for most spiritual, eh, Reverend?" said Elmer, on whom no flies rested for long. Dookie nodded, without, Quill thought, a great deal of comprehension.

"Well, Quill?" said Harvey. "You want to go on up and ask her now?"

"Ask her now?" Quill repeated dumbly.

"Yay!" said a couple of members from the far end of the table.

"Sandy Willis says the two of you are like that," said Harvey, crossing two fingers. "Or, folks, we can form a delegation, maybe me, the mayor . . ."

The thought of a chamber delegation descending on the Shaker suite made her head throb. "I'll go up and talk to her."

"When?" demanded Harvey. "She goes for this, and I know she's going to, there's a lot of planning to do."

Maybe, thought Quill, she could nip this in the bud right away. "I'll be back as soon as I can." She put the minutes pad in front of Miriam and fled.

Quill found Helena calm in the midst of chaos, ruling over the Shaker suite with a well-groomed iron fist.

"Poor you! Kiss-kiss!" Helena greeted her like Charles de Gaulle greeting the Germans in 1944. "Meet the minions. That's Tabby Fisher, doing Connie's hair, and Dwight Nelson, putting all those pretties onto Sandy. People? Sarah Quilliam, the artist. You remember her, took SoHo in a storm of oils about six years ago, then left for parts unknown. Did that dishy sheriff catch the guy who tried to murder you? Tab, the poor girl got shot at last night. And then there was a body in the bushes to boot. Just like home, *n'est-ce pas*? And no, dear ones, it wasn't an art critic, whatever you may think."

"Sawyourstuf'sgreat," said Tabby laconically. No question where Tabby was from. Her brightly hennaed hair stuck up in sophisticated clumps at the back of her head. She wore a white body suit, with no bra, a tunic embroidered GET STUFFED in scarlet thread, black leggings and purple ballet shoes. Intricate gold chains swung from each ear, brushing her shoulders. Dwight's provenance screamed Manhattan, too: his earrings were silver ankhs and his face only slightly less pale than

Tabby's. Quill felt a sudden, urgent nostalgia for Soho.

The two remaining members of the Bosses Club looked fabulous. Terrified, but fabulous. Dwight fussily draped fabric swatches over Connie's stiff shoulders, murmuring delightedly at the effect of a bronze almost the color of her skin, then scribbling on a small notepad hung around his neck. Sandy sat upright and immobile in a straight-backed chair as Tabby dabbed blusher on her cheekbones with careless expertise. Her brown-blond hair had been highlighted a soft gold. She sat on the edge of the couch near the mullioned windows of the Shaker suite, taking occasional, shallow breaths, as though normal body movements would destroy the effect of her makeover. Tabby's magic had taken ten years off Sandy's face.

"My gosh!" said Quill.

"What d'ya think?" said Sandy anxiously.

"I think you look fantastic. You both look wonderful!"

"Maybe we could take some pictures?" Sandy's voice was timid.

"I'll call downstairs and see if John can find a camera," said Quill. "This looks like so much fun."

"It's like a *dream*," breathed Sandy.

"Lord, don't wake me up," said Connie.

Sandy gave her a determined punch in the shoulder. They both broke into nervous giggles.

Quill made a quick call to John for camera and coffee. "Herbal tea for me, sweetie," said Dwight, frankly eavesdropping, "and maybe the teensiest glass of some wine. White. The sulfides in reds are murder for my head."

Quill completed the call and sat next to Helena. "They're awfully good," she commented, with a nod in Tabby and Dwight's direction.

"Um. The little bastards charged me double for coming up here to the boonies," said Helena, clearly bored. "You'll agree this called for drastic measures."

"Not really," said Quill. "We're not real downtown here— and do you really think that matters to your audience? I mean, it's a national show—you've viewers in the Midwest, the South, the Northwest. Not everyone wants to look like a *Vogue* insert."

"Aren't we Citizen Sarah this morning," Helena drawled. "Actually, my producer said the same thing. I'll tell you, after one look at this crew, I'd decided to cancel the show."

So it did bother her. The bowling jackets and the home perms. The Wal-Mart makeup. The question is, Quill thought, did it bother her enough to get rid of Dawn Pennifarm and shoot Dot Vandermolen? In the middle of the cheerful activity of the Shaker suite, it didn't seem likely. Unless there was another motive—one she hadn't discovered yet. "And you think your producer's right?"

Helena shrugged. "Doesn't matter, does it? I'm committed to do this damn thing. Unless they all miraculously disappear like this Dawn person seems to have done. I should hope." Her voice rose: "Sandy, darling, I ask you. Is that fantastic or is that fantastic. Thank Tabby, like a good girl."

Sandy shyly surveyed herself in a hand mirror. "My husband is going to shit a brick."

"And Kay?" said Quill.

"Kay?" The indifference in Helena's tone made Quill's palm itch to slap her.

"Kay Gondowski. The shy one."

"Oh! The one with no cheekbones whatsoever. Here's a treat for you. Connie? Tell our Sarah about Kay."

"She called last night," said Connie. "Said she was petrified to face the cameras. Asked Sandy and me to get her money and set it up in an account. I already talked to Mark Anthony at the bank, and he says she's got to have a signature card. Kay said she'll call either me or Sandy back tonight, and I'll ask her to send us one."

There was a tap at the door. Kathleen Kiddermeister wheeled in a cart, and there was a rush for coffee and wine. Helena yawned and beckoned to Tabby. "Either you or Dwight's *got* to do something instantly about my hair."

Quill sat on the couch next to Connie. "Did you talk to Kay yourself?"

"Yes, Quill. I did."

"How did she sound?"

Connie smiled warmly. "Scared."

"But you're sure it was Kay?"

"Who else would it be?"

And that, thought Quill, is the sixty-four-thousand-dollar question. A memory tugged at her, and she shook her head to clear it. "Kay told you to set her money aside for her, and she'd claim it later?"

"Look," Sandy interrupted. "You gotta know Kay, all right? This is one shy lady. That husband of hers ups and dies on her, and do you think I could get her to go down to the Croh Bar Saturdays just for a couple of laughs? No way. This is a lady that likes to sit, knit, and watch TV. Don't surprise me at all that she's ducked out of this."

"Have you talked to Myles about this?"

"God, no, Quill," Sandy flushed guiltily. "Who had time?"

Quill was silent.

"Myles found out anything about Dawn yet?" asked Sandy after a strained moment.

"No. Not yet. But he's good," said Quill confidently. "I'm sure something will turn up soon." She hesitated, then asked, "What do you guys think happened to Dawn?"

"Well, Connie knows her best, and she's clueless."

"But you all must have some theory."

"Sure. That no-good son-of-a-bitch Rickie. The whole town thinks he hit her over the head or blasted her with that damn shotgun and dumped her body in the river." She frowned. "You know what they say—don't pray for it 'cause you might get it? Well, it's a little like that. I'm not lying when I tell you, Quill, there's a third of a million for each of us if Dawn doesn't show up, with Dot and all. Isn't that a hell of a thing?" She shook her head. "You asked me last week if anything could have broken the Bosses Club, I would have laughed in your face. We were tight. Dookie Shuttleworth's always on about how the love of money is the root of all evil. I guess he might be right. My god! You hear that?"

The door to the Shaker suite burst open. Harvey Bozzel, Elmer Henry, Dookie Shuttleworth, and Esther West flooded in, if, Quill thought, four people could constitute a flood.

Harvey waved a camera like a cheerleader at the head of a parade. "Somebody call for a photographer?" Sandy jumped up with a shriek of joy.

John closed the door behind them, raised an eyebrow at Quill, and sat next to her on the couch.

"You think this is hilarious," said Quill.

A muscle twitched in John's cheek.

"You can't pull that silent man of the plains act with me, John Raintree. You're laughing your head off."

"I did try to stop them," he said. "You've heard about the Little Miss Hemlock Falls Beauty contest?"

"They voted to do it?"

"So the mayor tells me. It was a unanimous vote."

"Even Dookie?"

John thought a moment. "I believe that Dookie was under the impression he was voting for a guided tour of the church, conducted by the child our citizens voted most spiritual."

"Harvey," said Quill. "That bozo."

They watched Harvey.

"Oozing charm from every pore . . ."

"He oiled his way across the floor," John said, "I can't remember the rest."

"Dum-de-dum-barbarian," said Quill. "Which doesn't fit because he isn't Hungarian, and what did Lerner have against Hungarians anyway?"

Harvey snapped Connie and Sandy's picture rapidly, three times in succession. Then he gave a patently artificial start of surprise and maneuvered Sandy into taking photos of himself posing with Helena, shaking her hand, standing next to her, and finally with his arm around her, which she shook off with the ease of an expert. The moments dragged on. Dookie engaged in a serious conversation with Dwight; Elmer, reduced to incoherence by Tabby's braless bodysuit, stared at the floor and talked beauty pageant to the clearly indifferent makeup artist; Quill and John sipped coffee.

Observing the twitch under the actress's left eye, Quill bet Helena would clear the room of Hemlockians in under twenty minutes.

John refused the bet. "Ten or less."

"You've got to admire her technique," Quill added. "I couldn't empty a room like that to save my life."

Harvey (although he reappeared at the door twice before

his final exit) was the first to go, followed by Sandy and Connie, still moving as if their new looks would shatter at a cough. Dwight fluttered his fingers at Dookie and beat a swift retreat with Tabby. Only Dookie remained in innocent incomprehension, maintaining an amiable flow of conversation with Helena, until Quill, grumpily responding to John's encouraging eye, finally took a hand.

"I was just telling Ms-ah-urm that her colleague may be oddly dressed, but he has a most Christian interest in his fellow man."

"Although none at all in his fellow woman," said Helena nastily. "Has he has offered to 'make over' the boys choir at the church? Now, if you'll excuse me, Reverend."

"It is past eleven, Dookie," said Quill.

"Already!" Dookie cast an anxious glance at the ceiling. "I'll be down at the jail, Quill, if anyone should ask for me."

"He does a great deal of good work with the prisoners," said Quill defensively as Dookie made his gently aimless way out the door. "You might lay off a little bit."

"You tell your citizens to lay off me," Helena snapped. "Beauty contest? What fresh hell is this?"

"You mean the beauty contest?"

"Didn't I just say that? Christ! That clodhopper mayor and that *sleazy* asshole of an excuse for an ad man—" She broke off and looked pointedly at John standing silently at Quill's elbow. "Is there something I can do for you?"

"John's the general manager here, and what concerns the Inn, concerns him," said Quill. "And we need to talk about arrangements for your crew during the shoot."

"I'll be liaison for the beauty contest," John volunteered with a suppressed grin. "I hope to learn a great deal from you."

"Don't even think about sucking up to me, sweetie. You're dealing with a grand master. You, Quill, or your office boy here, are to tell those crazies that in no way, no how is any Little Miss Hemlock Falls Beauty Pageant going to appear on my show. Never, in this life or the next. And you tell that geek in the gray flannel suit—"

"His name is Harvey Bozzel," said Quill evenly, "and he

has the village interest at heart, Helena. His ideas can get a little out of control—"

"A kid's beauty contest? My god!"

"It is a little vulgar," Quill admitted, "but properly managed, it might not be too bad. I mean, it doesn't have to be awful. This is a nice place to live, and your audience would like to see happy kids just like anyone likes to see happy kids."

"I don't," said Helena with finality. "I don't like kids. Kids are not part of a Beautiful Life. Kids—"

"Have a talent for upstaging you?" suggested John.

Quill held her breath. Helena turned bright red. Glared at John. Noticed, Quill hoped, that he really was an extremely good-looking man.

"Nobody," said Helena, "upstages me. Not the cutest little bastard in the world."

"You can't see fresh-faced children in the rose garden here at the Inn?" urged John. "Drinking milkshakes at the Hemlock Hometown Diner? Playing ball by the edge of the falls?"

"I'm way ahead of you, pal." Helena crossed her arms in front of her chest and rocked back and forth on her heels. "I'll think about it."

"You will?" said Quill.

"Maybe a few shots—no audio, just background—of kids reciting their own poetry?" John suggested. "Or a ballet class? Or band recital?"

"No horrible little boys lipsynching street rap," said Helena.

"Certainly not," said John. "If you have the time, I could show you some of the places in the village that'd make interesting footage."

Helena looked up at him. She smiled. Took his arm. "Hey, why the hell not?"

Quill, standing in the middle of the Shaker suite, began to feel like a fifth wheel. "I'll just go see how the lunch trade is doing," she said.

Helena turned and regarded her with a steady look. "Tell your mayor I'm thinking about it. But I'm telling you, I get one two-foot Liza Minnelli in an icky little tux, and the deal's off."

CHAPTER 7

"My granddaughter," said Elmer Henry proudly, "sings 'New York, New York' so that you can't tell the difference from that singer what's-her-name."

"Liza Minnelli," said Quill. "I'm pretty sure that isn't what Ms. Houndswood had in mind."

She'd had no trouble rounding up those chamber members who had volunteered to be on the Little Miss Hemlock Falls It's a Beautiful Life Talent and Charm Contest Committee. Elmer and Harvey were waiting in the lobby to enlist Helena Houndswood's attendance at all (or any) meetings pertaining to the show. Helena herself slipped out through the kitchen with John to tour the village. Quill invited Elmer and Harvey into her office for a candid chat.

"She don't want us to say 'Beautiful Life' in the contest title, then?" said Elmer.

"I'm afraid not, Mayor. It's sort of a trademark of hers, you see, and while she's agreed to have the winners host a little tour of Hemlock Falls, she won't do any judging or feature the contestants. She won't sponsor it."

Elmer's belligerently expressed opinion was that if Hemlock Falls preteens were good enough for the village, they were good enough for the nation.

"That is not it," said Harvey with great authority. "She's thinking a whole new concept entirely." He rocked back in Quill's chair, contemplating the northwest corner of her ceiling. "I had a little chat with her this morning while we were taking the meeting in the Shaker suite. And I can't tell you what transpired, but it's going to be big. I mean really big. So here's what we do. We go ahead with the contest categories . . ."

" 'Little Miss Personality,' " said Elmer, consulting a scrawled piece of paper from his vest pocket. " 'Best Little Talent' and 'Little Miss Hemlock Falls' herself."

"Yessir," said Harvey in satisfaction. "Prizes to be offered by Frederick Bellini's Funeral Home and Peterson's Buick."

Quill found her patience wearing thin. "Harvey, if the town really insists on doing this, don't you think we should open it to little boys, too?" Neither man looked at her, which told Quill they'd discussed the possibility that she would bring it up.

"Women's Lib," said Elmer. "Well, I guess we got to consider you feminists. Now, I'm all for women's lib, Quill, or I should say"—(this with heavy jocularity)—"*Ms.* Quilliam, but I don't know as how we could get the town to support a beauty contest for boys. Now, if we had a category like Best Little Fisherman, or Best Little, I dunno, some more boy-like thing . . ."

"Best Little Bow Hunter?" Quill heard herself say. "Best Little Sport with a Shotgun? *Best little penis?*"

"Oh, my god," said Elmer.

"It's the gunshot wound," said Harvey. "Saw a lot of it with 'Nam."

"Harvey, you were never in 'Nam," said Elmer, "not even close."

"I didn't say 'in' 'Nam, I said 'with' 'Nam."

"Ayuh. You know what you need, Quill? A nice cup of coffee or something."

Quill went into the kitchen to get a nice cup of coffee or something.

"I'm losing it," she told her sister. "It's the gallery business all over again. One-way trips to remote mountain areas are starting to look attractive."

"Explain," said Meg.

Meg demonstrated the proper degree of outrage over the Little Miss Hemlock Falls Beauty Contest, loyally endorsed Quill's proposed category, and immediately began preparing cappuccino as a restorative. "I'm surprised you haven't fizzed out before this, Quill." She frothed the milk, blended in the coffee, and added cinnamon and chocolate. "There. Put your feet up. Think soothing thoughts. Are you thinking soothing thoughts? Maybe you and Myles should try to get away for the weekend. We can handle things here just fine."

Quill twitched in her rocking chair. "Every time I try to think soothing thoughts, I end up against that damn brick wall. Why can't I remember what happened last night? Where's Mrs. Whitman? I've got to talk with her about what she heard when she hung up the phone."

"On a hike, of course. What's this about hanging up the phone?"

"At the reception desk last night. Dina said I was on the phone when Rickie blasted the front door. I just can't remember who I talked to. I have this feeling it's important." She bit her lip. A tendril of memory came back. "Someone asking for directions?"

"Hanging up the phone is sort of an automatic response," said Meg. "I doubt that Mrs. Whitman would remember doing that last night. I certainly wouldn't; not with all the fuss."

"Dot's dead. Dawn's disappeared. Kay didn't show up for the party last night. It's all very suspicious."

"You were just like that as a kid," said Meg. "Remember that old couple that moved next door to us when I was in kindergarten? You told me that they were feeding a whole bunch of little people that lived in her basement. And you got me to sneak over with you at eleven o'clock at night to get evidence. Because she was carrying all kinds of fresh vegetables down there and you said it was to feed the little people. That's what you said to me then—'Meg. Something very strange is going on. Mrs. Nussbaum is feeding vegetables to the little people living in her basement,' and it turned out she was canning tomatoes!" Meg waved one finger in the air. "Now, the thing about Mrs. Nussbaum, Quill, is that you never did turn in that volcano project at school. The whole reason you made up that story about Mrs. Nussbaum was because you were afraid to put vinegar and soda together to make a bubbly little explosion. There's a word for what you do. Sublimation or something. Maybe avoidance. No. Displacement. That's it."

"You've been talking with a tennis-playing physician."

"No, really, Quill . . . Well, maybe a little. The question is, what's the real problem here? I mean, aside from the Horrible Helena and your flesh wound and the usual manic goings-on?"

"You have beady little eyes," said Quill.

"Come on, Quill. Give. Think about it."

"Myles wants to get married." She bit her lip. "I didn't mean to blurt it out like that. It just goes to show you how frazzled I am."

"Hm."

"You're not gasping with astonishment."

"Why should I gasp with astonishment? He loves you. In a lot of ways he's a traditional kind of guy. Why shouldn't he want to marry you?" Meg tugged affectionately at her sleeve. "Is that what's been making you edgy for the past couple of weeks?"

"It'd mean changes."

"Changes," said Meg. Her face clouded. She looked around her kitchen. She handed Quill a cup of cappuccino. The cup rattled in the saucer. "What do you want to do?"

"I like things the way they are. It's the 'or what.' "

"What or what?"

"What happens if I say no? Do we continue on the way we are? Or does Myles run off with a brunette? Or with Helena Houndswood? If I say yes . . ."

Meg cleared her throat. "You could build a little house near the rose garden." She smiled.

"Put up the trellis. Build a picket fence."

"So what are you going to do?"

"Nothing. Something. I don't know if I want to get married again. You know what life with Daniel was like. It's all too much to deal with."

"Maybe displacement is therapeutic. Don't think about it. If you don't think about it, your subconscious will solve the problem all by itself. Think business. Business is good. Helena Houndswood shows up and everyone's making reservations. All these New York types gossip, Quillie. Word-of-mouth like that is terrific for the Inn. Things are going to be terrific. Another couple of months and we'll be rolling in cash."

"You want to think about business? Great. John says we

have cash-flow problems. We can't wait a couple of months for cash to come in."

"So business is something you want to displace. Especially thoughts of immediate business. Especially when young Dawn's on the lam with that check." Meg took a large sip of Quill's cappuccino. "Okay, so the more I think about it, the more a certain degree of stress is inevitable in the following weeks. So here's what you do. Instead of thinking there's little people in our basement, or worse than that, two more dead bodies in addition to the one that's already there, and that Helena put them there, focus on a real problem that we can solve. What's happening with the Bosses Club? Who killed Dot and why? Where's Dawn Pennifarm and that forty-five hundred dollars? Men and money problems will make junk-yard dogs of the best of us. And you, Quillie, are the least snappish person I know. But here you are saying outrageous things to the mayor and Harvey and growling at the chamber people. So here's the plan, Stan. We talk to Connie and Sandy. We talk to everyone who saw Dawn last on Monday, including the Bloater. We even talk to Marge Schmidt, because she has all those connections at the bank, and she can maybe find out what Dawn's finances are. And whether she's got a secret stash of cash."

Quill retrieved the remains of her cappuccino, gulped it, and set it on the butcher's block with a thump. "That's exactly what we can do. I'll start with Rickie Pennifarm. I'll forget Helena. You're right, her involvement doesn't make sense."

"The Gourmet Detective."

"Artist as Gumshoe."

They shook hands.

"So what do we do first?" said Meg. "We make a list. Except that I've got the chamber lunch to fix, so we'll have a—what do you call it?—strategy session this afternoon."

"Dina and I have to give statements about last night at the sheriff's office after lunch. I'll interview Rickie Pennifarm then. But I've got free time now. I'll make a preliminary list, and we'll go over it tonight."

Quill decided that the best place for detecting was outside, in the rose garden, where the sun, fresh air, and blue sky would provide a calm center in the middle of any psychic storms. Mike the groundskeeper had built a gazebo overlooking the falls and surrounded it with Blaze, a reliable floribunda climber in the sometimes tough growing conditions of central New York. Quill settled back on the cushioned bench under the roof and watched the water through a spray of crimson blossoms. She kept a pocket-sized pen and notebook with her—for sketches, comments on Inn matters, requests from guests she encountered during the day—and she pulled it out and flipped through to a clean page. She'd asked Myles once about the success of his investigations; she knew his record of convictions as a detective in Manhattan was a goal for the New York police statewide. Crimes formed a pattern, he'd said, and each had its set of solvability factors. The point was to answer who, what, where, when, why, and how with proven facts. The trick was never to make assumptions, or operate on gut feel. Which was why, she, Quill, should stick to Inn management as a career.

She did a quick cartoon sketch of a wild-haired Quill marching side by side a Myles with an oversize sheriff's badge. Underneath the sketch she wrote:

Victim: Dot Vandermolen

Means: Rifle 270 caliber bullet. Kept in pickup truck with access to all suspects listed below.

Opportunity:

Rickie Pennifarm	(seen leaving by reliable eyewitness)
Sandy Willis	
Connie Weyerhauser	(all in vicinity of the Inn
Kay Gondowski	at the time of death)
Hudson Zabriskie	
Helena Houndswood	
Dawn Pennifarm	(????)

After a moment she added "X"? since part of solving any mystery had to take into account the occasional random tramp beloved by inept village constables in the English countryside.

Quill sat and considered motive. The truth stuck out like a red flag on a ski slope. Every single surviving member of the Bosses Club benefited when a member died. And no one in the Bosses Club liked Dot. That left almost all of the suspects with a motive, including Rickie Pennifarm, who may have thought that the more members of the Bosses Club he killed, the more money would be left for Dawn.

On the other hand, Hudson Zabriskie, far from having a motive, had lost a supervisor at a critical moment in production. At least, that was what Quill surmised from his distracted behavior. And the surviving members of the Bosses Club must know that they'd be suspects.

IMPORTANT she scrawled in capitals, Dawn's disappearance linked to Dot's death?

She had a lot to ask Rickie Pennifarm, if she could get into his jail cell and talk to him while Myles was away.

She turned to Dawn Pennifarm herself.

Who: Dawn Pennifarm, age 32. Supervisor at Paramount Paints ? years. Married, Rickie Pennifarm ? years, no children.

Then she wrote WHY? She thought a moment. What else did she know about Dawn? She'd been to Hemlock High School, as had almost all the workers at Paramount. She was tough. She was mouthy. She was a good worker, according to Sandy (who was loyal to the Bosses Club) but not according to Hudson Zabriskie, her ultimate boss (who was loyal to the much invoked "New York HQ").

Quill added the caption SOLVABILITY FACTORS and then wrote: Did she need money? Did she have debts? Did she have a record?

Then: WHAT REALLY HAPPENED? Fact: disappeared Monday. Assumption: $4500 of Inn money PLUS? Paramount money? That Dawn disappeared *with* the money, Quill figured was an assumption. And how, Quill thought, did Kay's disappearance fit into all of this? Her head started to throb. Quill wrote

INTERVIEW SUBJECTS and listed: Rickie Pennifarm; Hudson Zabriskie; Sandy Willis; Connie Weyerhauser.

"Quill? You busy?" Connie Weyerhauser stood outside the gazebo railing. "My husband and Sandy's husband are in at lunch talking with Howie Murchison about how we get the money. I left them to it. Just give me the check, I said. I'm going for a walk. You men figure it out and just give me the check."

"I'm glad you came out. As a matter of fact, I've been wanting to talk to you. Come up and sit down."

Connie hauled herself up the one step and settled at the far end of the bench.

"You look terrific," said Quill. "That makeover must have been so much fun."

"It lasted?" Connie patted her bangs carefully. "I've never done this before in my life. None of this seems real. I'm just hoping I can do it at home. I looked at all the makeup Tabby had in her cart. . . . Maybe I can buy a cart like that when I get my money. Barbie'd love it."

"How is she?"

"Oh. You know. The doctors . . ." Connie sighed. Her face shuttered closed. "They tell you one thing and then they tell you something else. There's a clinic for C.P. children in Buffalo. I was thinking maybe about taking her there, once I get the money. They have cures for all kinds of things these days. Dawn always said there was one kind of medicine for rich people and another kind for the working poor. Actually, there's three kinds, the third is for minorities. I was thinking now that I'm going to be rich, I could find out more about a cure."

"But you've got health insurance through the factory," said Quill. "Isn't her treatment covered?"

"Oh, yes. But Dawn always said there are treatments they don't want you to know about because of how expensive they are. The company doctor just says there's nothing we can do. I believe there's an operation somewhere that can get Barb out of the wheelchair." There was a terrific urgency in her deep slow voice. "Maybe in Switzerland. You read about all kinds of cures in Switzerland. And Mexico."

"Cerebral palsy's pretty tough," said Quill, a little help-lessly.

"You're telling me, girl?" Connie sighed. "Would you behave any different?"

"I think I'd probably do exactly what you're doing; look for something to help until I know that there isn't anything more I could do. The trick is knowing when to stop. When you've done all you possibly can. That'd be a tough one for me."

"That's so." Connie smiled. "And then this happens. I thought I'd done all I could, but now look. All this money, Quill."

"Dot's share is added to yours, then. And Dawn's if she doesn't turn up."

Connie moved restlessly, her gaze shifting. "I don't know what got into Dawn, running off like that."

"Did you see Dawn the day she disappeared?"

"Monday, you mean? Sheriff asked the same thing. We knew Helena was here, you know, so we were all excited about that. Didn't talk about anything else at break time."

"You knew Helena was here! This was on Monday?"

"We discovered she actually got here on Sunday. She got off the train with twenty pieces of fancy luggage, didn't she? And the station's right next to the Croh Bar. Rickie called and told Dawn. He'd stopped in at the Croh Bar, as usu-al. He was supposed to be in Buffalo, looking for work. I told Dawn that man was no good, and now look what he's done." She glanced at the bandage on Quill's temple. Quill waited for the expected inquiry. It didn't come. "He called Dawn right up at their trailer, then she called each one of us."

"So you knew you won Sunday afternoon?"

"Well, we didn't know for sure." Connie chuckled. "Dawn wanted to come right up here to the Inn and demand to know. But Sandy said we had to vote on it. So when we went to work on Monday, the Bosses Club voted to wait a few days, see what happened. We were a little scared to call on someone as famous as she is."

"So what did Dawn do on Sunday? Did she go see Helena?"

Connie, Quill discovered, had dimples. "Sheriff's gonna be

upset, you keep on poking around his investigations."

"I'm not . . ." Quill began with dignity, "well, maybe . . . I just . . ."

"As far as I know, Dawn did what she was supposed to do that day and nothing else. Monday, we worked the seven to three shift, like always. After, Dawn had to go to the Qwik Freeze for a benchmarking meeting, so I assume that's just what she did."

"To Qwik Freeze for a what?"

"You know, benchmarking." Seeing Quill's bewildered expression, Connie said, "Let's see if I can make it simple. When one business has a good process for doing something, another business visits to ask about the process. This better way of doing things is installed in their own business. The Monday second shift at Qwik Freeze has a worker rotation process, and Dawn, as one of the Bosses Club team, was supposed to talk to the workers to see how satisfied they were with the arrangement. It's part of our Paramount Quality program, to go to different operations and benchmark processes they perform better than we do."

Quill, somewhat fuddled, made a surreptitious note INTER-VIEW QWIK FREEZE and said, "So Dawn went to Qwik Freeze . . ."

" . . . to benchmark employee satisfaction with their rotation shifts," said Connie.

Quill decided not to write this down. She sent up a fervent hope that benchmarking had nothing to do with the investigation. "So did she go to Qwik Freeze?"

"She left the shift early and headed in that direction."

"The Qwik Freeze plant is right next to yours, isn't it? You're on that little crossroads between ninety-six and route fifteen."

"Mr. Zabriskie calls it the Hemlock Falls Industrial Park," said Connie. "Far as I can tell, it's two plants close together. Lord, Quill! Look at the time. I have to pick up Barb from the adult care center. You'll excuse me. And I forgot that I came out here for a reason; Doreen wants to see you."

"Thanks."

Quill found Doreen stacking clean towels in the large linen closet next to the kitchen.

"So. There you are," she said. She counted the towels by two, under her breath, recorded the number on the clipboard on the inside door, then laid one callused palm on Quill's forehead. "Huh!" she announced. "Thought so."

Quill felt her forehead herself. "You mean I have a fever? I don't have a fever."

Doreen locked the closet door with a deliberate click of the key and said with an air of disapproval, "Mayor thought you might. From that there gunshot wound. Told him I thought you was dee-lerious, saying strange things about this beauty contest. Ast me to give you some aspirin." Quill felt her cheeks go warm. Doreen withdrew a bottle from her apron pocket. "So do you want some? You look flushed."

"No. Thanks."

Doreen stuck the aspirin bottle back in her pocket and jiggled it.

"Is that why you wanted me? To give me aspirin?"

"Nope. It's this-here beauty contest."

Quill ran her mind over Doreen's family. She had a daughter with two young boys. Rowdy ones. "Your grandkids want to enter the contest? I told the mayor and Harvey that we should let little boys enter, too—"

"It ain't that. It's Mr. Whitman. The Fresh Air folks. They're fixin' to protest." Doreen sucked in her lower lip. "They ast me to let you know, they don't think it's fittin' or proper for young bodies to be paradin' out in dressy clothes and makeup. S'not fitting for young girls, is Mr. Whitman's message."

"The Friends of Fresh Air want to protest the beauty contest?"

"Right."

"I thought they were environmentalists," said Quill. "Not that I don't agree with them about beauty contests . . . I mean, I'm not violently opposed or anything, but golly, Doreen."

"Your body's part of the environment, too."

Doreen's logic, Quill admitted, was irrefutable, if a trifle unorthodox. But then, how orthodox were renengade Green

Quakers? "I'm not too certain how I can help, Doreen."

"Mr. Whitman thought maybe that there Helena Hounds-wood might give him and his group a bit of time on the TV show. Say a few words about how Hemlock Falls is to be left natural."

"I see," said Quill, who was sure she did. "Well, you tell Mr. Whitman. No, I'll tell Mr. Whitman that it's a free country and he can protest up Main Street and down again for all I care, but I'm *not* going to help him and his group get air time on *It's a Beautiful Life*."

"You think maybe that's not all they want?" said Doreen anxiously. "They ain't sincere?"

"I'm sure they're sincere," said Quill mendaciously. "But I'm also positive that anyone who gets within fifty yards of Helena Houndswood becomes absolutely addled and starts thinking TV stardom immediately."

"Addled," said Doreen with satisfaction.

"Don't tell Mr. Whitman he's addled. And for goodness' sake, don't give him aspirin for it, or call the funeral home, or do any of the things you do that drive me *crazy*, Doreen. I suppose you want to be on TV, too."

"No, ma'am," said Doreen with a sniff, "but I know some-body who does. Somebody who's right here in front of this linen closet."

"I don't want to be on Helena Houndswood's TV show!" Quill calmed herself with an effort. "I'm sorry, Doreen. I didn't mean to shout, I don't know what's gotten into me these days. . . ."

"You started the whole thing," said Doreen. "Astin' her to put the Inn on and all."

"You and John and Meg and that rat Harvey made me!"

"You can't make a body do what she doesn't wanna do," said Doreen virtuously. "Mr. Whitman even says you shouldn't keep the body from doing what it wants to do because it's unhealthy. Mr. Whitman says . . ."

Quill foresaw days, if not weeks, of "Mr. Whitman says." "Stop!" said Quill. Doreen stopped. Quill found herself with nothing further to add and went in pursuit of John to discuss his walk with Helena. He was, Doreen called after her, sitting in the lounge drinking sherry with That Ms. Houndswood.

John stood up as she joined them and pulled out a chair. "Did you get any lunch?"

"No. Not yet."

"I'll ask Nate for some soup. You look a little flushed. Mayor thought you might be starting a fe . . ."

"I am absolutely *fine*," said Quill. "Helena, how's the day going?"

"The usual. Squabbles among the staff. They find the Bosses Club hopeless. They are, of course." She was dressed in pale green, a fitted jacket over a long floaty skirt.

"That outfit is just terrific."

Helena flicked a dismissive eye over Quill's challis skirt and cotton blouse. "Well, one does like to keep up."

John handed Quill a bowl of onion soup and resumed his seat.

"God. That looks terrific," said Helena. "Your sister's pretty good, isn't she? It smells great."

"Would you like some?" asked Quill politely. "We can—"

"No, no." She patted her nonexistent stomach. "I'm on nine hundred calories a day. I don't know how you keep so skinny. I've seen you eat like a horse."

Quill, deciding she spent far too much time decoding messages, ignored the possible insult and asked if the Inn was to her lawyer and producer's liking.

"Marvelous," said Helena promptly. "It's inspired my next book."

"The Inn? Really?"

"The Inn. The village. The country life. What is the dream of every upper-class American? The life of a gentleman farmer. A beautiful farmhouse, centuries-old, filled with antiques. Velvet green pastures and an adorable red barn. A few of those lovely fluffy sheep in the barn. A sleek, gorgeous horse that one can ride through green fields. A herd of crimson and sunshine-yellow chickens peacefully walking about the front lawn. One of those friendly-looking cows with the big brown eyes. Fresh milk. Fresh butter. That thick lovely cream. Delicately browned omelettes from farm-fresh eggs. The pictures will be wonderful."

"Manure disposal," said Quill suddenly, remembering the potential for altercation between the farmers and the Friends of Fresh Air. "I don't think farming is all that easy a life, Helena. Besides, the farmers I know work like dogs."

"This is gentlemen farming," Helena corrected her. "All the latest equipment combined with an understanding of what it really means to live a Beautiful Life can make farming a pleasure, not a business."

"The reality may be quite different," said John, with such a sober expression Quill knew he was amused. "I worked on a farm when I was growing up here in Hemlock Falls, and it's not as easy as it looks."

"Nothing ever is," said Helena soberly, "which is why I've had my lawyer make arrangements to try it myself."

"Try it yourself?" said Quill.

"You looked amazed." Helena tossed her head and laughed in a way someone had probably told her was delightful. "You should know—my audience does—that what I write, I write from real life. So Harvey rented that lovely parcel down by the waterfall for me for a month. I move in tomorrow morning."

"You mean the Peterson house?" said Quill. "That's been empty ever since Tom Peterson went off to jail last year. His wife moved to Syracuse with the children."

"One of Hemlock Falls' oldest families, I understand," murmured Helena, "and quite wealthy."

"Well, yes," said Quill, "except that he made all that money by selling rejected shipments of meat to Third World countries."

"Every great family has its black sheep." Helena waved this aside. "I've looked the house over this morning, on my walk. It's lovely. Harvey is making the arrangements to move me and the animals in for a month. My guess is that this book will be another best-seller."

"The animals?" said Quill.

"The sheep, the cow, the chickens. Everything. My publisher will take care of all the expenses, naturally. A small John Deere tractor. A Land Rover. All the accoutrements for a Beautiful Life on the Farm. As I said. When I write, I write about what I know. What I've directly experienced."

"Are you going to have help?" asked Quill, fascinated in spite of herself. "I mean, I don't know much about farming, but those animals take a lot of care, not to mention the manure dispo . . . well, never mind."

"I will have advice, of course. I've put Harvey on retainer. He has offered to provide anything I need to support my research."

Quill, doubting that Harvey knew the difference between a chicken and a guinea hen, suppressed the pleasurable thought that Helena would no longer be drifting about the Inn with her predatory eye on Myles "Hunk" McHale. On the other hand, it was going to be harder to keep tabs on her in case she had an undisclosed motive for murder.

"You're moving out tomorrow?" said Quill. "We'll have to keep in touch."

"Thank you, darling. I'll have you and that marvelous sheriff over for a farm-style meal. But drop in anytime."

"I certainly will," said Quill.

Helena glanced idly over Quill's shoulder. "There's a little person waving dramatically at you from the doorway."

Quill turned around. "Oh, dear."

Dina marched up to the table with a shy glance at Helena. "Quill," she said urgently. "The deposition!"

CHAPTER 8

Quill made sure she had her investigation book, brushed her hair and swept on some blusher, then met Dina at the car. On the road she gave Dina a quick rundown on her plans to investigate Rickie Pennifarm.

"You and Meg're going to do what?" Dina's eyes widened and she turned in the passenger seat to shake her head at Quill. "Did you talk to the sheriff about it?"

"I don't know why everyone seems to think I should check out every little discussion with Myles." Quill signaled a left turn onto Main Street and pulled her battered Olds through the intersection. "All I want to do is talk to Rickie Pennifarm by myself for a few minutes. If you can keep Deputy Dave busy, he probably won't even notice."

"The sheriff notices everything," said Dina. "I don't think this is going to work."

"Myles won't be there. He's in Ithaca. Rickie's essential to the solution of the case. He's a solvability factor."

"Solvability factor," muttered Dina.

"But unless you distract Dave Kiddermeister, he's not going to let me in to see Rickie."

"And how am I supposed to do that?"

"You know, flirt."

"Flirt?"

"Flirt. Bat your eyelashes. Sit on his desk and adjust his tie. Cross your legs and let your skirt creep up over your knee. V. I. Warshawsky does it once in a while, even though it's against her principles. And if V. I. can do it, so can you."

"I'm a doctoral student, not a private investigator. And I'm wearing jeans. Besides, Quill, my generation doesn't flirt."

"We need that forty-five hundred bucks. Rickie's probably the only one who knows what Dawn did with it. We need it to pay your salary. Your generation spends money, doesn't it? To eat?"

"Right. Jeez. Well, okay."

"You'll distract him?"

"Do my best."

Dina subsided into a glum silence. Quill drove to the end of Main Street and paused at the entrance to the parking lot. The Hemlock Falls Municipal Building was a large wooden structure dating from the upper third of the nineteenth century and prey to the chief architectural sin to which those decades were heir: Carpenter Gothic. Even unadulterated Carpenter Gothic made Quill's teeth itch; but, like an uncertain lady experimenting with hair dye, the municipal building suffered from the contribution of strong solutions to a style which had been problematic from the start. It stood, a proud eyesore, at the end of Main Street.

Quill parked at the rear of the building in the space marked Official Sheriff's Business Only, responding to Dina's nervous query that they *were* on Official Sheriff's Business Only. "Besides," she said, "I told you Myles isn't here."

"So Deputy Dave is going to take our depositions?"

"Probably. You can handle him with one hand behind your back and a bag over your head. Just don't call him Deputy Dave. He hates it." Quill led the way through the labyrinth of dark corridors, low ceilings, and splotched linoleum to the door marked SHERIFF'S OFFICE AND COUNTY LOCK-UP, knocked, and walked in. Dave Kiddermeister (Kathleen's younger brother) immediately rose to his feet. The word for Dave, Quill thought, was dewy: he was blond, with a bleached Scandinavian fairness, young, and he perspired a lot. He blushed frequently, too, a distinct disadvantage when apprehending Saturday night revelers at the Croh Bar. Dewiness inspired invective. A desert sunset pink spread up to his hairline as Quill and Dina came in. He rose, stuck his thumbs in his belt, and frowned in a sheriff-like way.

"You ladies ready to give a statement about the incident of the night before?"

Nervousness made Dina bridle. "No, Dave, we're here to plead a parking ticket. And thanks for asking about Quill—she's just fine. And thanks for asking about me. I'm just fine, too."

The desert pink deepened to red. "Sorry, ma'am. Ms. Quilliam. How's your head? Doc Bishop said it was—"

"Only a flesh wound," said Quill. "No problem."

Dina circled the small office like a cat with sore feet. "So, is he here?" she whispered.

"The alleged perpetrator of the murder and the assault? Yes, ma'am."

"Ick." Dina settled into one of the plastic chairs with a shudder. "I don't hear him or anything. What's he doing?"

"Just sitting there, ma'am," said Dave. "You know, waiting for the sheriff and all." He looked thoughtful. "Got a hell of a hangover, pardon me, ladies."

Quill patted her skirt pocket to make certain she hadn't forgotten the investigation book, and wiggled her eyebrows at Dina.

"Dep . . . Dave," said Dina huskily. She rose to her feet and swayed in a seductive manner across the room. "I can call you Dave, can't I?"

Dina perched on the edge of his desk and crossed her legs, revealing fluorescent green socks. She smiled at the deputy, who grinned back.

Quill sidled toward the cell block door. "I'd like to see Rickie for a moment, Dave. Just to see how he is."

Dave's grin disappeared and his thumbs went back in his belt. He shook his head. "Can't do that, ma'am. Not allowed. On'y friends and relatives."

"Well, I'm a friend."

"You're the victim, ma'am."

"That's an even better reason," said Quill, who thought that Dave's view of which role was more important would have been significantly affected if he were the one with an inch-long wound in his skull, "Did Sheriff McHale say specifically that I couldn't talk to Rickie?"

"Well, no, ma'am, can't say as he did, but like I told you, on'y friends and rel—"

"Helena Houndswood asked me to give him a message about the money from the contest. . . ."

Dave took his thumbs out of his belt, dropped one shoulder, and lowered his head confidingly, the universal Hemlockian response to getting a good piece of gossip. "It's true then. They really won a million bucks? And that actress, Helena whatsis . . ."

"Helena Houndswood," said Quill. "Yes. She's staying at the Inn, you know. As a matter of fact"—Quill raised her eyebrows slightly to increase her air of innocence—"she wanted me to see Rickie, too. Just for a minute. It's possible she's considering . . . just considering, Dave . . . bringing the cameras in here to do a short segment on crime in Hemlock Falls. It's by no means a sure thing, but it's a possibility."

Dave looked around the office. "A TV crew, here? You mean like those True Cop Stories TV shows?" His cheeks, Quill noted, had achieved an interesting shade of mauve.

"But, Quill," Dina said, "Helena's TV show is about—"

"The biggest thing to hit this town in years," interrupted Quill solemnly. Dina closed her mouth and fluttered her eyelashes.

"We'd look pretty good next to those cops from Miami, I guess," said Dave proudly, "and Detroit. No flies on us here in Hemlock Falls."

"I guess you might call me a scout," Quill said, thinking, well, he might. He'd be wrong, but he might. "So I'll just take a few seconds, no more than that, to feel him out about this." Still talking, Quill marched confidently up to the steel door labeled Lock-Up, slipped through, and left Deputy Dave to Dina's wiles.

The county lock-up consisted of two steel barred cells with concrete floors that made Quill think of a dog pound. The air was sourly humid with cigarette smoke. Rickie Pennifarm was the lock-up's only occupant. He sat hunched on a horizontal gate covered by a mattress, dressed in soiled blue jeans and a red flannel shirt. Rickie was scrawny and small, with a straggling brown beard and mean little eyes. He inhaled the last of an unfiltered cigarette, stubbed it out carefully with his booted foot, and dropped it in the toilet.

"Mr. Pennifarm?" said Quill.

"Yeah." He got up and advanced to the side of the cell facing her. "You a lawyer?"

"Am I? No. No. I'm Sarah Quilliam."

"Yeah?" He squinted at her. "I guess you are. I seen you around. Oh!" His snigger trailed off into a cough. "You're the one I winged. Din't mess you up much, looks like."

"Not too much."

"So. What can I do you for?" He leered at her.

"We're looking for Dawn. You really don't have any idea where she is?"

"Fuck, no. You think I woulda shot you up if I knew where she was? Hell, I thought she was at that party spending the money she won, just to spite me. That bitch's got no sense of gratitude."

"When's the last time you saw her?"

"What, you the fucking sheriff's deputy? No? Wait. I got it. You're the one fucking the sheriff."

Rickie's laughter at his foray into wit left Quill unmoved. She'd had some pangs of conscience about her proposed method of interrogation; she abandoned them. "Helena, I mean Helena Houndswood, the actress, is up at the Inn making arrangements about the million dollars. If Dawn's disappeared, of course, you're her husband—"

"Fuckin' right!" He grabbed the bars with both hands. "Dawnie comes into a million, it's my million, too. I mean, I'm her fuckin' husband, for christsake."

"Well, it's not a million, you know. It's one fourth of that. Connie, Kay, and Sandy all share in the prize."

"One fourth," said Rickie. "Son of a bitch. That's a lot of money, right?"

"It's increased, of course, since Dot Vandermolen passed away."

"No kidding? Four-way split?"

Quill, increasingly sure that Rickie was innocent of at least Dot's murder, decided to spare him the effort of calculation. "Two hundred fifty thousand dollars."

"Two hundred fifty fucking thousand dollars. Yes!" He pounded his thigh enthusiastically. "So. Look. I may need a little advance. For my defense and all. You get this Helena Houndswood to come and see me? Maybe bring some of it in cash?"

"I'll ask her," said Quill, "but I'd like to ask you some questions first."

"Little trade-off, right? Fire away."

"When did you last talk to Dawn?"

"Sunday morning. Told her I was headed off on to Buffalo, looking for work. Lost my fuckin' job at the fuckin' Qwik Freeze on account of—"

"So you left her at home?"

"Yeah. Stopped at Marge's for some breakfast."

"And then you went to the Croh Bar."

"Couple of pops for the road," he said, his lower lip at a belligerent angle. "So what?"

"And you saw Helena Houndswood come off the train?"

"Yeah. Man, that's some babe." He shook his head. "Looks smaller than on TV, you know. Saw her, figured Dawnie oughta know. I mean, shit. What's the broadie here for 'cept to fork over the bucks? And I wanted what's owed me."

"You were broke, is that it?"

Rickie scowled, immediately defensive. "Who the fuck told you that? They're a goddam liar. I'm as good off as anyone in this shitheel town. Hell, I paid my truck off two months ago, and that trailer's practically paid off, too. We got enough, not that the bitch is any too free handing it out." He flexed his fist absentmindedly. "Guy needs some beer money, he should get some beer money. No damn wife of mine's gonna say no, either."

"Could Dawn have had a separate checking account?"

His mouth tightened into a mean line. "Could be. Wun't put it past her. We put our paychecks in the same damn account. She makes eleven twenty a hour; I was making fifteen. She'd wave that checkbook at me once in a while, bitching about my takin' out beer money."

"There must have been some opportunities to find extra money at Paramount. I mean, she was the bookkeeper. You

know, Rickie . . ." Quill glanced behind her. The steel door
was closed. She took a breath and plunged in. "If you know
about something Dawn did—maybe if you even helped her
to some extra money, if you talked to Sheriff McHale about
it, things might go better for the both of you. I mean, if
she's hiding out because she maybe took off with some extra
funds from Paramount and is afraid to come back to claim her
winnings, or something . . ."

"You mean I could get that money faster?" Rickie's little
pig eyes glittered. "If Dawn was like, a thief, she maybe
couldn't collect that million bucks. It'd come to me?"

"No, no no," said Quill, "that's not what I meant. What I
meant is you could sort of throw yourself on the mercy of
the court by confessing before the court had to go to all the
expense of an investigation. They go more lightly on people
who confess up front, I think."

"Yeah? I could use some lightening up, that's for sure. I
mean, what kind of fucking fool shoots the goddam sheriff's
fucking girlfriend? And now they think I shot up some broadie
I don't even know. Although," he said with a conciliatory air,
"I din't mean to hurt nobody. Least of all you. Anyways, I'm
standing here to tell you that Dawn never thought about being
a thief. Not Dawnie. An out-and-out slugger bitch, yeah, no
question. Whacked me more'n once with the fry pan, coming
home too late from the Croh Bar. Whacked me another time,
she finds out I been drawing a little extra from the checking
account for beer. Besides," he said with a very peculiar kind of
dignity, "we have our plans, Dawnie and me. I mean, we have
our disagreements, no question about that, but I was going to
Buffalo for a better job. We was going to start saving for
the kid, and then she ups and disappears on me. Bitch!" He
pounded one fist into the palm of his hand. To her amazement,
Quill saw tears in his eyes.

"I didn't know you had children," said Quill. Myles, she
was convinced, had no idea, either, and she had a sudden
chilling vision of toddlers left in the Pennifarm trailer overnight with no one to take care of them. "Is anyone taking care
of them? Can I check on them for you?"

"No kids. Not yet, anyhow. Dawnie has a bun in the oven.
Not that she thanked me," said Rickie bitterly. "Said she don't

want no drunk for a father. She thought maybe I'd fuck it up or something."

"You mean Dawn was pregnant," said Quill.

"Yeah," said Rickie proudly. "Our first. Three months along."

Quill threw another involuntary glance over her shoulder. "About yesterday, Rickie."

"What about it?"

"I found . . . the body, you know. Dot Vandermolen."

"So?"

"I guess the bullet that winged me might have come from that rifle?"

"So fucking what? I didn't do it. I wasn't anywheres near that place. Sure the truck was there, but I keep that Remington right where it's supposed to be, see? In the gun rack in the back. And so what if some damn fool comes along and borrows it? When I get my hands on that bastard . . ." His lips curled back from his teeth. "And I got an alibi. I was down to Frank's, getting gas in a can. No matter what that fuckin' sheriff thinks I done, I didn't do that stupid bitch."

"Dot," said Quill. "Dot Vandermolen."

"I run out in the woods!" raged Rickie, his hands white-knuckled on the bars. "I run outa gas in the fuckin' woods and I walked off down the fuckin' road to the fuckin' gas station and I didn't fire no rifle!"

"I see," said Quill.

Quill concluded the interview with a few vague promises to give Helena Houndswood the opportunity to offer Rickie an advance on his two hundred and fifty thousand, and returned to the office. Dina was leaning over Deputy Dave's shoulder, looking at his gun. She greeted Quill with a cry of relief.

"Rickie claims he was getting gas?" said Dina. Quill had added her short and unremarkable statement to Dina's, and they were driving back to the Inn. "That's pretty thin. What about Dawn? You think he killed her, too?"

"I don't think Rickie's killed anyone. For one thing, he talks about her in the present tense. Even though my gut feel says Dawn's dead, and he's the likeliest suspect, I still don't think he did it. Being married to Rickie—and she was pregnant by the way—it gives her even more of a motive to take the money and run. But it doesn't make sense. Why make off with our forty-five hundred dollars when she was convinced that two hundred thousand dollars had gotten off the train with Helena Houndswood? On the other hand, with his pickup truck parked right there, and unlocked, *anyone* could have picked up that rifle. And there were a lot of people in the woods that day. Sandy. Kay. Connie. Helena herself." Quill brooded, and absentmindedly turned right under the sign on the intersection that said NO TURN ON RED.

"Uh, Quill," said Dina.

"What? Oh! Was that red? Darn." Quill braked. A horn sounded. Quill waved at Elmer Henry in his 1980 Seville. Harvey was seated next to him. Neither man waved back.

"Uh, Quill!"

"What, Dina?"

"You probably didn't drive too much being from Manhattan and everything, but we shouldn't be sitting in the middle of the road like this."

"Oh. You're right, of course. Sorry." Quill shifted into Drive and mused on. "Unless Helena did it. Killed Dot and bought Kay and Dawn Pennifarm off."

"Helena Houndswood!" said Dina, scandalized. "Why?"

"Dina. You've met Dawn. And the rest of the Bosses Club. I don't know if you'd met Dot, but she was a pretty tough cookie. Suppose you're Helena Houndswood with a reputation for appealing to the crème de la crème, and here the china contest winners turn out to be Dot, Sandy, Connie, Kay, and Dawn. Now. You find out who they are. You realize that Connie is well spoken and attractive, but she's black. And don't you tell me that racism isn't alive and well and thriving from Manhattan to Tacoma. She's clearly not a candidate for Helena's screwy notions of who gets to lead a Beautiful Life. Ditto Sandy Willis, for separate reasons. Kay Gondowski and Dawn are intimidated into keeping their mouths shut, and they leave town. But Dot . . ."

"A shouter?" said Dina. "An activist?"

"And almost as mean as Rickie Pennifarm himself. If you were Helena Houndswood, wouldn't you try and do some damage control?"

"Wow," said Dina thoughtfully. "No offense, Quill, but it's just an opinion, right? I mean, you don't have any proof."

Quill parked in front of the Inn's main door. "I'll get proof. But not before I've identified the solvability factors and eliminated the nonessential facts. This will lead me to a logical conclusion."

"These solvability factors," said Dina, "you've mentioned them before."

"They're facts that lead to the solution of the crime," said Quill. "You collect all the facts pertaining to a crime, and then you determine which are the ones that lead to the solution, and those are the solvability factors."

"How do you determine which fact is the right one?"

"Analysis," said Quill firmly. "Are you getting out?"

"You're not coming in?"

"No."

"I think everyone from the chamber's left. I mean, the only ones who were really mad at you were Miriam and Harvey and Elmer and Howie."

Quill stared at her. "Really mad at me? Why?!"

"The chamber minutes."

"The chamber minutes. Oh, dear," said Quill guiltily. "I have this kind of weird shorthand, Dina, and it was probably impossible for Miriam to interpret them."

"They interpreted it just fine. The drawings were real clear, I guess. So were the captions. You're awfully good, Quill, as an artist I mean."

Harvey on the pitchfork. Marge in flames. Quill slid down in the driver's seat: the matchmaking note about Miriam and Howie Murchison. "They saw it? All of them?" she said after a moment.

"Yep. So I can see why you might want to stay away from the Inn for a while. Miriam's waiting for you."

"I'm not afraid to go into my own Inn," said Quill, which wasn't the literal truth. "I'm going to Paramount to talk to Hudson Zabriskie. I'm gathering evidence."

"Jeez," said Dina. "The Bloater. See you in a couple of days, then."

"Very funny."

Dina got out, then leaned in the open window. "You know, I was thinking that maybe I could solve this with you and Meg? It was kind of fun, being a femme fatale with Deputy Dave. But I don't know, Quill, Rickie Pennifarm is like the scum of the earth. And Hudson Zabriskie . . . I mean, ick! Nice guy, but we're talking geek city."

Quill decided a modest smile was in order. "Not everyone," she said, "has the motivation to be a detective, Dina. Which is fine."

"And besides, it takes time." Dina sighed heavily. "The orals for my dissertation are up in three months. Keep me up on your progress, though, right?"

"Right."

The drive to Paramount was short. Quill kept an eye out for Harvey and the mayor, stopping carefully at every red light. She pulled into the employee parking lot and sat for a moment, wondering who had the chamber minutes now, and if the chamber members would consider a free eight-course gourmet meal as sufficient apology. "Never apologize, never explain," somebody had once said, which Quill thought perfectly ridiculous: she was going to have to apologize all over the place if she wanted to keep any friends. "Head wound" or "post-traumatic stress syndrome" might do as an explanation. Quill tried to think of Famous Detectives who'd used "head wound" as an excuse for rudeness, and failed utterly. "Order and method," said Quill aloud. "Use those little gray cells." She took out her Interview book, recorded the substance of her interrogation of Rickie Pennifarm, adding a note: Take Miriam shopping? Call Howie and grovel? Bag Harvey! Then listed the next set of Things To Do.

1. Where was Hudson at the time of Dot's shooting?

2. Verify Dawn's last seen/last day activities?

3. GET MONEY!

Quill had never been inside the Paramount Paint Factory, although she'd passed it innumerable times and it was hard to overlook. The building was long and low, the size of several football fields end to end. Each section of aluminum siding was painted in a different Paramount exterior color, beginning with Cryst-All White, through the red-yellow-green-blue-violet of the color palette. The Qwik Freeze plant a quarter of a mile away was bigger and employed more people, but Paramount loomed a lot larger in the town's collective imagination. Although when she thought about it, this may have been because of Hudson himself and not the startling appearance of the factory building. Hudson was widely popular despite his esoteric dyslexia, perhaps even because of it; frequently, the only rational response to Hudson's linguistic vagaries was a genial, uncomprehending nod. Hudson never made any real enemies because no one could tell if he was voicing an unpopular opinion or not. More to the point, as a subsidiary of a Fortune 500 company, Paramount pay scales and benefits were better than Qwik Freeze, whose local farmer-owners were notoriously thrifty. Hudson benefited from the halo effect.

Quill went through the front door and into the reception area. There was no one at the front desk, but a large sign read VISITORS WELCOME! PLEASE SIGN IN! with an arrow pointing downward to a visitor's book. Quill wrote her name, then pushed a bell labeled RING FOR ASSISTANCE, and sat down to wait.

The reception area was furnished in what Meg called Business Plastic: bucket chairs and teetery end tables with fake geraniums resting on an exceptionally clean linoleum floor. The walls were off-white, and displayed Paramount's "COMMITMENT TO QUALITY," an award for "EXCELLENCE IN EXTERIOR LATEX" and a plaque for the U.S.A.P.M. Race for the Rainbow First Prize for a paint called Crimson Blaze, displaying a virulently orange-red paint sample.

"You sap 'em," said Hudson, coming through a door marked NO ADMITTANCE. "Two years in a row."

"Hi, Hudson," said Quill.

Hudson veered aimlessly to the plaque. "Dutch Boy couldn't touch it," he said with visible pride.

"U.S.A.P.M. The United States of America Paint Manufacturers," said Quill with sudden insight. "How wonderful, Hudson. It's an important prize, I take it."

"Without question." Hudson smoothed his mustache. "My process, you know. Leadless. Nothing to do but promote me, they said."

"How in the world did you get that marvelous orange-red without using lead oxide?" asked Quill. "It's amazing!"

"Teamwork," said Hudson. He beamed. Quill noticed he had a very nice smile. "The Bosses worked under my leadership. Enormous savings, not using lead. OSHA's happy. UMC's down. New York's delighted with me, just delighted. No contaminants, you see, at least, not that we can tell."

"What did you use instead of lead oxide?" Quill's professional curiosity was aroused.

Hudson looked at her helplessly. Quill made a mental note to ask Connie Weyerhauser whether Hudson knew anything at all about the process that had brought them to the attention of New York.

"Well, it's wonderful," said Quill. "I'm sorry to interrupt your workday, Hudson, but I thought maybe I could pick up that check?" She stopped herself, aware that she'd rushed her fences. Nothing made Hudson more hopelessly twitchy than the mention of money. Hudson was oblivious, contemplating his plaque.

"Trying to get the color of fire," said Hudson, complacently observing the framed sample of Crimson Blaze. "You're a painter, too, they tell me. Of course, pictures are different, but paint's paint."

"Artist's colors *are* a bit different," said Quill diplomatically. "The process—"

"The process! How right you are! Paint is *not* paint, Quill. Why, there's a very well-known oil-base manufacturer, and I'm naming no names, mind you, but I'd swear they'd put their label on anything! Soybean substitute!" Hudson snorted in patent disgust. "Very few people really understand paint, Quill. People who really understand paint, really love paint, who know about the value of paint to our culture, know why I'm so concerned about the cost of our lunches. Would you like to see the improvements I've brought to the Hemlock factory?"

Great detectives, thought Quill, frequently conducted their investigations along unobvious and seemingly irrelevant lines. Look at Miss Marple. "Sure," said Quill.

Hudson barged through the NO ADMITTANCE DOOR rather like a golden retriever begging for a walk, treading backward to face Quill waving his arms back and forth like twin tails. "It all begins," he said seriously, "with the exoskeletons of tiny creatures who died hundreds of thousands of years ago." He inhaled, choked, and apologized, "Sorry. I got so excited I swallowed my spit."

Quill was disarmed. She followed him meekly through the factory, which was huge, noisy, and very clean. Quill heard about diatomaceous earth, cut out of the Adirondacks in ten-ton chunks and thrown into Paramount's sixteen-foot-wide, sixty-foot-long ball mills, to be ground to the consistency of talcum powder, then mixed with calcium carbonate, mica, and zinc oxide, the latter, Hudson told her sternly, an expensive mineral that Certain Companies skimped on. Not Paramount, which was, if Quill didn't mind a little jest, paramount.

Hudson was rather endearingly fond of oil-based paint. "They'll ban it eventually, you know," he said wistfully. "If I hadn't come up with my orange-red process, we'd have to be obsolescing the whole line in five years. It's a pity."

Quill, who loved the fiery depths of color, agreed, but added practically, "Latex is much safer."

"Latex!" Hudson's scorn was clear. "Let me tell you about latex! More expensive, but will customers pay for it? Absolutely not. So the profit margin's lower. I have to work that much harder, which I don't mind, of course, not at all. Terrible coverage. Awful stick. Fades. Disgraceful. Nothing," continued Hudson earnestly, "will touch your basic oil-base."

"Hmm," said Quill, for lack of a comprehensible response. Cursed with a memory only erratically retentive, Quill later found herself able to quote the properties of "hiding" pigments like titanium dioxide (which gives paint its quality of coverage), zinc oxide (which makes dried paint hard), and how "certain manufacturers who shall remain nameless" cheated on the quality of oil-base paint by using the lowest-grade linseed oil—sometimes achieving the nadir through the use of a soybean substitute.

"You would think," she said to Meg that evening, "that I could remember stuff like your recipe for ratatouille, or the combination to the office safe, but no, my brain stores the fact that pigment is seventeen point six percent of paint."

"I gather that the rest," said Meg solemnly, "is solvents."

"Hamlet, sideswiped." Quill settled back into a rocker next to the kitchen fireplace. "Actually it was kind of interesting. Those ball mills are filled with fist-sized stones. The mill rotates, the rocks tumble, and ten-ton chunks of rock are reduced to the consistency of talcum powder in about eight hours. I was thinking a little teeny ball mill would be fun in the kitchen. You know, you could grind up spices and what not."

Meg, who was grinding nutmeg to a powder with a mortar and pestle, stopped and gave her sister a dubious look. "Aside from genius ideas about innovative kitchen equipment, did you get the money?"

"I didn't get the money."

"Why didn't you get the money?"

"Because Hudson talked so much about mineral spirits and kerosene and how his process for making oil-based orange-reds is leadless that I didn't get a chance. He claims that he won't know if the money's missing until he talks to the bank, and I asked him to talk to the bank, and he picked up the phone and then started to fill me in on how stones from Normandy are the only ones you can use on a ball mill without cracking. Which I thought was pretty interesting, by the way." She ignored Meg's eye-rolling and said, "I did, however, pin him down about Dot and where he was at the time of her murder. He gave Kay Gondowski a ride home from the Inn. So she's his alibi. If she shows up." Quill frowned, the faint memory troubling her. "I think he thinks Dawn stole the money. But he waffled. And he clearly doesn't want to pay up, which is why he's saying he's not sure, and he has to call the bank. But he thinks she took it. He said he's suspected her for a long time of petty thieving. There's *always* a certain amount of small stuff in a business, but lately, Hudson said—well, he didn't exactly say it, but I gathered as much—that there'd been a lot of complaints about money missing from the women's locker room. The workers all have to wear white lab coats and change their shoes and shower off. They have a locker room for men and women, and the women's locker room has been where the thefts have occurred. The Bosses Club will be crushed if Dawn's a petty thief. So, in fact, will Rickie Pennifarm, who thinks his sweetie is incapable of it. But that's what it looks like, at least. Hudson also thinks Kay and Dawn just up and quit. Hudson said he's already received budget approval for five new supervisory positions from New York. He says Connie and Sandy are going to quit, too."

"Hudson didn't tell us anything very useful, did he? You're awful at pinning people down," Meg observed without rancor. "On the other hand, you're pretty good at caricature, from what Miriam Doncaster tells me."

"Uh. That."

"It's great when you squirm. If they haven't burned the minutes book, I'd love to see it. So Dawn seems to have done a permanent bunk. Maybe we don't need the forty-five hundred as much as John thinks we need the money. The Inn is stuffed full, Quill. The dining room's booked through the weekend. Nobody from the Chamber, of course, since there's a temporary boycott due to your minutes book. I take it you didn't leave your Investigator's Book lying around for Deputy Dave to find and marvel at?"

Quill pushed the rocker into motion, to avoid a descent into adolescent behavior involving phrases of the "Shut up, stupid," "Who's stupid?" "You're stupid" variety. "Well, maybe Hudson wasn't all that useful. But Rickie Pennifarm was. Now, here's what we know from Dawn's creepo husband." She summarized her conversation with Rickie Pennifarm, gratified at Meg's horrified expressions of sisterly concern: "You talked to this guy alone!" Then, "How could she stand being married to him!" Then, thoughtfully, "So they weren't broke."

"But she's pregnant. And it makes sense to me that she grabbed money from everywhere she could to get away."

"God!" Meg shuddered. "What a father the kid's got to look

forward to." She emptied the nutmeg into a glass bowl, opened the freezer, and pulled out a large beef tenderloin. She dumped it into the Cuisinart and watched the meat pulverize with a thoughtful expression.

"So what do you think?" asked Quill.

"Steak Tartare's a big seller when the dining room's full."

"No, I mean about the investigation."

Meg added salt, pepper, and a dash of vinegar to the glass bowl, turned off the Cuisinart and dumped the beef into the spices. She began to shape the meat with her hands. "Rickie's alibi is tissue paper. He could have shot Dot by mistake before or after he went to get gas. It looks like Dawn Pennifarm has run off with as much cash as she could pull together. When she hears about the million bucks, she'll probably be back. If she's lucky, Rickie'll be sent up the river for twenty years for murder." Meg nodded in the direction of the newspaper folded on the counter top. "There's a paragraph in *USA Today* about the win. She'll see it. And she'll come home with some story or other. It looks like the case is closed, Sherlock."

"But what about Kay?"

"Connie heard from Kay, didn't she?"

"So she said."

"It's consistent with Kay's character. That she'd take off and hide."

"What's consistent, Meg, is that all these women are connected to Helena Houndswood, who has every reason in the world to buy them off."

"Bullshit." Meg thumped the beef.

"I take it that means you don't think Helena Houndswood is behind the planned disappearance of the Bosses Club one by one."

"I never did think that. You thought that. What I thought is that we could find Dawn and get our forty-five hundred dollars back. Now I think we have to wait until Dawn finds us."

Quill leaned her head against the rocker back and closed her eyes. "Helena is leaving tomorrow. Although it's just down the hill to the Petersons' old house. If there's anything funny going on, it's going to be harder to keep an eye on her."

Meg shaped the finely ground beef into a large ball, covered

it with cheesecloth, and put it in the cooler. "I don't know
a thing about what's-this-he-called-it retrograde amnesia, but
that whack on the head seems to have given you a *thing* about
Helena Houndswood."

"I don't have a thing about Helena Houndswood. I have a
thing about one woman dead and two women missing after
winning more money than they've ever seen in their lives."

"Then we should be looking at Connie and Sandy as suspects, right? I mean, they have the most to gain." Meg wiped
her hands on a kitchen towel. "God, my hands are cold after
handling that meat."

Quill stiffened.

Meg turned to the sink and rinsed her hands in warm water.
"And I don't believe Connie's capable of hanky-panky. Sandy,
now, she's a possibility . . . except that there's a logical explanation for both incidents. Tell you what, let's try displacing
stress with some good old sex. Much more fun than detecting,
sex. I was thinking that maybe you and Myles and Andy and I
could go to Syracuse next Friday and have dinner somewhere
else, for a change. . . . Quill, are you all right? What's the
matter?"

"That's what Kay said. 'God, my hands are cold.' Meg! I
remember! It was Kay I was on the phone with when Rickie
shot up the front door. Kay Gondowski!"

CHAPTER 9

"That's all you remember? 'My hands are so cold'?" Myles was dressed in a rumpled tweed sport coat and a blue workshirt. He slouched against the kitchen fireplace, his evidence case at his feet.

Quill nodded. The bullet wound itched. She rubbed it with a tentative finger. "That's it. It's a funny sort of memory, like an electrical short. Sort of sputtery. I've tried and tried to remember more, but I can't."

"But you're sure it was Kay."

"Positive."

It was after eleven. The kitchen was deserted except for the four of them. Quill sat on one side of the long counter, John and Meg on the other. Quill had sent most of the young staff home; the sole remaining diners were a young couple on a tour of the Finger Lakes who'd gotten lost on their way to Canandaigua.

Meg fiddled with a plate of salmon sandwiches she'd made while they waited for Myles. "You said you found some evidence at Kay's house? But no Kay?"

"No Kay. I did find this. Recognize it?" Myles set the evidence case on the counter and removed a sheaf of manila files.

"It looks like the minutes of the team meetings for the Bosses Club," said Quill. "I saw it yesterday in the conference room."

"In whose possession?"

"Connie's. Connie Weyerhauser." Quill paged through the file. There was an incredible amount of paper; page after page of notes, accounts, printed material from various government agencies. "She was Dawn Pennifarm's backup on the team."

"It was Connie who told you Kay called her to say she'd left town because she was too frightened to show up."

Quill, uneasy, nodded reluctantly and attempted a diversion. "Boy! Look at all the stuff you have to do to handle lead oxide!" She pulled out a Materials Safety handling sheet from OSHA. "Masks for the workers, gloves, vents. No wonder the Bosses Club leadless process is saving so much money."

Myles refused to be drawn. "John, I'd like you to take a look at how Dawn handled purchasing."

"The General Ledger's in there?" said John with a frown.

"Just the inventory accounts."

John spread the files on the counter, took a pencil from his pocket, and began to leaf slowly through the pages.

"So did Rickie Pennifarm confess to killing Dot yet?" demanded Meg. "That alibi of his is pretty shaky, if you ask me."

"I tend to believe it," said Myles. "It's the airtight alibis that bother me. Frank Talbot sold Rickie five gallons of gas yesterday afternoon sometime between five and five-thirty. He doesn't remember precisely. Rickie was drunk, he said, and wanted a ride back to the truck, which Frank wasn't inclined to give him."

Meg made a noise indicative of disbelief. Quill bit her lip.

"Hm," said John. "Well, well, well. Myles. How would you feel if your supplier charged you two thousand dollars a ton for iron oxide?"

"I don't know," said Myles. "Bemused?"

"Suspicious." John looked up, a faint grin creasing his face. "That's red clay, basically. A pigment. According to the Bosses Club, it's the ingredient that replaces lead oxide to get that orange-red color. It's cheap, I know that. Nowhere near two thousand dollars for a ton."

"Iron oxide?" said Quill. "To replace lead oxide as a pigment?"

John ignored her. "There's a second inconsistency. The proportion of pigment versus solvent is roughly one to five. But the amount of iron oxide ordered is far more than the gallonage for the whole factory. At least on paper."

"Where's the iron oxide shipped from?" said Myles.

"The wholesaler's address is Queens, New York," said John. His brow furrowed. "Queens. Now where have I seen that address before?" He raised his eyebrows. "By god! Makepeace Whitman!"

"The Fresh Air People!" said Quill. "You're joking! The guy wholesales clay?"

"Well, somebody has to," said Myles, amused. "I don't suppose it's inconsistent with his interest in fresh air. Everyone has to have a hobby. John, if you had to guess, what would you say is going on here?"

"Embezzlement," said John. "Not on a huge scale. Don't hold me to this, but . . ." He withdrew his pocket calculator from the breast pocket of his sport coat and rapidly punched in numbers. "If I extrapolate from this one month, April, somebody pulled three or four hundred dollars out of Paramount. Multiply this by twelve and it's a little less than four thousand a year."

Quill opened her mouth. Myles held up his hand to forestall her comment. "It's not enough for Hudson Zabriskie to be involved, Quill."

"That's not what I was going to say," said Quill indignantly.

"Well, it's what I've been thinking. Hudson's responsible for the Bosses Club, and for the P and L at the end of the year. What do you think, John?"

John shook his head. "No way. It wouldn't make sense for Hudson to engage in this kind of petty theft. He makes well over a hundred thousand a year. . . ."

"He does!" gasped Meg.

"How do you know?" asked Quill.

"Benchmarking," said John. "Most of the large businesses in town share salary figures. It gives an idea of how much we have to pay local employees."

"Bench what?" asked Meg.

Quill patted her arm. "I'll explain to you later."

"So it's not worth Hudson's time. Certainly not worth the risk. But it might be worth the Bosses Club's. The women's wages average a little less than eleven hundred a month, and an extra three or four hundred pays a lot of groceries. On top of that, it's unlikely that this scam would survive an audit. And Hudson's way too smart for that."

"A hundred thousand a year," marveled Meg. "He's such a dope!"

"He's a dope running a subsidiary of a Fortune 500 company." John shrugged. "What can I say."

"Have you bench whatis chefs' salaries?" Meg demanded. "Quill . . . a hundred thousand a *year?!*" Quill opened her mouth again. "You were going to say that I'm not worth a hundred thousand a year," said Meg furiously. "Well, I'll have you know that a good chef in Manhattan is worth five times that. Ten times that!"

"That's not what I was going to say," said Quill. "And you're priceless, Meg. John, that iron oxide . . ."

"I took a cursory look at the figures," said Myles. "Do you agree that both Dawn and Connie Weyerhauser may have been involved?"

John paged through the figures again. "It's a good guess."

"Sufficient grounds for an arrest?"

John nodded. "I can work up a paragraph for you for a warrant."

"Myles, no!" Quill clenched her hands. "This is absurd. There's no way that Connie Weyerhauser could be mixed up in this!"

"I know you're upset, Quill—"

"If you pat me on the head," said Quill through gritted teeth, "I'll hit you."

"Quill," said Meg. "Settle down. Look at the facts. Connie left the Inn at four-thirty, just before Dot was killed. You told me yourself that Dot was threatening to look at those files. Worse yet, every time a member of the Bosses Club drops out of the picture, Connie gets another piece cf that million dollars. It's a pretty strong motive."

"I suppose you're going to tell me she stuck Kay Gondowski in a refrigerator somewhere," said Quill, stiff with anger. "And that Sandy Willis is next."

"I didn't think that either Kay or Sandy had access to these files," said Myles. "But I'm wondering why Kay had them. And yes, I'm concerned about both the women. Which is why I'm going to pick up Connie now."

"Wait!" said Quill. "What about Helena Houndswood?"

"What about Helena Houndswood?" said Meg, exasperated. "Honestly, Quill."

"She was in the woods at the very minute Dot was murdered," said Quill. "And she could have passed right by Rickie Pennifarm's truck, swiped the rifle, and killed Dot."

"Except she hadn't seen any of the Bosses Club at that point," said Meg. "How would she know who to shoot?"

"That's where you're wrong," said Quill. "I have proof that she knew about the Bosses Club the Sunday she came into town . . . well . . . not proof exactly, but a strong suspicion. *And* she said she was going upstairs to take a hot bath, and she lied about that—she was out, probably shooting Kay Gondowski. And she's got a motive, Myles. She thinks these women could end her career. I know she does. And besides . . ." Quill stopped suddenly and folded her arms, determined not to discuss the puzzle of the iron oxide until she solved it herself.

"Besides what?" said Myles.

"Nothing."

"Stubborn," said Meg. "It's just like that time with Caroline Addison, Quill."

"It is not like the time with Caroline Addison."

"What about Caroline Addison?" asked Myles.

"They don't want to hear about Caroline Addison," said Quill.

"I do," said John.

"Caroline Addison—" said Meg.

"Meg!"

"—was the meanest, rottenest waitress at the country club when we were in high school. Quill and I waitressed at the club in the summers. And the deal was, all the waitresses put their tips in a big jar, and we split it at the end of each shift. Caroline never put in any tips, and we all said that it was because Caroline kept hers and then took some of ours, but no, Quill didn't believe it. She said we should leave Caroline alone because it would be just awful for Caroline to have to admit nobody gave her any tips because she was a rotten waitress. It would be even worse to accuse her of being a thief. Which she was. Instead, Quill started giving her little hints about how to be a better waitress, and Caroline got pissed off and socked her. So I socked Caroline. And we all three got fired. But that's Quill. Stubborn in defense of the helpless. Caroline Addison was about as helpless as a rattlesnake.

"And Myles, the same thing is happening here. Quill likes Connie. She feels sorry for Connie because she has a daughter with CP and a hard life. I do, too. But it looks very much like Connie's in the middle of this, Quill. And you don't like Helena Houndswood because she's not an underdog. She's an upper dog. She's about as upper dog as you can get." Meg, seeing Quill's expression, continued rapidly, "And now she's really mad at me, so I'm going, going, gone to bed." She backed out of the dining room doors and disappeared.

Quill picked up the salmon sandwiches with a purposeful air and aimed them at the sink. The plate landed on the rinse side with a crash.

John put the Bosses Club files into a neat stack with a grin.

"Where is Helena?" asked Myles with a conciliatory air.

"Harvey took her to Ithaca to look at tractors," said Quill shortly.

"Tractors? Why would she want a tractor?"

"She's moving into the Peterson house for a month. She's going to write another book. Farming: It's a Beautiful Life."

Myles gave a shout of laughter. John bit his lip.

"I'm serious," said Quill, smiling in spite of herself. "She's going to get a horse, a cow to milk, some pigs. And some chickens."

"Chickens!" John nodded at Myles. "I was there. It's true." John burst into outright laughter.

"What's wrong with chickens?" asked Quill. "I sort of like chickens."

John shook his head, helpless.

"It'll be interesting," said Myles. His smile died. "I'm leaving now, Quill. I'll check in with you later."

"You're going to arrest her?"

"I've got probable cause, Quill. And I have one dead woman, and two missing. And a fourth to worry about. Sandy Willis. Every time a member of the Bosses Club disappears, Connie benefits that much more. No, I'm not sure. But I've got cause to wonder."

John, murmuring vague excuses, went to bed and Quill was left glaring at Myles alone. "Please wait, Myles. You have to talk to the Whitmans, right? And where are you going to get an arrest order this time of night? You'll have to go to Ithaca and raise a judge and by the time you get back it'll be morning. Why not wait tomorrow?"

"Quill, I . . ."

She reached over and drew his hand to her cheek. "You're wrong about this. I know you're wrong. Come up to bed with me."

He put his arms around her and rested his chin on the top of her head. "You're right, I suppose. A few hours isn't going to make any difference. And Judge Anderson is going to be a little more receptive to the warrant if I catch him during chambers." He drew back and took her chin in his hand. "You go on up. I want to give one of the deputies a call."

"You're going to have Connie's house watched," said Quill.

"Give me twenty minutes."

"Okay," said Quill. "Okay."

"What is so funny about chickens?" Quill asked Myles sometime later. She lay with her head against his chest, both of them propped up in bed, looking out the window at the summer moon.

"You've never raised chickens?"

"Of course I've never raised chickens. I was brought up in Connecticut. In the suburbs. You've never raised chickens, either, Myles, have you?"

"I knocked around a bit after college. Spent some time in Central and South America. Worked in a lot of places for my keep. Poultry farm was one of them. Chickens are . . ." He paused, and silent laughter reverberated in her ear. "Messy. Very stupid. There's nothing meaner than a chicken. People who raise chickens eat a lot of chicken. Not out of necessity. Out of revenge."

"Oh, ha, ha." Quill sat up and drew her hair off her neck. "You never told me that before."

"You never asked." He stroked her cheek. "If I'd known about this compelling interest in chickens . . ."

"I don't mean chickens. I mean about Central America. You just don't . . . talk to me, Myles. I find out things about you by accident. From other people." The atmosphere in the darkened room changed. She felt him withdraw. Quill tried to keep her tone light. "I never knew a thing about your stellar career as a SuperCop in Manhattan, for example, until your partner . . . what's his name . . ."

"Billy Nordstrum. Smilin' Bill."

" . . . Came to visit and you two started reminiscing and I discover you're some kind of legend in Manhattan." She continued: "I don't know anything about your first marriage, either."

"You could talk to my first wife, I guess."

"Myles! That's just the point." She got out of bed and walked out onto the balcony, water mist rising from the falls cupping the stars and shrouding her view of the moon. She folded her arms around herself and shivered slightly. Myles moved through the darkness, and embraced her from behind, burying his face in her hair.

"It's an ordinary story, you know. Most failed marriages are."

"That's not true. You know that's not true. Failed marriages tell a lot about people."

"All the more reason to talk to my first wife."

"You're serious. Is it that hard to tell me yourself? I feel . . . awkward . . . asking you. I'm afraid you don't trust me. I feel as though I should be doing more to prove you can trust me."

Myles was silent for a long moment. "You're such a gentle woman, Quill. For all your fierce defense of your stray lambs and black sheep."

She reached around and jabbed him in the side. "Gentle, huh? Of all the condescending, fat-headed things to say . . . Do you think I can't take it? That's an insult, Myles, and pretty damn chauvinist. The fragile little woman bit! I thought you were past that."

The phone rang, cutting through the two A.M. quiet with a shrill insistence. Quill moved quickly into the bedroom, stubbed her toe, and knocked the phone off the stand. She picked up the receiver with a muttered "Hell!" to hear Deputy Dave blushing over the wire. "Uh . . . Sher'f there, Ms. Quilliam? Sorry to disturb you, but it's an emergency."

She handed the phone to Myles, then switched on the light and stood watching his face. He listened silently, then said, "Give me twenty minutes," and hung up. He looked years older.

"Bad news," said Quill.

"Sandy Willis. Automobile crash on fifteen."

"Myles! No! Is she all right?"

Myles shook his head.

"She's not dead? Oh, Myles. Oh, this is terrible! Roy? The children?"

"Roy's at home with the kids."

Distractedly Quill began to dress. "There must be something I can do. You must let me help."

"There is. I'm going to the scene to relieve David. I want you to go over to the house and talk to Roy. Find out why she was driving on route fifteen alone at two in the morning. Wait there for me, and then I'll take him over to the morgue. He'll have to do the identification."

"Me?" said Quill, dismayed. "You want me to help with the investigation by interviewing Roy within an hour after his wife's been killed?"

"I know he'll be upset," said Myles quietly. "Sometimes that's the time to get the truth out of people. You've got a way with people, Quill. And I need the facts. There's been one too many coincidences involving the Bosses Club."

Myles took off in his car with efficient, quiet speed. Quill followed him down the drive and out onto the highway at a more sober pace.

Sandy and her family lived on East Lane, a one-street-long development a half mile from the Paramount plant. The plant had opened in the late twenties, just before the Depression, and five stone and lathe houses had been built for the plant managers and supervisors at the cul-de-sac; in the booming fifties, more than a dozen one-story ranches built by one of the enterprising Petersons extended the length of the street. Another handful of cheap, prefabricated houses had been added during the decade-long boom of the eighties. One of the latter had a patrol car parked in front. The mailbox read WILLIS.

Quill pulled the Olds to the side of the road and sat for a moment, gathering the courage to go in. Lights shone in every room of the house, spilling out onto the lawn. The house was sided with aluminum clapboard, alternating with brick facing in front. A tricycle was upended on the sidewalk, and the lawn was unevenly mowed. But there were flowers in homemade planters on either side of the short sidewalk, and cheerful print curtains at the windows.

Quill went up the short, concrete walk to the door. Daisies and marigolds bloomed from wooden half barrels on the porch. She rang the bell and waited. Roy Willis jerked open the door. He was in jeans, barefoot and bare-chested. Behind him, Quill heard the wail of a young child. A second child, who sounded somewhat older, scolded in a singsong voice: "Timmy's face is dirty, Timmy's shirt is dirty, Timmy's butt is dir—"

"Quiet!" Roy yelled, turning back to the living room. He swiveled back to Quill, regarding her mutely.

Quill stepped inside. Dave Kiddermeister stood uneasily by the television set, his Stetson in his hand. He was pale. He greeted Quill with a relieved smile. A toddler, no more than two years old, Quill guessed, lay on a tattered blanket in the middle of the carpeted floor, crying and waving his legs in the air. A little girl of perhaps five or six stood next to him, holding a Barbie doll by the hair in one hand, and sucking her thumb with the other. Both were in pajamas. Roy picked his daughter up and cradled her in his arms, his eyes fixed on Quill's face.

Quill cleared her throat. "If you'd like," she said without preamble, "I can help you get the kids back to bed."

"He needs changin'." Roy indicated his son with a jerk of his chin. "Sandy should have been home by now. It's her night. We trade off nights for changing the baby, see. On account of we work different shifts, is why I do it."

Quill glanced at Dave. He shrugged helplessly and said in a low voice, "He can't seem to understand about the incident, ma'am. I told him. Took a swing at me and then ran around and got up the kids. Called me a liar."

"Well, you are a liar!" shouted Roy. "You're a goddam liar!" Both children burst into tears. Quill sent Dave to find clean diapers, picked up the toys scattered on the couch and floor, then lifted the baby onto one hip. Dave reappeared with a box of Pampers and a washcloth. "I can do that, ma'am," he said.

At Quill's doubtful look, he smiled. "Seven kids in my family, and I was the oldest." Quill surrendered the baby, then gently took the little girl from Roy's arms.

"Are you sleepy, honey?"

The child nodded.

"Can you tell me your name?"

"Brenda."

"Can you show me where your bedroom is?"

Brenda gestured with the Barbie doll. "Up 'tairs."

Quill carried her upstairs to a tiny bedroom decorated with colorful posters and a handmade quilt on the small bed. "Mommy did it," Brenda explained. She wriggled and Quill set her down. She ran to a gaily painted box and flung open the lid. "You wanna play Barbie?"

"Not right now. Aren't you sleepy, Brenda?"

"I'm waiting for Mommy. I can play until she gets home to put me to bed."

Sandy must have a sister, thought Quill, or a mother. Someone needed to be here. "Do you have a grandmother, Brenda?"

"Grandma June."

"Does she live around here?"

"Yes," said Brenda, then, "no."

Dave must know, Quill thought.

She got Brenda to lie down, "just to *pretend* to go to sleep," and went quietly downstairs. Roy sat slumped on the couch. Dave was waiting by the front door, his hat firmly in place. "The little guy's asleep," he said, "and I have to get back to the . . ." He darted a glance at Roy, who sat staring at nothing.

"Brenda said there's a grandmother. Her name is June."

Dave nodded. "Sandy's mother. She lives over to Trumansburg. Ought to be here in another twenty minutes. You'll wait with him, because I've got to get back to the . . . you know."

Dave left. The silence in the room was profound. Quill found the kitchen and made coffee. Feeling cowardly, she stalled until the machine stopped perking. She carried the carafe and three mugs back to Roy, and set them on the coffee table. He took the filled mug without looking at her.

"June will be here soon," said Quill.

Roy nodded.

"She . . . um . . . worked tonight? Sandy? The three to eleven shift?"

Roy nodded a second time. "Got home about a quarter to twelve." Tears began to run down his cheeks. Quill's throat filled.

"She came home? She went out again?"

Roy's gaze shot to the telephone on the TV set.

"She got a phone call?"

The tears rolled silently down his cheeks and splashed onto his bare chest. Quill blinked rapidly and lowered her head. It was hard to look at him. Stories about great detectives rarely told you how hard it was to look at people in trouble. "Do you know who the call was from?"

"Kay."

"Kay Gondowski?" Quill set her mug carefully on the table. "Do you know what she wanted?"

"Sandy," he said simply, "Sandy was laughin'. Told her she was a scaredy-cat. 'You ol' scaredy-cat, you,' she said. And then she told her about the makeover and all, and how good Kay was gonna look after Dwight got hold of her." The tears ran down his cheeks. His grief was simple. Uncomplicated. He breathed with a sound like a sea bird calling from a long way.

"Did she go out to meet Kay?" asked Quill carefully. "Did she say where Kay was?"

"Sandy said Kay got scared. Just took off in that old Plymouth of hers and drove instead of coming to the party last night. Stopped at some motel and liked to froze to death 'cause she didn't bring no clothes to sleep in. Wanted Sandy to bring her some stuff. Sandy said okay, tell me where you are, I'll come get you." Roy's voice rose higher and higher, and the words began to spill out of him like the water spilled over Hemlock dam. "Sandy said isn't it just like that girl to get scairt of good fortune and run right off. Sandy said only Kay Gondowski would win two big ones and run off like some rabbit. That was Sandy, you see. She always knew everything about everybody. She always could tell what people were gonna do and then she could tell them how to get it right. Sandy said she'd bring Kay back here to stay with us for a while and that was Sandy all over. 'I'll take care of it,' she said. 'Don't you worry, I'll take care of it.' She put a nightgown and sweater and a toothbrush in a plastic bag to take to her." He was sobbing. Quill bit her lip hard and pinched her knee.

The doorbell rang, and Quill bolted for the front door. It opened as she grasped the handle, and a woman who looked like Sandy would have twenty years from now walked into the room. Behind her was Myles.

"Roy!" she cried. "Oh, Roy! My little girl."

Myles drew Quill outside and shut the front door behind her. Quill drew three deep breaths.

"Rough in there," Myles said after a moment. "Are you all right?"

Quill nodded, grateful for the cool air.

"We'll give them a minute. Did you learn anything?"

Quill steadied her voice with an effort. She moved away from him and looked out over the lawn until she felt more in control. "Kay called her about midnight."

"Kay Gondowski?"

"Told Sandy she was at a motel outside of town. Sandy went to get her. What happened, Myles?"

"Did she tell Roy which motel?"

Quill shook her head. "Was there another car?"

"Yes. A red Ford Cortina. This year's model. It's a rental car. We found it abandoned about a quarter mile down the road. It was set up to look like a hit-and-run. I've got Syracuse running a computer check. You're sure Roy doesn't know the name of the motel."

"It can't be too far from here," Quill said, after she summarized her talk with Roy Willis. "I mean, the night of the party, I got that call from her about what . . . a quarter to nine? So assuming that she had checked in at a motel, she should be two to three hours from here. Good grief, Myles, how are you going to check all the motels within an eighty-mile driving distance? This time of year thousands of people are vacationing in the Finger Lakes and taking the wine tours."

"That's what APBs are for," said Myles absently.

"You told me APBs are no substitute for legwork."

"They aren't. But I haven't got the manpower. The county mounties will help, but I can't count on it." He'd been speaking almost automatically, his mind elsewhere. He seemed to come to a decision; his gaze sharpened and he took her chin in his hand. "Why don't you go home and get some sleep."

Sandy's mother opened the door. She held Roy by the elbow. Her eyes were wet. "Roy says he's got to go with you?"

"Just down to the county hospital for a while," said Myles.

"You'll bring him right back?"

"I'll bring him right back."

"Is there anything I can do?" asked Quill. "Would you like to go with him, June? I'll be happy to stay with the children."

"Don't want to see her," said Sandy's mother. "I can't. Roy'll do it. He's tough." She patted his arm. He looked dully at her, then without a word went down the narrow sidewalk to Myles's car and got inside.

Quill got into the Olds and drove home.

When Quill looked at the Inn, she saw it through colors composed of paint from an infinite palette in her head; her mind's eye edited for the rightness of composition. Every view could be made perfect in her mind. There had never been a time when her painter's connection to the Inn had failed her, when she saw shapes and atmosphere that could not be translated into a painting in her head. Until now.

The Inn was alien ground to Quill when she walked up the drive to the front door. On summer nights the moon was high, bathing the grounds in silver light, and the sounds of the peeper frogs by the river were a musical undercurrent to the rushing water. Tonight, the building and the gardens were shrunken, diminished, the colors flat. She unlocked the front door and went inside, circling through the dining room, the kitchen, the lounge, the conference room, waiting until the place lost its strangeness and became familiar again. On her second slow wandering through the foyer, she found herself noticing small irrelevant details in an effort to push back the guilt she felt. She blamed herself for this. If Myles had gone to arrest Connie . . . would Sandy be alive? Quill blinked back tears. Mike the groundskeeper had sanded the front door and filled in the gunshot holes with spackling compound. The splintered edge of the reception desk had been glued in place. He'd even found time to refill the giant Chinese urns with roses, purple spar, and early lilies. Quill switched on the overhead lights and sat on the couch by the cobblestone fireplace. The cream-colored wall by the staircase had been repainted. Spotches of blood showed through. Quill shivered and closed her eyes.

"You okay?" Meg appeared at the top of the stairs. "I heard you and Myles leave a while ago." Quill sat up and wiped her cheeks with the back of her hand. Meg was dressed in a long purple T-shirt with a bunny logo. Her feet were bare. She padded downstairs and sat next to Quill. "Out for a midnight snack?"

"Mike did a good job in here," Quill said.

"It's a good start." Meg surveyed the wall critically. "I know he repainted that wall. But the blood shows through."

"Blood eats through paint. He'll have to sand it off. Otherwise, it'll be a constant reminder of my flesh wound."

Meg smiled faintly. "How come *you* know so much?"

"I'm a painter," said Quill. "Just ask Hudson Zabriskie. Paint is paint. He's a painter, too, he says."

Meg slipped an arm around her shoulders and hugged her. "My sister the artist. So what happened? You look grim."

"Sandy Willis was killed in a hit-and-run tonight. Myles asked me to go over and see Roy."

"You're joking. Oh, my God. That poor woman." Meg jumped up and began to pace up and down the foyer. Her bare feet slapped on the wood floor. She looked angry. "This is crazy. It's too much coincidence. Way too much coincidence. What's Myles going to do about it?" She made a face. "He doesn't think Connie's behind this, does he?"

"He can't. He just . . . can't. They found the other car at the scene, and he's checking that out. Roy said Kay Gondowski called the house and asked Sandy to come and get her; that's why she was out so late. Kay supposedly said she was checked into a motel. Myles is going to put an APB out on Kay. Meg!" Quill lowered her voice to a whisper. "Helena Houndswood rented a car, right?"

"Right."

"What kind?"

"A red one."

"No! Was it a Ford Cortina?"

"It was red! How should I know a Ford Cortina from a Porsche? Now, monkfish from lobster, no problem."

"What time did she get in tonight?"

Meg shot a glance upstairs. "I don't know," she said in a low voice. "I went to bed when you guys did, about eleven-thirty. She wasn't back by then."

The front door opened. Quill jumped. John walked in, a pair of jeans hastily pulled on over his pajamas, his sockless feet encased in well-worn tennis shoes. "Quill?" he said. "I wondered why all the lights were on."

"It's not all the lights," said Meg. "It's just the foyer lights. Keep your voice down."

"It looks like all the lights from my apartment."

"That's all you can see from over the carriage house is the foyer, and stop worrying about the utility bills, John."

John settled onto the coffee table. "I know you, Meg. All that irrelevant chatter means something's up. What is it?"

Helena Houndswood appeared at the top of the stairs. She was in a brocaded bathrobe. Her feet were in slippers. Her hair was uncombed. She rubbed her eyes and yawned. "What the hell's going on down there? Is it a party?"

"Quill," Meg hissed, sliding next to her on the couch. "She's in full makeup. Nobody goes to bed in full makeup."

CHAPTER 10

"The whole story sounds incredibly suspicious to me," said Meg. "I don't believe a word of it. Helena's tame lawyer claims he dropped the rental car off in the Hertz lot and used the Jiffy thingummy . . . ?"

"The Rapid Return," said Quill. "Let's not talk about it for a while, okay, Meg?" Quill admitted to herself that she was tired and confused, and didn't want to discuss the events of last night at all. Meg, on the other hand, not only looked as though she'd had a full night's sleep (which she had, barring her late-night discussion with Quill) but was in one of her talkative, chatty moods. Mikhail, the Russian *sous* chef, had made sour cream and caviar scrambled eggs. Quill took a bite and attempted a diversion. "I think we ought to put these on the menu."

"He's pretty good with a skillet," Meg agreed. "So the lawyer uses the Jiffy thingummy and hops the late train to New York City and somebody steals the Cortina out of the lot and runs into Sandy and kills her? And Myles buys this bag of baloney? Sure! And now poor Connie's locked up."

"She couldn't account for her whereabouts at the time Sandy was killed. She claims Kay called her, too. That Kay gave her the same story she gave Sandy. When she got to the hotel—it was the Dew Drop Inn, Meg, if you can believe—she woke up the owner to find out why nobody answered her knock at room five, and he said it was because nobody had checked into five all week. When

Connie came home, the deputies were waiting for her and they took her."

"Is Connie sure it was Kay on the phone?"

"She said if she hadn't thought it was Kay, she would have stayed in bed with Roosevelt where she belonged." Quill, with the memory of Roy Willis's bewildered face in her mind's eye, was guilt-ridden. She tried a diversion. "Any idea when the *L'Aperitif* people will be by to review?"

"Oh, not till the end of the year," Meg said dismissively. "You've been right about La Helena all along, Quill. I admit it She could have imitated that little voice of Kay's. When I came downstairs this morning, she had acres of luggage in the foyer, and you wouldn't believe how she sucked up to me about the food. 'The best of the best, darling,' she said. 'I'll be up a couple of times a week for dinner. Couldn't live without it.' Couldn't live without it? Then why is she moving out?" Meg twirled her fork indignantly. "A murderer *and* insincere."

"She's moving to the Petersons' farmhouse this morning. She probably doesn't want to cook for herself since she's committed to feeding the chickens and the horse and the cow."

"Yes, but now? With the TV show coming up in two weeks? Of course," Meg answered herself, "she doesn't have to lift a finger to do the show. She's got all those 'little people' to do it for her. All she has to do is show up and chat. That woman chats at the drop of a hen's egg. I think she's leaving because she's heard about how we solved that murder last year and she wants to escape your eagle eye."

"She's got an excellent alibi for last night," Quill said. "Harvey swore on a stack of King James Version Bibles that they'd been in Syracuse until well after midnight."

"Harvey," said Meg with disgust. She poked at the potato soufflé on her plate. "There's too much cheese in this. And Mikhail used milk instead of cream." She jabbed at it until it deflated.

"Harvey's an idiot," Quill said. "But he's a good-hearted idiot. I don't think he'd lie to cover up a murder, Meg."

"Not a murder. Vehicular homicide." She swallowed a piece of sausage and screwed up her face. "Somebody in there went ballistic with the sage. I've gotta get back." She jumped out of her chair. "My guess is Helena got tanked up—how else could she stand six hours straight of good old Harvey?—smacked into Sandy, and coerced that tame lawyer of hers to help her out of it. And she could get Harvey to lie about the time she returned. You know she could. I think you're right. She killed Dot and did something awful to Kay and Dawn, and now, poor Sandy. So I say, go ahead and nail her." She paused with her hand on the swinging door to the kitchen. "But not until after the TV show. She wants to feature my soups."

"My sister the cynic."

"Your sister the realist. At least she's out of your hair, and mine. Although I have my doubts as to how long she's going to stick at gentleman farming. Andy says she has no idea what she's getting into." She pushed her way into the kitchen and came back out. "Where's the activity sheet?"

Quill, thinking of her "X" suspect, was vaguely aware of Meg's insistent finger in front of her nose. She wondered about Kay Gondowski. If Connie were convicted of a capital crime, she couldn't benefit from it—Kay would take the entire million.

"Quill! The activity sheet!"

"Oh, god. I forgot."

"How am I supposed to plan the meals today without an activity sheet? You know I can't run a decent kitchen without the activity sheet! And will you ditch that goofy new format you developed? I liked the old one: number of guests, meetings, lunch, dinner. Real simple. Now! Now! Now!"

The doors banged shut. Quill ate the rest of her eggs, drank her grapefruit juice and gave serious consideration to the missing Kay Gondowski. There was a hot brioche, made from dough Meg had prepared two days before. She ate that and surveyed the dining room. There was an independent witness to Kay's existence. Mrs. Whitman. Six of the tables were occupied by the Friends of the Fresh Air. They had the flushed, sweaty look of people who'd been up at the crack of dawn, marching through the hills and moraines of the country-side surrounding Hemlock Falls. Their Friends of the Fresh

Air! T-shirts came in sizes ranging from small to, if the lady crunching her way through a mammoth bowl of granola mixed with yogurt represented a clue, extra-extra-large. Makepeace Whitman caught her eye and gave her a modest wave. His wife smiled. Maybe she ought to try the natural look, Quill thought: Mrs. Makepeace's gilt hair was drawn back in a modest bun. Her large blue eyes glowed with health. Her cheeks were blusher free and delicately pink.

The kitchen door banged open. "Well!" Meg demanded, hands on hips.

"The only meeting today is a subcommittee of the chamber. The Hemlock Falls Clean It Up! Committee."

"And?" said Meg dangerously. "Reservations? Dinner? Lunch? *Tea?!* How full are we? And conventions at the Marriot? Are we going to be hit with an overflow? *Quill!*"

"Meg?!" Quill shouted back. "I'm going to finish my breakfast first!"

"Okay," said Meg.

"Okay," said Quill. They grinned at each other. Quill got up and made her way to the Whitmans' table.

"Toxins," said Makepeace Whitman, by way of greeting.

"Yes," said Quill, with every appearance of comprehension. "I hope you had a good walk this morning? The weather is just beautiful."

"Pollutants," said Mrs. Whitman, her mascara-free eyelashes pure and silvery in the June sunshine, "affect the neurotransmitter fluid in the brain."

"Leads to all sorts of instability," said Makepeace agreeably. "Your . . . sister . . . is it? Would she like to join our group?"

"The sun just flushes all the toxins out of the system," added Mrs. Whitman. "It's God's way of purifying our bodies."

"I know it may not look like it," Quill said, "but she's actually in a pretty good mood. Did you enjoy your breakfast?"

"Wonderful," said Makepeace. "The cooking is marvelous. We understand that Helena Houndswood is going to feature the Inn on her show. As a matter of fact, I was going to speak to her about our group. Do you think she could find time to talk to me? Perhaps I could invite her for tea?"

"Or one of our lectures," said Mrs. Whitman. "A very dear, dear friend and supporter, a veterinarian, is giving a lecture on our feathered sisters and brothers at four."

"Birds," said Makepeace helpfully.

"Ms. Houndswood has moved to a farmhouse in town for a month to write a book," Quill said, "so I'm afraid I won't be seeing much of her, if at all. If the opportunity arises, of course . . ."

Makepeace Whitman pressed her hand in an understanding way. "You and your sister must be relieved," he said sympathetically. "I could tell from the outset, Ms. Quilliam, that your heart and mind are more in tune with nature than one might suspect. Ms. Houndswood, alas, represents much that's artificial and frivolous about our society. Whereas, you! Perhaps you would like to join us."

"May I sit down?" asked Quill, whose thoughts had been diverted by Whitman's *whereases*. "I mean yes, thank you, I'd love to join you for a moment."

"Indeed!" Makepeace pulled out a chair, and courteously stood while Quill sat down. "Any questions you have, we'd be glad to answer."

"There's two. Not about your environmentalist movement, which I think is wonderful, but about the night before last, when the shooting occurred."

"Oh, yes." Mrs. Whitman drew back as if confronted with Styrofoam.

"You hung up the phone at the reception desk? When it was off the hook?"

"I believe I did."

"Did you hear anything? You know, put your ear to the receiver?"

"Oh, no!" said Mrs. Whitman. "I would never do that."

"It's just the usual reaction," said Quill, "and I don't believe you were listening in, or anything like that, it's just that it would be very helpful if you could identify the voice on the end of the line."

"I never listen to the phone. I never use the phone."

"You don't?" asked Quill politely.

"Electricity," said Mrs. Whitman, "just pours out of the receiver. It's why I hung that phone up. It's very bad for the brain."

"Oh," said Quill.

"There was a second question?" asked Makepeace Whitman. "We have some literature on our group. . . ."

"Iron oxide," said Quill. "Does your company ship iron oxide to Paramount Paints?"

Mrs. Whitman shrieked, "No! You promised!"

Makepeace Whitman flung his spoon furiously into his yogurt plate.

Mrs. Whitman sobbed, "You swore! You swore you would stop the rape!"

"Now look what you've done," hissed Makepeace. "A perfectly legitimate business and . . . dear. Dear." He patted his wife's hand. She bared her teeth at him. "We use very gentle backhoes. And we replace as much as—"

"Tearing great gouges of earth flesh from Her sides!" screamed Mrs. Whitman. "You bastard!" She shoved her chair back and ran from the room.

Mr. Whitman, with a despairing look at Quill, ran after her.

Meg poked her head out of the kitchen doors. "What the heck was that!"

Quill, conscious of the shocked diners, carefully picked up the dirty dishes from the Whitmans' table, carried them to the doors, and thrust them into her sister's hands. "Sometimes," she said, "investigations can get a little rough."

"A little rough? It sounds like you ran them over with a bus."

"Never mind." Quill pushed Meg into the kitchen, letting the doors swing behind them. "Meg, I've got to break into Paramount Paints tonight. After the plant is closed."

"Is Myles going to like that?"

"He's not going to know anything about it. Are you with me?"

"Sure. Why can't we go now?"

"We can't let anyone know. Just act normally."

"Okay. Normally I'd want the activity sheet. Will you get it for me, please?"

Dina was sitting at the reception desk, looking woeful as the last of Helena Houndswood's luggage was carried out the door to the Inn van. Mike the groundskeeper was sanding the bloody spot from the wall, a bucket of paint beside him. Mike was short, dark, and Italian, a gardener and a son of a gardener, he'd said when Quill hired him three years before. "It's in the blood. Us Sicilians were born to garden. It's like, genetic."

"I'm glad Mike's doing this," said Dina by way of greeting. "That blood spot was giving me the creeps. Like that scene from *Macbeth*, you know?"

"Is she gone yet?" asked Quill.

"Ms. Houndswood? She walked down the hill about twenty minutes ago. Peter's taking the luggage down. It's not going to be the same without her around here."

"She's not all that far away," said Quill gloomily. "Have you got the activity sheet?"

"Yeah." Dina tugged it from beneath a pile of papers. "It says you're supposed to be like, in a meeting?"

"Me? Here. Give me that. Hemlock Falls Clean It Up! Week," Quill read. "Bozzel, Henry, Shuttleworth, Schmidt, Doncaster, Quilliam. Ten A.M. I'm not a member of the Clean It Up! committee." She frowned. "Harvey isn't, either."

"They changed it," said Dina. "It's now the Clean It Up! Beauty Pageant Committee."

"Oh, damn."

"One good thing, though."

"What's that?"

"They aren't mad at you about the minutes book anymore."

"You sure?"

"Yeah. They think that they have to suck up to you so Helena Houndswood will keep the beauty contest winners on the show."

"That's ridiculous."

"That's what I told them," Dina said earnestly. "Harvey was all for getting you off any committee where you took notes. And Miriam said she hoped you went and gained twenty pounds. 'Wait a minute,' I said. 'You're talking about my boss. She's a great person. You don't have to suck up to Quill just because she and Helena are like best friends,' I said."

"What did they say?" asked Quill anxiously.

"Harvey said he'd forgotten that you and Helena were so close, and maybe they should be careful of how they treat you."

Quill thought about this for a moment. If Harvey had lied to save Helena Houndswood, wouldn't he be cocksure about the TV show? Did Helena even need Harvey to establish an alibi? She'd been so tired by the time Myles had finished questioning Helena last night that she hadn't gotten Sandy's time of death straight. Maybe she could weasel something out of Harvey.

"Quill?" said Dina insistently. "So you see? It worked out okay. You can go sit in that meeting and they'll be nice as pie. They're meeting right now. You'd better go."

"Dina," said Quill, "you don't have to defend my honor. Really. As a matter of fact, I'd rather you didn't ever again."

"It's the least I can do," said Dina. "You're the best boss I've ever had."

"But I'm not Helena Houndswood's best friend! And I don't *want* to be on any more committees!"

"They're even going to let you take notes again," said Dina. "How's about that?"

"I take terrible notes. That's what started this whole mess in the first place. Here's what we do. Esther West is just dying to be on the Beauty Pageant committee, right?"

"She is?"

"Of course she is. She loves things like this. Remember how much she enjoyed directing the Hemlock History Week play? Call her, Dina. Tell her the Beauty Pageant committee is meeting right now, and to get on over here in, say, about an hour. That'll give me time to talk to Harvey in, a subtle way. Then Esther can take my place, and I can get down to investigating this properly."

"Why? I thought you were going to give investigating up. That's what you said when I saw you before breakfast. So you've decided not to give it up. Why not?"

"Lots of reasons," said Quill vaguely. "Just see if you can find Esther, okay? If she's not at her shop, try her at home.

And if she's not at home . . . I don't know what to do if she's not at home."

"Maybe Sheriff McHale could put out an APB?"

Quill contemplated her receptionist for a long moment. Dina's brown eyes were clear and innocent. She even had a dimple. She was getting a Ph.D. in limnology. Quill decided that a doctoral student in fresh pond water ecology was probably naive about such matters as APBs. "It's not quite that important, Dina. But I'd really truly appreciate it if you can get Esther to this meeting. If you can't, about eleven o'clock come in and tell me there's an emergency."

"Got it. You don't want to be on this committee. So what kind of emergency shall I make up?"

"Anything short of a kitchen fire. It'd be pretty obvious to those guys that we're not having a kitchen fire."

"I'll think up a great one if I have to," Dina assured her. "But I'll get Esther here, too."

Quill went to the conference room wondering if the Cornell Management School for Labor Relations had a course in Quelling the Imaginative Employee.

"Hey, Quill!" Harvey exclaimed as she walked into the meeting. "You're looking terrific this morning."

A chorus of enthusiastic "hellos" and "good to see yous" came from the members of the Clean It Up! Beauty Pageant Committee. Quill nodded to Marge, Miriam, Elmer Henry, and Dookie Shuttleworth as she sat down in the chair Harvey drew out for her.

"Can I get you some coffee?" Harvey asked solicitously. He went to the sideboard where Kathleen had set out the coffeemaker and mugs, as she always did when there was a chamber meeting. "We decided that you and Meg shouldn't have to put out for free coffee for us, so Elmer put out a little cash jar." Coins clanked as he rattled it. "It's a quarter."

Marge snorted, "She ain't going to pay for her own coffee, Harvey. Sit down, Quill."

"I appreciate being invited to sit in on the committee, guys, but—"

"We'd like you to be secretary," said Elmer heartily. "Take all the notes you want. You can draw all the pitchers you want, too." He thrust a notebook into her hands and proffered a pen.

"Really, Mayor. Thank you very much, but—"

"You're a little late, but that's okay," said Harvey generously. "I'm the chair of this committee, by the way, so when I say it's okay that you're late, it's okay."

They waited, expectant. Quill sighed. Sat down. Opened the notebook. Wrote Cl/Beu/Comm at the top of page, then Members: and rapidly sketched flattering caricatures of Dookie, Marge, Harvey, the mayor, and Miriam.

"Lovely," said Miriam, leaning over Quill's arm.

"Is there a first order of business?" asked Quill.

"Haven't gotten to it yet," said Harvey somberly. "We were discussing the car crash last night."

"Awful," said Marge. She blew her nose furiously. "Betty and me both liked Sandy. That little shit of a husband is still in the slam, though, right? So he didn't do it. Sure like to find the sucker that whacked her."

"Dreadful, dreadful," murmured Dookie.

"They say," said Quill cautiously, "that Helena Houndswood's car was involved."

"Stolen out of the lot," said Harvey. Quill watched him closely. He was as pompous as ever, but there was no trace of guile or deceit in those protuberant eyes. "I was with her all evening, you know, finding a John Deere tractor in Syracuse. We stopped for dinner at a little place I know of, there. Got back after midnight."

"You took her car," said Quill.

"Mine's in the shop," said Harvey. "Would have been glad to drive, but . . ."

"That old Caddy of his ain't fancy enough for her," said Marge Schmidt shrewdly. "What, Quill, you think old Harve here was involved with killin' Sandy?"

Quill saw the change in Harvey's face the moment the penny dropped. "Hit and runs happen in every town, in every state in these United States," said Harvey indignantly. "Kids, usually, driving stolen cars. That's what Sheriff McHale thinks, and that's very probably what happened. Tragic, but an inevitable part of driving in America. And for your information, Quill"—

he leaned forward, his self-importance temporarily forgotten—
"Helena's lawyer took the late train back to the city when we
came back and left the car in the lot. My guess is some kids
were waiting in the bushes, just hoping for something like this
to happen, and as soon as the train left the station, they broke
open that Rapid Return box, stole the keys and were off like
a flash. You should see that box. Smashed all to hell."

Clearly, no one had heard that Myles had arrested Connie
Weyerhauser. It wouldn't be long before word got out, or,
Quill figured, for gossip to indict, try, and condemn her.

Harvey sat back in his chair, the flush on his face subsiding.
"I'd like to get to the first order of business—Elmer, you have
that gavel?"

"Subcommittees ain't allowed to use the gavel," said Elmer
promptly. "It's the mayor's gavel."

"The gavel should be for committee heads," said Harvey
persuasively. "Now, I know you keep it with you at all times,
Mayor. . . ."

"Kids, my foot," said Miriam, who'd been in a brown study
since Harvey had put forth his car theft theory. "I heard that
Sandy got a phone call from the killer just before she went
out. Did Myles say anything to you about it, Quill?"

Quill hesitated. Myles seemed to have relaxed his rigid rules
about her participation in his investigations. And he hadn't said
to keep what she knew confidential. On the other hand, maybe
the confidentiality was implied.

"I heard she and Roy had a fight over the money," said
Marge. "Sandy slammed out of the house to cool off."

"What did I tell you, Mayor," said Harvey loudly, "no one's
paying attention to the next order of business."

"Gavel's not going to help you, boy," said Elmer. He dug
into his mayoral briefcase. Reluctance in every line of his
body, he handed the gavel to Harvey, who promptly smacked
it loudly against the table.

"For heaven's sake, use the rest," said Miriam. "You'll
wreck the finish. Somebody said you were over there last
night, Quill. At Roy's."

"Just to sit with the kids while Myles took Roy to the
sheriff's office."

"This meeting will come to order!" Harvey beat a tattoo on the table with the gavel.

Miriam leaned close to Quill and whispered, "They don't think Roy had anything to do with it? Did he tell you who called Sandy?"

Quill decided that, one, Roy would probably tell anyone who asked about Kay Gondowski, and two, that she was behaving as badly as Harvey over the gavel. "Kay Gondowski called her, Miriam. Apparently she'd gotten so flustered at the idea of all that money and attention, she just left town to give herself some breathing space."

"Kay Gondowski caused the wreck?" said Elmer. "My god, what's the town comin' to!"

"What does Kay say about it?" demanded Marge. "She say she made that phone call?"

"I don't think Kay's shown up yet," said Quill.

"If this meeting isn't called to order, I'm calling off the Beauty Pageant and you can just handle Clean It Up! Week all by yourselves," said Harvey loudly. "We've got important issues here."

Dookie *tsked*. Marge scowled. Miriam looked at him with exasperation.

"These things are important, Harvey," said Quill. "You're right. But it's natural to be concerned over Dot, and Sandy and Kay. And Dawn Pennifarm, too. I mean, these are the women who made all this possible, in a way. Helena Houndswood wouldn't be here if it weren't for the china contest, and if she weren't here, we wouldn't even be considering a beauty contest."

"I don't see that that follows," said Harvey. "No, I don't see that at all."

"All three of these girls were members of the Bosses Club, right?" said Marge.

"Yes," said Miriam.

"They split the money equal?"

"Yes," said Quill.

Marge crossed her arms over her considerable bosom. "And what happens to the money if there's only, say, one winner?"

Quill doodled on the pad.

"The heirs get it, or what?"

"The money's not assignable," said Miriam. "It's like a tontine."

"Like a what?" demanded Elmer.

"A tontine. The survivor gets it all."

There was a long silence.

"How'd you know that? About not being assignable," asked Marge.

"I had a discussion with Howie Murchison over it," said Miriam primly. "I just happened to drop by his office—he'd invited me out for coffee—and happened to mention it."

"Hell," said Elmer. "Pardon me, Rev'rund. So all these gals have a motive to knock each other off."

"Maybe we'd better get back to the agenda," suggested Quill. "The sheriff's handling all this."

"Question is," said Harvey, "does he have enough manpower? I happen to know—this is in strictest confidence—that he's put in a request for three more men in next year's budget."

"That's not in strictest confidence," said Elmer. "Town budget proposal's published in the *Gazette*. Everybody know Myles needs more men."

"Maybe we could help," said Miriam.

"I don't think Myles . . ." Quill began.

"Just a minute, Quill." Harvey put his hand up authoritatively. "We have a motion before the committee."

"We do not," said Quill.

"Hang on. Hang on. A concept's coming to me." Harvey got up and paced around the room, hands thrust in his trousers pockets, head down. He flung his head back, closed his eyes, then opened them. "I've got it. We'll form a citizens' committee. There's all kinds of national precedence for a citizens' committee. A committee to Stop Crime. Composed of tireless volunteers from the community, this band of citizens cries Stop! Stop the crime. The violence. The rape of our women."

"Well, now," said Elmer, "I'm not sure that a citizens' committee is legal."

"Isn't nothing illegal about it, Mayor." Marge explored a back tooth with her tongue and looked thoughtful. "We look for the bodies, for example. They get volunteers to search for the bodies all the time, with missin' kids and so on."

Harvey, who'd been circling the conference table like a large dog in search of a hydrant, clapped a hand on Marge's shoulder. "True, Marge. That's very true. There's a lot of publicity about it. National publicity."

"Screw the publicity," said Marge. "I want to find out who did this. We find out if anyone seen Kay. The last time they seen Dawn, and where she was headed. Whether anyone saw Sandy on route fifteen last night. And like I said, we search good and hard for the bodies. This has gotta stop." She lowered her chin and looked around the table, unsmiling.

"We will find out what has happened to these three women," said Harvey in a radio voice. "With Myles as understaffed as he is, it can only help. We are the Citizens Against Rampant Crime. C.A.R.C. cares."

"You don't think we should . . . um . . . check with him about it, first?" said Quill.

"Mayor?" said Harvey. "I'd like to authorize you to contact Sheriff McHale about permission to support the sheriff's investigation through the medium of my citizens' committee, because C.A.R.C. cares."

There was a respectful silence.

"I'll do it," said Elmer, "I'll get hold of him right now. I can use the phone in the hall, Quill?"

"Of course. But, Elmer . . ." Quill chewed her lip. "Could you maybe not mention my, um, involvement? I wouldn't want him to think that I was . . ."

"Horning in on the investigation like you done before? Don't worry about a thing, Quill. I'll be real tactful." Elmer walked majestically out of the room, preceded by his belly.

"Might as well get some business done while he's gone," said Marge in a practical way. "About those assessments for Clean It Up! Week. How's everyone doin'?"

"Clean It Up! Week's at the end of the agenda." Harvey frowned. "Next item on the agenda is contest rules for the Little Miss Hemlock Falls contest."

"Any kid who wants to can enter," said Marge promptly. "How are we doin' on Clean It Up! Week? We want the town to look good for that TV show."

Harvey thumped the gavel. "I've drawn up a complete list of agenda items. While the mayor is carrying out my instruction, we are scheduled to discuss the beauty contest categories and the dress code, and establish the panel of judges, and time limits of the entertainment. You can't accomplish anything without pre-work, Marge. And then there's the budget."

"What budget," said Elmer, returning.

"For the expenses," said Harvey. "As chairman of this committee, I think it only right that we get a professional job done and that we retain a professional firm."

"And what professional firm would that be, Harve?" asked Marge with spurious interest.

"There are excellent firms in Syracuse," said Harvey, with an air of disingenuousness, "and of course one or two in Buffalo. Why don't you leave the selection up to me?"

"Why don't I put a fox in my henhouse?" said Marge. "Well, Elmer, what'd the sheriff say?"

"Says fine with him," Elmer said unhappily.

Quill sat up abruptly. "Fine with him? He really said that?"

"Thought maybe Harvey could arrange to have some C.A.R.C. posters printed, too." Elmer sat down, clearly disgruntled. "Thanked me for coming up with a civic-minded idea."

"He did?" said Quill.

Harvey cleared his throat modestly and raised his hands in a deprecating way. "No charge for this idea, folks, unless we take it national."

"Asked me to work up a schedule for the search. Wants a twenty-four-hour rota, concentratin' on the swamp."

"The swamp?" said Miriam. "Does he have any reason . . . why the swamp?"

"Said it's as good a place for a body as anywhere else."

"Does Myles think we'll find a body?" demanded Marge.

"Well, no," Elmer admitted, "no, he didn't. Said it's a good idea, though, on the off chance that Harvey here is right. This citizens' committee of Harvey's . . ."

"Actually," said Harvey, "if you don't mind. It was Miriam's idea, Quill. I'd like that in the minutes. That Miriam thought of this, not me."

"The heck it was my idea," said Miriam. "C.R.A.P., sorry, C.A.R.C., the citizens' committee was your idea, Harvey, and I'm certainly not going to slop around in a swamp at two A.M. for bodies which our own sheriff doesn't expect to be there. Maybe we should vote on this."

"All in favor of Harvey's idea to search the swamp for bodies say 'aye,' " said Elmer, grabbing the gavel and whacking it on the table.

"Aye," said Dookie, into the quiet.

"Nays?"

The "nays" carried it.

"All right, then," said Elmer, "we get on with the agenda." He took the agenda from Harvey's hands. "Okay. Any progress from the citizens who're sp'osed to Clean It Up? Courthouse is comin' along good. Only thing left that I can see is the post office. Quill, you go along and encourage Vern to finish up. You can tell him, official, from the mayor about the pride we all have in this town, and how it's their civic duty to make a good showin' on Helena Houndswood's TV show. All in favor?"

They were unanimous, except for Quill, who was glumly sketching Vern Mittermeyer throwing cans of Paramount paint from a flying buttress she'd placed atop the post office. There was a little tiny Quill on the ground, ducking the spatters.

"Motion carried," said Elmer with satisfaction. "Now we're gettin' somewheres. Beauty contest, next. Harvey? We ain't budgeting a nickel for advertising. Got that? This is a volunteer town, and we're doing a volunteer beauty contest. Anyone here have any experience with beauty contests?"

Quill looked at her watch: three minutes after eleven. No Esther. And no Dina. She raised her hand. "Esther West has had a lot of experience running town productions," she said. "I move to have Esther West appointed to this committee."

"Absolutely not," said Harvey. "This pageant needs a professional touch, and with all due respect to Esther, she's never run a project as complex as this one before. Why, she'd want to direct it and everything. And I can just see the faces on those guys from the Helena Houndswood show when she drags out that *Complete Guide to Television Production* video. I mean, she's a great gal. A great gal. But anyone who's learned all there is to know about TV from a tape out of a catalog . . ."

"Be a lot like somebody learning about advertising from *The Complete Encyclopedia of Advertising Terms and Expressions,*" said Miriam with a wink at Quill.

Harvey fidgeted in his chair. "Professionals use reference works," he said earnestly. "I'll admit that . . ."

"Quill?" Dina appeared at the conference room door, frantically waving a slip of pink paper. She'd removed what little cheek blusher she used and powdered her face to a pale beige. She leaned against the doorframe, panting slightly. "Please. Disaster has struck!"

Quill got up from her chair, avoiding Miriam's skeptical eye. "I was afraid this might happen," she said with an apologetic smile. "It's probably going to take a long time. Miriam, could you take over the notes?"

"I'll take the notes." Esther marched into the room, her eyes sparkling. "Thank you so much, Quill, for inviting me to be on the committee. I'm so sorry I'm late, Harvey, Mayor. But I didn't hear about it until just now." She waved her handbag excitedly. "I ordered the *Complete Guide to the Miss America Beauty Pageant,* and I was just down to the post office. It came overnight mail. It's got some terrific ideas."

"Vern paintin' right along?" asked Elmer alertly.

"Nope. He's cursing a blue streak," said Esther. "Didn't see too much progress."

"Well, Quill's goin' to stop by there today and push him," said Elmer. "Right, Quill?"

"And I'd better get to it," said Quill cheerfully. She excused herself and went out into the hall.

"Was I dramatic enough?" asked Dina.

"Oh, yes," said Quill absently.

"It's just a phone message from Sheriff McHale," said Dina, handing her the pink piece of paper. It was damp and slightly crumpled. "So what do you think? I figured if I just left it like, mysterious, then it might be more impressive. Were you impressed?"

"I'm impressed," said Quill. She took the slip of paper.

"I'm back to thinking maybe this detecting business is all right. You know, first seduction, now mysterious lady in black. Except that I'm wearing jeans."

Quill read the note: "If you're not on swamp patrol, what about an early dinner?" She stuck the note in her skirt pocket and moved down the hall to the back of the Inn, Dina following.

"So, since I'm back on the scent, what's next?"

Quill said "nothing," figuring a bit of subterfuge was in order if she was going to plunder the Paramount office that evening.

"Nothing?"

"Nope. Investigation's temporarily suspended. I have to run to the post office. If the sheriff calls, looking for me"—Quill paused, one hand on the back door—"tell him I'm in the swamp."

She stepped outside into the vegetable garden and let the door slam behind her.

A dirt path curved around the side of the Inn to the falls, and from there through a copse of beech, hemlock, and crepe myrtle to the village. It would take her to the west end of Hemlock Falls, without passing through the birch woods, where Dot had been killed.

Quill walked past the Peterson place and paused to look over the fence. The farmhouse had originally been part of a forty-acre parcel that Norm Peterson's father had deeded over to the town thirty years before. About five acres were left; a portion of the lot was taken up by a charming cobblestone farmhouse, trimmed in white, and a small hay barn, painted the traditional red. About three acres had been left fenced for pasture. A brown and white cow (which Quill recalled was a Guernsey) grazed peacefully next to a nervous looking horse. Quill clucked and held out her hand. The horse, which was brown and big, dashed up to the fence, reared, whinnied, and dashed away again, its eyes rolling. Quill wondered if Helena could ride. In the farmyard she heard the clack and squall of a herd of chickens and caught a glimpse of a large straw hat trimmed with purple flowers of some kind. It was Helena herself, moving among the chickens, flinging some sort of grain to the ground. A loud and angry "Fuck!" floated through the air.

Quill grinned to herself.

A few more minutes' walk took her to the west end of Main.

Quill rounded the corner of Main and Maple to find Vern slowly at work sanding and painting the red trim. An open bucket of Paramount Paint's Exterior Latex Crimson Red sat beside him.

Quill said hello. Vern grunted. The weather was fine for June, although a bit warm. Sweat rolled down his face, which made him look like a damp turtle instead of a dry turtle.

"How is it going, Vern?"

"This paint stinks."

"I've never minded the smell of fresh paint myself," said Quill, "although I know it bothers some people. The red's nice and . . . and . . . bright."

"Nice and screwed up, you mean," said Vern. "That Hudson's allus going on about how fabulous his paint is, right?"

"He does like his paint," Quill admitted in the vernacular. "How do you mean screwed up? Lloyd was having problems, too."

"Looky here." He stepped back from the window frame. "See what I mean? It stinks."

Quill peered closely at the frame. The red paint was mottled, stippled on the sanded wood. She frowned. "Did some sawdust get into the can, maybe?"

"Just opened her up," said Vern. "I sanded first, *before* I opened her up."

Quill looked into the can. The surface of the paint was smooth, unmarked. . . . She looked back at the window frame. She looked at Vern. There were no cuts or bruises on his skinny arms or freckled hands.

Who would have thought the old man would have had such blood in him?

"Hey," said Vern. "You can't faint on federal property." He grabbed her arm. "Siddown. Get your head down." He pushed Quill onto the bench under the lamppost.

She took several deep breaths. Her vision cleared. She straightened up, her breath harsh in her throat. Vern didn't move. Just looked at her, eyes like a lizard's in the sunlight. Quill shivered.

"Stop," she said. "Stop painting right now."

CHAPTER 11

"What d'ya mean, there's blood in the paint?" Vern let Quill sit on the hard plastic chair inside the post office ("Can't stop you, I guess"), and after a silent communion with the postal gods, brought her a glass of water. Quill examined the glass as though it were a foreign object and set it on the floor beside the open paint can.

"Vern, did you cut yourself when you were painting? Did some of it get into the can?"

Vern examined his freckled, paint-spattered arm with deliberation. "Broke off the nail opening the lid." He offered a grimy forefinger for her inspection. "Gotta file a disability claim. Might not," he added generously, "depending."

Quill started to ask how freely the finger had bled, and stopped herself. There was no way Vern's finger could account for the amount of blood disfiguring the coated trim. And besides, Lloyd had had the same problem two days before. A horrible possibility was growing in her mind. She shivered.

"Can't change the temprachure in here," said Vern belligerently. "Set by the guv'mint. You cold, you go outside."

"Lloyd said this paint came from Paramount?"

"Picked it up myself, on Tuesday. Connie Weyerhauser gave it to me. Part of an overrun on Crimson Blaze, she said. No charge." He shifted his wad of gum from one cheek to the other. " 'Course, now I see why it come free. Like I said at the chamber meetin', this stuff stinks."

Maybe Vern meant it literally. Her heart quivering, Quill leaned over and inhaled. There was, unmistakably, a faint coppery odor underlying the fresh scent. Abruptly she got up and moved away, as one might from a dead animal in the road. She should call Myles. Except Myles was out scouting motels for Kay Gondowski, and she'd undoubtedly get Deputy Dave, and the whole town would be engaged in frantic speculation by nightfall.

"Would you like me to return the paint for you, Vern?"

"Eh?"

"You know, take it back. Get you another—what, three gallons?"

"Not of the Paramount stuff, thank you very much. They're not an approved United States guvmint supplier anyways."

"What if I took this and we bought some Dutch Boy, or something. From Nickerson's."

"Ain't in the budget."

"I'll tell you what. If you can give me a ride back to the Inn, we can stop at Nickerson's and have them put the paint on the Inn account. You can choose any paint you want. I'll just take this back to . . . I'll take it with me. That is, if you can leave the post office."

Vern threw his thumb over his shoulder. "Lloyd's on duty. It's my day off."

Quill, who had recovered herself a little, smiled and said it was civic-minded of Vern to come in on his day off.

"Ah, that's okay," said Vern expansively. "Gotta file for overtime, of course."

Some thirty minutes later Quill, appalled by the cost of three gallons of name-brand exterior latex paint, was in the kitchen. The cans of Paramount Crimson Blaze stood on the newspapers spread on the floor. Meg and Doreen had been in the kitchen testing various recipes for gazpacho when Quill had come in. All three of them now stared at the cans in horrified fascination.

"There can't be a body in the paint can," said Meg after a moment. "I'll tell you why. Those ball mills you described to me—they're filled with special round rocks all tumbling together to break up the chunks of mineral?"

"Yes," said Quill. "You can put a three-ton chunk of diatomaceous earth into a ball mill, and about sixteen hours later, you get stuff the consistency of talcum powder."

"But minerals are dry and brittle. Bodies aren't. I'll show you what I mean." She went to the huge built-in refrigerator and pulled out a raw Rock Cornish game hen. "See?" she said, wielding it aloft. "Guts included." She dropped it into the Cuisinart and turned the dial. The hen spun around, blades chopping futilely at the rubbery skin. Meg switched it off. "You get goo. And not very good ground-up goo, at that. These are sharp blades, too, not rocks."

"You freeze the meat before you chop it, right?"

"That's my point," said Meg in exasperation. "Now if the body were frozen, I'd say, yeah, maybe this is a unique, first-time ever, one-of-a-kind way to dispose of somebody, but come on, Quill. You think somebody stuffed Dawn Pennifarm into their home freezer, hauled her out, took her into the plant in the dead of night and dumped her in the ball mill?"

"The Qwik Freeze is right next door," said Quill. "You tell me."

Meg's eyes widened. "God!" She ran her hands through her hair and circled the kitchen in agitation. "God! Somebody shut her in the nitrogen room at the Qwik Freeze, spun that dial down to twenty degrees below centigrade, and froze her stiff."

"It's possible, then."

"Oh, yeah. I mean, they handle tons and tons and tons of green beans that way, flash frozen. God."

"You bin watching too many Terminator movies or what?" said Doreen. "No body parts in that paint can that I can see. You'd get little bits and pieces. Teeth and such like."

"You haven't seen what those ball mills can do," said Quill stubbornly. "But we can drain it through a sieve and find out."

"You drain it through a sieve," said Meg.

"See? You both think I'm right. You think that Da . . ." Quill stumbled over the name. "Somebody might be in there."

"All the saints!" said Doreen obscurely. She knotted her apron firmly around her waist, went to the cupboard and removed a sieve, then selected a large stockpot.

"Not that one," said Meg. "You're not going to ruin a perfectly good stockpot with red paint. Not in my kitchen."

"For god's sake," said Quill. "We can buy another stockpot from Nickerson's. I'll get it myself."

Doreen took the stockpot, the sieve, and the open can of paint to the sink. Meg and Quill stood at each shoulder as she carefully poured the paint through the sieve.

"Smooth as paint," said Doreen in satisfaction, "I told you."

"That doesn't mean anything," said Quill. "The paint's sieved before it's canned."

"They check it for contaminants, don't they?" asked Meg. "If there'd been anything in the paint that's not supposed to be there, they would have found it at the factory."

"It's all automated. And they check for dirt, not blood. Maybe they wouldn't find it. Maybe the person who put the body into the ball mill runs the quality assurance line. I don't know."

Meg gazed at the counter, picked up a spoonful of gazpacho, gazed dubiously at the tomato-red color, and set it down again. "Baloney."

"Those ball mills can reduce an automobile to metal grit in about a day," said Quill impressively.

The three of them drew a little closer together.

"Maybe you should put the paint back in the can, Meg," said Quill in a hushed voice.

"You put it back. You brought it here."

"And their shoes!" said Doreen, rolling her eyes skyward, in apparent reference to the aforementioned saints. She upended the stockpot and poured the red liquid back into the can. She set the can inside the pot, and placed the sieve upside down over the lid. "Somethin' weird in that paint can, I'll tell you what it is—rodents."

"Rodents?" said Quill.

"Mouse. Or a rat." Doreen stuck out her lip and shook her head. "You two get crazy ideas, I'll tell you. All kinds of stuff gets into food, don't it?"

"You could be right," Quill admitted.

"Din't raise two kids and outlive three no-good husbands without bein' right," Doreen grunted.

"Let's put the whole thing in a box and cover it up and call Myles," said Meg.

"That shows *some* sense," said Doreen scornfully. "I got boxes in back." She marched out of the kitchen.

"So the question is, 'What bloody man is that?' " said Meg, "unless it's What bloody rat is that?"

"Rodent," said Quill gloomily. "What if we're crazy?"

"What if we're not? What if that's where all the missing women are ending up? Is that why you wanted to break into Paramount tonight?"

Quill blinked at her. She'd forgotten the iron oxide. She said aloud, "What's iron oxide got to do with the body in the paint can?"

"Earth to Quill!" said Meg. "Non sequiturs not appreciated. What about the iron oxide?"

"Well, I tried to tell you last night, but you were too anxious to bring my youthful defalcations to the attention of Myles and John."

"People without defalcations in their past are boring, boring, boring," said Meg airily. "So tell me now."

"For one thing, I doubt very much you can use it as a pigment substitute for lead oxide. Not without changes in the mixing process. I think that iron oxide is just plain old rust, isn't it?"

"Beats me."

"Anyway, it didn't sound right to me. And then when John found that the address for the supplier was the same as the one for Makepeace Whitman, I asked him about it."

"Makepeace Whitman supplies minerals to Paramount Paint?"

"Well, he's got to do something for a living. And his wife had a really peculiar reaction when I asked him about it."

"Which was?"

"I told you. Peculiar. Something about raping the earth. Which would make sense if Makepeace were engaged in a business that polluted, but iron oxide isn't a pollutant. At least, I don't think it is. My courses in paint chemistries were oriented more toward how to make colors than how the stuff is manufactured. But Paramount has those material safety sheets that OSHA makes you post? I wanted to get a look at them."

"Why do we have to break in to do it? Why not just go down there and ask them?"

"Because if something funny is going on, and women are being murdered, you don't just walk into the place where the funny stuff is happening. How many times have you read a Gothic novel and thrown it across the room because the heroine was so stupid she went into the basement? And everyone up to Chapter Seven had told her, 'Don't go into the basement!' There's too many questions about Paramount Paint just to walk in there and ask to see the files. Why should Hudson give them to us anyway? It's none of our business. Now there's even more of a reason to break in tonight. Who knew about the embezzlement from the inventory invoicing? What does Makepeace Whitman know about the orders for iron oxide?"

"You're going to end up proving Connie Weyerhauser's responsible," said Meg. "Are you ready for that? Nobody else has a motive and an opportunity both."

"Kay Gondowski does," said Quill. "And let's not forget Helena Houndswood. And if the iron oxide's a red herring, I just want to get the question cleared up. I don't know at this point whether it's a solvability factor or not."

Doreen came back into the kitchen carrying a large wooden box marked Moët & Chandon. "This'll do." The housekeeper placed the stockpot and the remaining two gallons of paint in the box and hefted it. "Storeroom? Or you gonna take it down to the sher'f's office?"

Quill hesitated.

"Storeroom," said Meg. "By the time Myles gets back into town, we'll have the whole thing nailed down."

Doreen shook her head and lugged the box to the storeroom. She set it down with a loud thump and returned, her lips thinned to a stubborn line.

"Now"—Meg dusted her hands briskly—"first job is to find out whether there's a body in the paint can, right?"

"Right," said Quill.

"Second job is to break into the paint factory and find those sheets you were talking about."

"Materials safety handling sheets. Like the one that was in the Bosses Club file which described how to handle lead oxide."

Doreen gave a loud snort, sat at the counter, and picked up her soup spoon.

"You're going to eat that stuff with a soup-colored corpse in the same room with us?" demanded Meg.

"Perfectly good soup." Doreen swallowed and considered, "Might be the last I get if you two end up in jail for breaking and entering."

"The third job," said Quill, ignoring Doreen, "is to talk to Connie Weyerhauser."

"You think Deputy Dave is going to fall for Dina's mysterious-woman-in-black act again?" said Meg. "I don't. I think he'll throw you right out of the jail."

"She's not in jail," said Doreen. "Howie Murchison sprung her. She's at home. Warn't enough evidence to keep her in."

"There you are," said Quill. "I'll go talk to Connie, and you call Andy Bishop."

"Me call Andy Bishop? Why?!"

"Because he can test the contents of the can."

"I don't want to call him. You call him. I'll go talk to Connie Weyerhauser. If I call him, he'll think I'm encouraging him."

"You don't want to encourage him?"

"Yes. No. I don't know."

Doreen took her empty soup bowl to the sink. "Rest of the world like you two, we wouldn't have any kids." She put her hands on her hips. "I got more important stuff to do than lookin' for rodent parts. You need me for anything else?"

"You don't want to be in on this investigation, Doreen?" asked Quill.

"Told the Friends I'd go on a hike with 'em this afternoon. Fresh air'll do me good. 'Sides, if I know you two, you'll be crawlin' around Paramount in the middle of the night lookin' for bodies and findin' rodents, and I like my sleep, thank you very much. You let me know what happens." Doreen hung her apron on its peg. "I think you should tell Sheriff McHale. You two want to go banging round that there factory, it's all right by me."

"Doreen? Before you go?"

"What, Quill?"

"Could you find out, just sort of casually, how the Whitmans came to choose the Inn for their FOFA convention?"

"I know that already. What d'ya wanna know for?"

"It could be important."

"I ain't betraying the Friends," said Doreen with dignity. "You'll know in due course, says Mr. Whitman, due course. So I say, that's for me to know and you to find out. Ha."

"Doreen," said Meg. "If you know how they heard about the Inn, you're duty bound to tell us. And you'd better tell us."

"You din't ast me *that*. You ast me if I know why they chose this-here Inn. How they heard 'bout us is different."

"Well, how'd they hear about us, then?" said Quill.

"Beats me." Doreen shrugged. She left, banging the back door shut.

"I'm going to push gazpacho up her nose," said Meg.

"If there's a link between the iron oxide, the embezzlement, the murders, and Makepeace Whitman, Connie should know. Or at least be able to point me in the right direction."

"Do you think she'll talk to you?"

"I'm going to try. In the meantime . . ."

"All right, all right, all right," Meg grumbled. "I'll call Andy." She went to the wall phone, picked it up and hung it up again. "What if Doreen's right? You read all the time about insects and whatnot that get into food. Why not into paint? Three parts rodent hair per million or whatever."

"Call Andy. That's the only way we're going to know for sure."

Meg lifted the phone and hung it up again. "What if you were right from the beginning? What if it's Helena? Let's say the iron oxide is the red herring. It was Helena Houndswood's car that was implicated in Sandy's death. The day Kay Gondowski disappeared, Helena said she was going to sit upstairs in the hot tub, and we both saw her come into the Inn at six forty-five, dressed in the clothes she'd worn that afternoon. And she passed Rickie Pennifarm's pickup truck just before Dot was killed. And none of this started happening until she rolled into town on Sunday. Sunday, let me remind you, was the day Dawn Pen—"

"Who's to say these things are all connected? Call Andy," said Quill inexorably. "I'm going over to see Connie. I'll be back in a few hours."

The phone book listed Connie and Roosevelt Weyerhauser's address in a section of Hemlock Falls not far from Sandy Willis's home. Quill debated on whether or not to call, then decided she would have a better chance of talking to Connie if she could see her face to face.

The Weyerhauser home was a small, stucco and beamed cottage dating from the twenties. The yard was neatly mowed. A wheelchair ramp had been built to the front door. Quill parked in the street and walked up to the house. A curtain on the front window twitched closed. She pushed the doorbell. The front door was plain leaded glass, and it was hard to see through the ripples. There was a long wait. Quill pushed the doorbell again. There was a faint shuffling sound, and eventually, Connie herself opened the front door. The skin under her eyes was purple with fatigue. She looked shrunken; her tunic top hung loose on her large frame. There was a gray tinge to her magnificent mahogany skin. She smelled of grief. Wordlessly she backed away from the door, and Quill went in.

The living room was covered in wall-to-wall Berber carpet in a neutral beige. There was an absence of knickknacks and small tables. A wheelchair was placed in front of the TV set, which was on without sound. Barbara Weyerhauser sat curled in it, head resting to one side on the back, her painfully thin arms and wrists in an *S* position.

"Are you all right?" Quill asked Connie.

"For now."

"I'll just say hello to Barbara. Maybe we could talk a little?"

"Back porch."

Quill went to the wheelchair and kneeled down. Barbara rolled her head and smiled, making her "Hello" sound.

"It's good to see you again," said Quill. "Your mother told me you're at the Adult Center most days during the week. Do you like it?"

Barbara made her "yes" sound and Quill smiled. "I'd like to talk to your mother for a while. Do you mind if we go out on the back porch?"

Barbara moved her head side to side in agreement. One finger pressed her buzzer.

"We'll come if you call," said Quill. "I'll see you later."

She followed Connie to the back porch. A ramp ran from the decking to flowers in raised beds. "She likes the roses best," said Connie. "And the bees. Loves the bees."

"She told me she was sorry Mike had taken the bees' nest from under the gazebo the last time she was at the Inn," said Quill. "She said she'd never been stung."

"Only a matter of time, isn't it?"

"Meaning we're all destined to get stung? Maybe you're right. This seems to be one of those times for you."

"Looks like."

"Connie, what's really going on?"

The dimples Quill had seen before shadowed briefly on her cheeks. "You messing in the sheriff's investigations again?"

"Was he right about the embezzlement? About Dawn?"

Connie nodded slowly. "Yes, he was."

"Connie, were you involved?"

"Hard to say I wasn't."

Quill, shocked, made a movement of protest.

"Oh, not in the way you think. I knew about it, is all, I didn't take any of the money. Never took any of the money."

"How much of this have you told Myles?"

"All of it." She sighed, her eyes shadowed. "You want to hear? I'll tell you everything I told Sheriff McHale. Dawn was always a little crooked. A little sly. And Mr. Zabriskie . . ." She shook her head, the shadow of the dimples back. "Sometimes I don't think that man's elevator goes all the way to the top. Anyway, he was set on this leadless paint process for the orange-red oil-base paints. Hard to get that color, you know, without lead oxide, but it's dangerous to handle. And expensive. When New York decided to cut expenses through this empowerment training . . . you know, handing off decisions usually made by the big shots to employee teams, Hudson got all excited. Took it into his head that he could save

on research, that the Bosses Club could come up with a way
to get that color without using lead oxide. Well, we couldn't,
of course."

"But you did."

"No, we didn't. What we came up with was this scheme of
Dawn's. We get the supplier to label the lead oxide *iron* oxide,
which he did, because his markets for lead oxide were shrink-
ing. Now. Lead oxide's expensive, upwards of two thousand
dollars a ton. But Dawn was smart. She got the supplier to
accept eight hundred a ton, because it was crooked, you see.
And she billed Paramount twelve hundred more a ton and took
the difference."

"Hudson didn't notice?"

Connie laughed. "Not a thing. Then New York imposed
new profit quotas, and Hudson got himself all of a dither and
gave the Bosses Club an output to cut costs."

"An output?"

"You know, a job for the team to do. The way this stuff
works, the boss isn't supposed to look at how the team decides
to cut costs, just whether or not we did it. We kind of leaned
on Dawn, then, to stop the double-billing. Our jobs were at
risk. Kay and I were the most vulnerable. Kay doesn't have
much in the way of savings, and she's paying off some heavy
medical bills for her husband."

"But Hudson never found out about the substitution?" said
Quill.

"No, ma'am." Connie was empathetic. "Just loved the
awards and the bonuses he got for running an efficient
plant. And why should he ask? Things were going just
fine."

"Until Dawn disappeared."

"That's right."

"And you don't know what happened to her?"

"Last I saw of Dawn Pennifarm, she was headed to the
Qwik Freeze to do benchmarking." Her eyes shifted. Quill
had a sudden conviction she was lying.

"Do you know the supplier for the lead?"

"Mr. Whitman. That crazy group of his is at the Inn."

"Do you know why he chose the Inn for his convention?"

"He was squawking pretty hard about Dawn upping the prices on him. Dawn just said, let him scream. She did mention that he was going to come up here to talk it over."

The Whitmans, Quill recalled, had arrived at the Inn on Tuesday. Which wasn't to say that Makepeace hadn't come into town earlier, shoved Dawn into the cold room at the Qwik Freeze, and dumped her body in the ball mill Monday night after the plant was closed. He was in the woods on a hike when Dot had been murdered, too.

"Connie, do you have any idea who's committing these murders?"

Connie looked at her, alarmed. "What murders? Sheriff McHale didn't say anything about murders. There's been a lot of talk in town about Rickie and Dawn. Do you mean Dot? We all thought that was a hunting accident."

"I think someone's being very clever," said Quill. "There are only two bodies, Connie, but four women are missing." She watched Connie closely.

Connie's hands twisted in her lap. "But Dawn's run off. And Kay's at her son's. And Sandy . . ." She shuddered. "And I get the money," she whispered. "I get the money. No. No. It can't be. It can't be!" she burst out finally. "Who?!" Then with horror: "I'm a fool. Sitting here counting that extra money and being a fool. All the Bosses Club!" She half started out of her chair.

"Well, that's the question, isn't it," said Quill with the voice she'd used when Meg was little and had scared herself. "Let's be objective about this, Connie. Why would someone want the Bosses Club out of the way?"

"She was angry, that woman," said Connie jerkily. "Said she was going to find some way to take it away. Dawn said we'd sue her. Dawn said we'd call the papers, and those reporters for *A Current Affair*."

Quill held her breath and let it out softly. "You mean Helena Houndswood?"

"She was looking for the Hall on Monday. Asked at the post office, I guess. Asked who I was, and did I live in the big farmhouse down in the park."

"Peterson's," said Quill. "She's there now."

"Vern said I worked at the plant. This must have been, oh, about three-thirty on Monday, just at the shift change. Dawn was going home in that rusty old Buick of hers and saw her come out of the post office. So Dawn pulls over and starts asking her, did we win, and it wasn't just me that won that million, it was all of us. I guess there was a fuss. Ms. Houndswood sat in that old Buick of Dawn's and took on something fierce." Connie sighed heavily. "Dawn called me, soon as she got home. Said she told her off, good. Said not to worry, she'd made some kind of deal with Helena about the money. Not to worry? Of course, we worried. We knew Dawn's kind of deals. We were all just waiting to see what she was going to do. And Wednesday, when you came in to tell us that we'd won. Well!" She smiled a little. "You saw how we reacted. Relief, mostly. We were sure Ms. Houndswood could find some way to hold up that money."

"God," said Quill.

Connie grasped the sides of the lawn chair, her knuckles a pale cream. "You think she killed them? You think she killed them all? Do you think she's going to kill me?"

"God," Quill said again helplessly. "I don't know."

"I'll tell you one thing, I'm not stepping out of this house. I'm not going anywhere without Roosevelt. And I'm not letting anyone in."

"There's another possibility," said Quill. "We'll have to tell Myles all this, of course. But until he gets back . . . just let me ask you this: Did everyone from the Bosses Club join in the . . . um . . . scam?"

"What? Taking the money from the double billing, you mean? Everyone knew about it. Sandy took some once in a while, when things got tight. I don't know about Kay, or Dot. I'd say Kay wouldn't have understood. I'd guess Dot was in on it, but I don't know. It wasn't something we talked about, Quill. And it wasn't something we were proud of. When we had that output to reduce costs—nobody took a dime except Dawn." Her face set. "You may not believe me."

"Connie, if you knew about the embezzlement, why didn't you do something?"

"Your sheriff knows."

"Myles?"

Connie had been looking at the far end of the garden. She switched her gaze to Quill's face. Her eyes were terrible. "You tell me what happens to me and mine if I lose my job. You tell me what happens to people that blow the whistle. You tell me, Quill. Who's going to give me another job with health benefits to cover Barb? Where would we go? You tell me that."

Quill came back to the Inn to find Meg sitting by the fireplace dressed in a skirt and blouse. "You look great." She sniffed the air. "And you used my Andiamo."

"It smells better than my Blue Grass."

"It's also more expensive than your Blue Grass."

Quill moved restlessly from the counter to the sink and back again.

"What's the matter, Quillie?" Meg drew a sharp breath. "Connie didn't confess, did she?"

"Not to killing Dot. Or Sandy. Or Dawn. No. She confessed to being helpless. What are we *doing* here, Meg?"

"Waiting for Andy Bishop to come and tell us if there's a body in the paint can." She watched Quill with an air of concern. "You mean, running the Inn? Staying out of the action in New York. To give you a more sober answer, I'm getting better and better as a chef. But you?" She hesitated.

"What?"

"You're not painting. You haven't picked up a brush in three years. Not seriously, at least. And you're not deciding about Myles. I think what you're doing is taking care of me. Which is a pretty dumb way to spend your time when you could be working. Really working."

"I am really working. I'm working like Connie's working. That's worthwhile."

"Well that depends on your world view, I guess. And look at the results. She's in big trouble, isn't she?"

"She is," said Quill shortly, "but only because she was caught between two terrible choices when she did what she had to do."

"Am I interrupting something?" Andy Bishop came through the dining room door. His hair was freshly combed. Quill, touched, decided he had stopped by the men's room on his way in.

"Yes," said Meg.

Andy's face fell. Quill frowned at her sister. "Of course you're not. We're glad to see you. Have you had lunch? It's a little late, but we've got some pâté? Maybe some soup?"

"Sounds great," said Andy, his eye on Meg.

She ignored him, unfolding herself from the rocker. "Have a seat. I'll get you something. Quill? You want to make some coffee? I'll have caffè latte."

"Sure. Andy?"

"After the pâté, maybe." He sat at the counter, eyes still on Meg, and began to chat, in much the same way, Quill bet, that he eased a sulky child into accepting an injection. "So, what's up? Meg said you had some questions about blood? Let me tell you all I know about blood. I see your reception area is still blotted with that little accident you had a few days ago, Quill. Which reminds me." He got up from the counter and peeled the bandage at her temple back with gentle fingers. "You must have had a remarkable surgeon. Looks great." He pressed the bandage back into place and resumed his seat. "About your foyer wall. Your guy Mike's going to have to replace the sheetrock there. The blood's soaked into the wall, and serum protein is pretty resilient stuff. I can see by your expression, Meg, that you are absolutely fascinated. I can also see that you are puzzled. What, you are asking yourself, is serum protein? Well, it's part of blood, ladies, and courtesy of my course in Hematology one-oh-one, I can tell you that blood is made up of all kinds of interesting things. Plasma. Red blood cells. White blood—"

"We think Dawn Pennifarm's been ground up and put in the paint can," said Meg.

"I beg your pardon?"

"I'll get the can," said Quill. She went to the storeroom for the box, and by the time she returned, Meg was sitting close to Andy at the counter.

He rubbed the paint between his thumb and forefinger, sniffed the contents of the can, and listened to Quill's summary of the events at the post office.

"Hm," he said.

"Do you think we've totally lost our minds?" said Meg defensively. "Is Doreen right? Do you think this is a rodent?"

"No," said Andy. "And serum protein would make those blotches on the post office, Quill, just like the blotches on your foyer wall, there. And there's too much of whatever it is to come from Vern's cut finger. There is absolutely blood in this paint. Have you talked to Myles—of course not. We're going to solve this ourselves, aren't we? I remember how envious I was last year when you two solved the History Days murder."

Meg flushed. Quill grinned; this guy, she thought, was in love, no question about it.

"I'll run a few tests at the clinic. Now, there's a problem. I'll be able to tell you if it's human blood, but . . ." He picked up one of the unopened cans of paint and read aloud, "Black iron oxide. Silicates. Two-four-five-six tetrachloro-Isopthalonitrile—betcha you didn't think I could pronounce that, did you? That's what medical school will do for a guy. Acrylic resin, glycols, and water. These babies are going to break down the identifying factors in the blood. So I'll be able to tell you what is in the can. But not who."

"There must be some way," Quill insisted.

"DNA typing. DNA strands survive practically anything. But then we'd have to have a sample of the victim's DNA to compare it to."

"How could we do that?" asked Meg. "I mean, if the body's in the paint can, how do we get a sample?"

"If it's a woman, there's a bare possibility that she's had a pap smear recently. If that sample's still around, then we can use that. Have either of the purported victims been to the doctor recently?"

"We don't know," said Meg.

"Dawn Pennifarm must have," said Quill. "Her husband said she was pregnant. The employee records at Paramount might show us."

"And we have a way of getting those," said Meg with a rather mischievous smile.

"If it's breaking in to Paramount, like Quill and John broke into Peterson's warehouse last year, then I have a better way," said Andy. "I do the comp claims for Paramount, you know. Physician of record. Let me check the files, okay? I don't want you two padding around that plant at two in the morning, especially if this"—he tapped the paint can—"is what we think it is. Too dangerous."

"Don't go into the basement," said Meg.

"What? Never mind. If Dawn was pregnant, she must have gone to Pete Dubrovnick in Syracuse, he handles most of the obstetrics-gyn work for the employees. Let me check with him, and see if we can come up with a tissue sample. In the meantime, you have an empty spice jar or something? I'll just take a bit of this and let you know." He eased off the stool.

"You'd do that for us?" asked Meg. "No questions asked?"

"Well." He leaned over the counter. His lips brushed her cheek. "There's a price."

"I'll go find John, or something," said Quill, "while you guys discuss the price."

Quill withdrew to the dining room. Several of the staff were setting up for afternoon tea. She waved at Kathleen Kiddermeister and asked for John.

"Last time I saw him, he was headed for the office. Quill? Is Helena Houndswood going to eat here tonight? Everyone's asking for her."

"Did you check the reservations list?"

"Yes." Kathleen's face dropped. "She's not on it."

"Then probably not."

"It's been so exciting having her around here."

"Yes," said Quill.

She found John absorbed in the calculator when she walked into her office. She sat on the couch facing the desk, guiltily aware she hadn't spared much time being fiscally responsible. "How's it look?"

"The cash situation?" He sat back and rubbed his eyes. "Not good. We're into the reserve line of credit. We're going to have a serious case of the cash shorts next week." He tossed the pencil he'd been using to punch the calculator keys onto the desktop. "No luck as far as Hudson giving us that check?"

"Not so far, but I haven't really tried," said Quill. "I'll give it another shot. But, surely with all this business we've booked, the bank will give us a loan?"

"Bankers loan you money when you don't need it. It's an oath they take when they buy their three-piece suits."

"What about Mark Jefferson at the Security and Trust?"

"I talked to him. We need a total of fifteen thousand to carry us through July. It's too small an amount."

"Too small?"

"Yes. They hold our mortgage. If we were in serious danger of defaulting, they'd lend us the whole half million. But we're not in danger of defaulting. What we need is fifteen thousand to carry us over the hump of the next three weeks. The risk to the bank's mortgage is low; the risk involved in extending an unsecured loan to us of fifteen thousand is high—at least that's what their actuarial tables say."

"That makes no sense at all," said Quill, indignant.

"It does if you're a banker. You know the options: we may have to close down for a couple of weeks, recruit volunteers to staff the Inn, beg the suppliers to wait more than ninety days for payment for laundry and food stock. The bank knows they're first in line to be paid, Quill, if we go belly up. They're just as happy to let our suppliers take the risk, rather than them taking the risk for the suppliers. You see what I mean?"

"Let's picket," said Quill, who always regretted missing the sixties.

"Let's find another lender. Half the problem is that Hemlock Falls Security and Trust is the only game in town. They can afford the hard line. This is my fault, Quill. I should have gone to Syracuse or Rochester for the mortgage. The banks there are larger, and more willing to absorb possible losses."

"I was the one who insisted that we use a local lender," said Quill. "You warned me. What do you want to do now?"

"Well, we're not as notorious as we were last year. I'll go into Syracuse tomorrow and talk to Chase. See what I can scare up."

"By the notoriety, you mean the murders?"

"That, and the business with the Board of Health."

"But you always told Meg—"

"You know Meg. The restaurant and hotel business is first and last built on reputation. If she'd known how worried I was over the temporary closure, we'd have had to put her on Prozac. The situation's dire, but not critical. Helena Houndswood's going to help us a lot. I know you don't like her, Quill, but her endorsement is going to tip the balance for any loan we might get. If you don't mind, I thought I'd stop down to her place tonight to see if I can use her name with the bank. Maybe get a written assurance that the show will be shot here."

"No," said Quill, "I don't mind."

He smiled slightly. "You do. I can tell. But that's the way the world works."

"John. If she were discredited or something. What would the chances of getting the loan be?"

"Poor to awful. Why?" He quirked an eyebrow. "You're not still on the gig about her knocking off the Bosses Club, are you?"

"Who, me?" said Quill.

CHAPTER 12

Quill went upstairs, took a shower, threw on a pair of shorts and a T-shirt, and sat on her balcony with her investigation book on her lap. Twilight came and deepened into night. Sounds of guests arriving, leaving, walking through the gardens drifted through the air. Her rooms were located over the kitchen; one end of her balcony formed the roof over the back entrance, and she heard the chatter of the *sous* chefs; Meg's voice raised in occasional outrage; bouts of laughter; the clink of pots and dishes. The sound of the falls wound through it all, and it was the best tranquilizer she knew, and it didn't work. Finally she tossed her pencil into the pot of dianthus near the French doors and called the sheriff's office: no, Myles hadn't checked in yet, but a message could be gotten to him right away. No, Quill said, no message.

Quill was switching through television programs that seemed increasingly stupid when Meg tapped on her door and pushed it open. Her face was both somber and excited.

"Andy called. It's human."

"Oh, my God," said Quill. "Does he know who? Not Dawn!"

"Not yet. He's going over to talk to this Pete Dubrovnick tomorrow. He said Dawn had an amniocentesis; that'll give us the tissue sample we need to match the DNA. Unless it's Kay."

"I called Myles's office. He's not expected back until Sunday."

"He'll miss the Little Miss Hemlock Falls beauty contest," said Meg. "Poor him. But it gives us two days to solve the murders. I've figured it out, Quill. It's—"

"You haven't figured it out, Meg. You couldn't possibly. You don't know everything Connie told me this afternoon." She told her. Meg, curled up on one end of the davenport, clapped her hand over her mouth, and yelled "Jeez!"

"So I don't think we should break into the Paramount factory. Andy's going to get the information anyway. I think we should break into the Peterson farmhouse."

"Okay," said Meg readily. "What are we looking for?"

"Evidence. Connie said that Dawn had given Helena something or done something that would guarantee they got their million dollars."

"What kind of something?" asked Meg skeptically.

"Well, I don't know, do I? Maybe she had figured out some kind of blackmail. Maybe she was just putting off Dawn until she had time to kill her. I won't know until I look."

"So when are we going to do it?"

"She's supposed to be at some chamber lunch tomorrow—"

"Not here!" Meg's eyes glittered dangerously. "There's nothing on the agenda sheet in the kitchen."

"No, down at the diner. I'll wait until she's out of the way, and then get in through a window or something. I'll bet she keeps a lot of files. Doreen said she had tons of paper and whatnot all over her room."

"And then what?" asked Meg. "What about Makepeace Whitman? Let's say that the story Dawn was going to give Helena was about pollution. If Dawn threatened to expose his substitution of lead oxide for iron oxide, he could be in real trouble with just about every government agency in the state. In the country."

"Makepeace is a prime suspect," said Quill. "I think you should join FOFA tomorrow and follow him around on his hikes. It's Saturday, and you don't have to be in the kitchen until dinner."

"Trudge around Hemlock Falls wearing one of those stupid T-shirts?" said Meg.

"Just try to find out if he came into town earlier this week. Be subtle."

"Okay. I'll do it. I just hope they don't have any lectures on insects of North America. I hate stuff like that."

"I'll see you at breakfast, then."

"Sleep well, Quillie." Meg reached over and hugged her. "We'll talk about stuff when this is all over."

"What kind of stuff?"

"You know, stuff."

Quill went to bed and dreamed of clocks. Dozens of them, the sound of their ticking merging into the roar of a ball mill. In her dream she approached the clock face, a huge, frightening combination of digital numbers and thick black hands. The hands descended, second by second. She reached up to grab it, stop it . . . stop it, and woke up with a jerk. Her alarm was ringing. The sun was shining through the French doors. She showered and put on a pair of cotton jeans.

She stood on the balcony and brushed her hair, the early sunshine warm on her face and arms. It was a very Grieg-ish scene, with the pale violet-pink of dawn submerged under the rising tide of stronger morning light, the finches and the barn sparrows arguing mildly in the poplars. Even the chickens busy on the fresh-clipped lawn were pleasing to the eye.

Except the Inn didn't have any chickens.

Quill frowned and leaned over the railing. Three of them—hens, she guessed—were right below her on the lawn. The asphalt drive leading away from the back door to the rear parking lot was covered with suspicious-looking piles. The jerky movement of the tarragon in the breezeless air indicated the presence of several more chickens in the herb garden.

The back door slammed. There was a sliding, scraping thud, then a shout: "Hellfire!"

"Doreen!" Quill leaned over the rail. Her hair swung into her eyes, and she brushed it away. "Doreen, are you all right?"

"Durn things!" Doreen marched out on the lawn and peered up at her. Her bun was askew. Chicken manure smeared the side of her white apron. Her expression rivaled that of the monk who took such umbrage at the innocent Brother Lippi. "If the Friends hadn't taught me 'bout the sanctity of livin' creetures, I'd be getting me an ax," she said.

"Where did they come from?" asked Quill. "Oh. Of course, Helen Houndswood's gentleman farm."

"There's chicken shit all over the place!" Doreen tramped determinedly across the lawn, flapping her apron at the chickens. This occasioned a curiously lethargic panic, demonstrated by a tentative jerk forward with one clawed foot, a frantic look from side to side, several distressed clucks, and a resumption of the foot into its former position.

"We should catch them and return them," said Quill. "Get a box. I'll be right down."

She knotted her hair on the top of her head and briefly debated the best components of a chicken-catching outfit. Shorts and a T-shirt should offer fewer opportunities for chicken droppings, and she changed out of her jeans.

Shorts, however, offered more flesh to chicken beaks. "Jeez!" exclaimed Meg, who'd joined them in the hunt. "The little suckers are nasty!" She shoved the last hen into the wire milk case Doreen had unearthed from the storeroom and held a garbage can lid over the top. "We need a bunch of heavy boards, or something. They're going to wiggle—*Ow!*" She sucked the back of her hand and scowled at the crate. A flat black eye glittered balefully back.

Doreen, who'd thought ahead, had rummaged several thick planks from the garden shed. She slid them over the top of the crate with a tender regard for those birds who refused to duck. "There. Your legs look a treat. Better get iodine on 'em."

Quill looked down at her bare legs, peppered with beak marks.

Doreen hefted the crate. A chorus of indignant clucks and screeches assaulted them. "I'll get the pickup and take 'em on back to Peterson's. You got any messages for Ms. Houndswood?"

"No. Just make sure she's going to that chamber meeting."

"Anything else? Doc Bishop find anything in that paint can?"

"Um," said Quill.

"Rats, right?" Doreen stumped toward the parking lot and pickup truck, the chickens protesting fiercely at every step. Or maybe, being chickens, Quill thought, simply squawking for the heck of it. Myles had been right about them—stupid and mean. "Be back in a few minutes."

Meg suggested breakfast, and they retired to the kitchen.

"So, you're going to break into the farmhouse?" said Meg. She slapped a bowl of blueberries on the counter and reached for the heavy cream.

"Yep. And I figured out what to look for. I'm convinced those phone calls supposedly from Kay were phony. Helena made at least four phony calls. One to Sandy the day before, to lead us to believe that Kay was still alive, the second to Sandy's home, to get her out on the road so she could smack her with that rental car, the other to Connie. Helena's got that cellular phone, and the phone company keeps records of all the calls made on cellular phones. I'll get the number from the farmhouse, and we can get hold of the records."

"She wouldn't be that stupid," said Meg. She apportioned the berries into two bowls and handed Quill a spoon.

"This murderer is taking risks," said Quill. "Look at what happened to Dawn. Frozen to death, transported across the parking lot to Paramount in the dead of night, and tipped into the ball mill."

"So how would she know where to put the body?" asked Meg. "How many people know about the ball mills?"

"Brought them chickens back," said Doreen as she came in the back door. She pulled out a stool and sat down with them at the counter.

"That was fast," said Meg. "About the ball mills . . ."

"What?" said Quill, who didn't want to answer Meg's question, because it pointed to Connie as the murderer. "Weren't they her chickens?"

"They was her chickens, all right," said Doreen grimly. "The last of the herd."

"Flock," corrected Meg. "Wasn't she around? Out in the barn, I suppose, doing picturesque things with the cows."

"Out in the driveway," said Doreen. "Doing you're not goin' to believe what with that fancy Jeep."

"You mean the Range Rover?" said Meg. "It did seem kind of excessive to buy a brand-new Range Rover for her project.

I mean, what farmer do you know that can afford a brand new Range Rover?"

"What was she doing with the Range Rover?" asked Quill.

"I drove up the hill, carrying them chickens," said Doreen. "They was squalling fit to bust. Fit to wake the dead and pecking each other like you wouldn't believe. I said," Doreen pointed out with a consciously virtuous air, "a prayer over 'em. And there she was."

"Helena Houndswood?" asked Meg.

"In that-there Jeep. Running back and forth over this big flat garbage bag."

"Over a garbage bag?" said Quill.

"Me, I thought she was recycling. She come up that little hill to the house gunnin' that Jeep—"

"Range Rover," said Meg.

"Like some Nazi tank driver. *Wham!* She'd hit the bag. Then she'd back up. All the way down that little hill. Then gunnin' back up and *Wham!* right over the garbage bag."

"Cans?" said Quill, confused, "she was flattening cans?"

"Chickens. Flattening them chickens. Or what was left of them."

"She ran over the chickens!" said Quill. "Why?"

"Well, I ast her that. Why she'd go and flatten one of God's innocent creatures with that there Rover. 'Innocent my ass!' she says. You look what they done to me. 'What they done?' I says."

Quill glanced under the table at her pecked and iodined legs. "Pecked her, I bet."

"Pecked her good. And she slipped and fell in the chicken poop like I done, and sprained her ankle all to golly. 'They stink and they're stoopid,' she says to me. 'And don't you go tellin' nobody. Chicken is not part of a beautiful life,' she says, and she whomps that ol' garbage bag in the Dumpster and stomps off. So I brung our chickens back."

"Uh, Doreen," said Quill. "I don't really want those chickens. Do you, Meg?"

"Nossir," said Meg. "Me, I think Helena Houndswood has the right idea."

"You watch your mouth, missy!" said Doreen. "Why do you want to go and punish one of God's innocent creetures?"

"What's this 'God's innocent creatures' stuff," complained Meg. "Did I miss something?"

"One of the Friends of the Fresh Air lectures," said Quill glumly. "The 'Friends' extends to all living things, I guess."

"Including chickens?" Meg rolled her eyes.

"What I want you to do with them chickens is to let them run free on the grass, just as God made them. They deserve to enjoy the sunshine and the fresh air, like all of us."

"Doreen," said Meg, with winning candor, "I don't want those chickens. Except maybe to stew. You don't want those chickens. You fell flat on your whatsis this morning because of those chickens, and my goodness, what's going to happen with the guests? Those Friends of Fresh Air of yours will be slipping and sliding all over the *lawn*, for Pete's sake. No. No chickens."

"You refuse sanctuary to them chickens?"

"I refuse what?"

"Sanctuary," interrupted Quill. "You could take them to the church, Doreen."

"The church?" Meg shook her head back and forth, as if trying to clear it.

"Take the chickens to Harland Peterson's," said Quill. "You know, the farmer that sold them to Helena Houndswood in the first place. He'll put them back with their relatives."

"He'll cook them," said Doreen indignantly.

"Well, probably," said Quill. "I don't care what you do with them. Take them home with you, if you want. Just don't let them roam all over the lawn."

"I know what to do," said Doreen. She rose, adjusted her bun with grim determination. "I seen my duty, and I'm doin' it."

"Jeez," said Meg as Doreen stumped off. "Do you suppose Helena really squashed those chickens like that?"

"Doreen wouldn't make it up." Quill shuddered. "Now, if she could do that to chickens, Meg . . ."

"Oh, I don't know. Somebody told me once that chickens are so brainless that if they look up to see if it's raining, they'll drown because they forget to look down. No, that's turkeys. Whatever. I'm a cook, Quill, and one of the things I cook is chickens. So I don't see Helena's disposal of her chicken problem as a major character flaw. Actually, given the kind of person she is, it was a typical tidy solution. I mean, obviously, these chickens were going to embarrass her big time. It's a neat, tidy way to dispose of an annoyance without making a big deal of it."

"Sure," said Quill skeptically. "I'm going down there now. And you're going to join Doreen and the nature hike, right?"

"Oh, right. Well. Guess I better get going." She sat, unmoving. "Quill?"

"What?"

"It might not be Helena. It might be someone else altogether."

Quill said, searching through her purse for the keys to her Olds, "Who else could it be?"

"I don't know. But one thing that's struck me about this murder is the need to absolutely conceal the body or bodies from identification. I mean—why else go through this elaborate stuff? The murderer had to get Dawn or Kay or both of them to the Qwik Freeze, then take the frozen body out and over to the ball mill. All within a space of what—two to three hours in the dead of night and eluding the security guards. All this to obliterate the corpse. Think about it."

"What do you think?"

"I don't have an answer," said Meg. "I'm just raising the question."

"Some help you are."

"Why are you so upset? All I'm saying is just thi—"

"Stop," said Quill. "It's perfectly fine for you to help with this investigation, but if you're simply going to be an obstructionist, forget it."

"You don't know what to think about it, do you?" said Meg. "Ha. Some Hawkshaw. Me, I'm going to think about it, and when I've come up with the answer, I'll let you know. Deal?"

"I'll come up with the answer before you do," said Quill. "So sure. Deal."

"Quill?"

"What?!"

"Ask yourself what *really* happened to Kay Gondowski."

Quill drove the Olds to the Peterson farm, thinking about it. Why would there be a need to destroy the body? And what *had* happened to Kay Gondowski?

The old farmhouse looked like the cover of a very expensive coffee table book. Quill half expected to see letters across the velvety grass reading: HELENA HOUNDSWOOD PRESENTS: IT'S A BEAUTIFUL LIFE ON THE FARM, or whatever it was that she was going to call her next best-seller. The Range Rover wasn't in the driveway. The yard was conspicuous for its lack of chickens. Quill got out of the Olds, went to the front door, and plied the brass door knocker vigorously. No answer. She walked around the back of the house, passing by the Dumpster. A large curiously flattened green Hefty bag lay on top. Quill hesitated. Miss Marple would have looked in the bag. Miss Marple, however, didn't have a housekeeper whose word was as good as Doreen's.

In the back of the house Quill saw that the horse and the cow had been fed large armfuls of hay and were chewing away in their paddocks. The pig was there, too, gloriously smelly, but only, Quill figured, because it was too large to fit under the Range Rover. Quill went back to the house and peered into the ground-floor windows facing the red barn. The Peterson kitchen was gorgeous, with custom cherry cupboards, granite countertops, and pine flooring. Mrs. Peterson had ruthlessly modernized it some time before Norm's commitment to the state slammer for criminal activities. There was a stack of empty Lean Cuisine boxes in the sink and a teacup near the coffeemaker.

Gingerly, Quill tried the back door. It was locked. She tried the kitchen window next. It opened easily. Quill, her heart pounding, hoisted herself up and went inside.

The house smelled faintly of Giorgio. Quill poked through the trash in the kitchen waste basket: tea bags, coffee grounds, and remains of a tube of Retin-A. The living room was as neat and impersonal as a magazine ad, the braided rugs on the hardwood floors placed equidistant from the walls. Recent copies of *Publishers Weekly* and *W* lay on the coffee table.

The Peterson den had been converted into a temporary

office. A laptop computer was open on the desk; a plastic file case, the sort that had a handle and could be carried, was open beside it. Quill, glancing around her with the furtiveness of a cat burglar, which, she thought, she was, gingerly flipped through the manila folders.

Helena was an organized woman, which didn't surprise Quill at all. Anyone who did twenty-seven television shows a year, published a book a year, and appeared at all the celebrity functions necessary to keep her in the media's eye had to be organized and fearsomely productive. There was a file on the china contest. Quill found biographical notes on Connie, Dot, Sandy, and Kay. They were short descriptions, rather acerbic, but otherwise unrevealing.

There was an outline for a book, simply labeled "Farm." She'd made an entry that morning: "Bag chickens," which made Quill grin and shake her head.

The file behind it was called "A Sharper Eye." Quill opened it to a series of faxes from someone named Max, who appeared to be Helena's agent. Helena's responses were on bond. At first perusal, Max came across as servile, obsequious, and fawning, agreeing to everything Helena suggested. Just, Quill thought, the sort of person she would have expected to be the actress's representative. As she read on, she realized Helena was begging him to find a credible alternative to her TV show. People, she complained, were not taking her seriously. Her audience share had dropped thirty-two percent in the past twelve months. And Max, in prose as oily as Göring's must have been to Hitler's, was telling her it was hopeless.

" . . . even for someone as loved by the audience as you are, another investigative news show is not going to fly. *60 Minutes, 20/20, PRIMETIME* have carved up what small market there is . . ."

" . . . Look at Julia. Eighty-three and still beloved. Forty-six is not the end of the world. . . . (forty-six? Quill was astonished) . . . you're a fixture with your fans. . . ."

"Fixture?" Helena had responded. "So's a toilet. I've run across an interesting problem here. Lot of resonance for the Greenpeace types. It's a hell of a story. Wallace is seventy-two, right? Unless the bastard's planning to die on the air, I want you to make some inquiries about my replacing him. This could be the feature that gives me an entrée."

That was the last fax. It was dated the day before. Quill reread the messages and found no clue as to what the story was that would "have a lot of resonance for the Greenpeace types." Whatever was going on had to be related to FOFA and Makepeace Whitman's substitution of lead oxide for iron oxide. Dawn said she'd fixed it, Connie had said. Dawn said the cash prize was in the bag, she'd made a trade. And here was confirmation. "Damn," said Quill, since Helena now had every possible motive to keep the Bosses Club alive. Quill closed the file, replaced it, and began thumbing through the correspondence file for the cellular phone bill. She found it for the prior month and copied the account number on a slip of paper. With any luck, she could figure out a way to get the record of calls made in the last week. John, she bet, would have an idea.

A squeal came from outside. Quill jumped. Her heart thudding painfully, she peered cautiously out the window. One of the pigs was digging in the lawn. She slipped quietly out the back door and into the car. The pig went "hrunh" and trotted toward her, eyes alight. Quill pulled out of the driveway and into the road.

"So much for being a burglar," she muttered aloud. Clearly, the next step was to confront Helena with the fact that she had evidence relating to a suspected homicide, and she had to cough up or suffer the consequences. Just as clearly, Helena would want to know how Quill had come by the information. Quill wondered what the penalty for breaking and entering was. So far, the only witness to her felony, if it was a felony, was the pig, and all things considered, she'd rather keep it that way. Maybe Meg would have some answers.

"Meg's still out with the FOFA people," said Dina when Quill got back to the Inn. "So's Doreen."

"Where's John?"

"Syracuse. He left this morning."

"Right. I forgot." Balked, Quill drummed her fingers on top of the reception desk. "Makepeace Whitman and his wife are on the hike, aren't they?"

"Yes," said Dina. "They left about an hour ago. They hike until teatime. Those guys are some hikers, Quill. But they never seem to get sweaty. They're the cleanest hikers I've ever seen."

"Would you hand me the master key, please?"

"Quill. You're not going to . . ."

"Going to what!" Guilt made Quill snappish, and she apologized. "Anyway, it's just a room check, to see how housekeeping's doing." Dina handed over the master key. Quill slipped it into her pocket and went upstairs. Great detectives, she was beginning to realize, had to cultivate character traits like nosiness and deception that made them less than desirable inn managers, much less prospective wives for sheriffs. Peter Wimsey was always plunged into guilt over the whole ethics thing, but kept determinedly on in the course of bringing criminals to justice; on the other hand, Harriet loved him anyway.

Makepeace Whitman's room didn't provide a single clue to prove his culpability in the environmental disaster Helena had alluded to in her fax. The only thing Quill discovered was that he and his wife traveled with remarkably few possessions and used a lot of towels. Quill relocked the door and went downstairs to her office, where she brooded for three hours, concluding only that it was unlikely Helena Houndswood was behind the killings, that Connie still had the best motive extant—and that she *really* wanted to find Kay Gondowski—prospective heir to a cool, clear million. When Meg banged into the office, she greeted her with a sigh of relief.

"So, how was it?"

Meg, in shorts and a grubby tank top, sank into the couch with a groan and untied her tennis shoes. "Awful."

"Awful?" She cast a critical eye over her sister. "How come you look like you've been rolling around in the Peterson barnyard, and they look so clean all the time?"

"They must take a lot of showers." Meg groaned. "Boy, my legs hurt. And I jog, Quill! Those people are fanatics. We tramped all the way down to the end of the gorge. And they're worse proselytizers than the Moonies at the airport. 'I wouldn't know what it was really like until I joined,' they said.

'My body wouldn't get the full benefit of the fresh air until I was a member.' Aaagh!" She shook herself like a puppy. "Spare me. And I didn't learn a damn thing about Makepeace Whitman's business. Just that he believes in benign use of the earth's resources, and his company turns rock quarries into parks and a whole *load* of baloney. This was *not* one of your better ideas. Next time *you* go on the endless tramp through the woods and listen to bozos going on and on and *on* about God's feathered friends. I tell you one thing, they were some kind of pissed off when Doreen got up to 'testify' and told them about Helena running over those chickens. They were ready to storm the Bastille, or, in her case, the Peterson farmhouse. Starving French peasants have nothing on them, I'll tell you. I hope you got something, because I'll tell you, I'm up the creek without a paddle." She glowered. "Stuck in a sinking canoe with crazies. And no life jacket. And no *food*! We walked for four hours without so much as a cookie. You better spill what you found fast, because I'm about to raid the refrigerator big time."

"I found something, but we're in the same canoe, so to speak. I'm not sure what to do next. The 'trade' that Dawn made with Helena to assure the Bosses Club win was a hot story on some kind of environmental disaster."

"So Helena's off the suspect list."

"I suppose so," said Quill with reluctance, "but I got the account number for the phone bill all the same."

The phone rang with one short, two long, that meant the call was for the office and not the reception desk. Quill picked it up.

"Quill? This is Andy Bishop. We're on the way to identifying the body in the paint can."

"Meg's here," said Quill. "I'm going to put you on the speaker phone." She punched the button and set the receiver in the cradle.

"Am I on? Are you there, Meg? I talked to Pete. He's sending the amniocentesis sample Dawn Pennifarm had taken over, so we can try and match the DNA. It's odd, though, a woman as young as Dawn having the test. Pete said it showed the fetus had a number of birth defects. I won't bother you with the medical jargon, but they're tetraogenic. That is, there's a strong probability the defects originated from environmental causes. And the results from the autopsy on Dot Vandermolen are back. She had a grade-three lung cancer. Are we moving along here?"

"Environmental?" Quill drew her breath in sharply. "Of course! And the clocks! The timing's off! That's it! Could a long-term exposure to lead do that?"

"I'm not sure about the lung cancer, but the evidence is pretty clear about the fetal defect."

"That's a yes?"

"Yes."

"Then that's it. Thanks, Andy." She rang off.

"That's what?" demanded Meg.

"Hudson Zabriskie."

"*Hudson*!? The Bloater!? He didn't even *know* about the lead oxide!"

"Bull," said Quill, inelegantly. "He runs the factory. And I don't care how stupid everyone thinks he is. He's got the best motive in the world, Meg. His entire career would come to a screeching halt. He'd lose everything if Helena exposed him on TV. It fits, Meg. Dawn's pregnant, about to blow the whistle. He's not sure how many members of the Bosses Club know about it—so he picks them off one by one. . . ."

"And he knows Connie's not about to testify against him because of her daughter—and even if she *did*, she genuinely doesn't believe he knows anything."

"I'll bet he would have tried for her in the end, solved," said Quill grimly.

"Solved but not proved," said Meg. "He's going to get away with it."

Quill, silent for a moment, said finally, "I guess we break into Paramount after all. I'll do it tomorrow. The factory's closed on Sunday. And Hudson will be at the beauty contest. He's a judge." With a frown, she flipped the scrap of paper carrying Helena Houndswood's cellular phone account number into the waste basket. "It's the dream about clocks, Meg. I broke into the wrong file. The proof we want is at Paramount."

CHAPTER 13

Quill and John piled out of the Inn van in the high school parking lot. They'd had trouble finding a parking spot; most of the town had turned out for the preliminaries of the Little Miss Hemlock Falls Beauty Contest, and the lot was jammed.

"There he is!" hissed Meg. She poked her elbow into Quill's ribs. Meg stopped, staring at Hudson, one foot up on the curb. Quill tried to look elaborately unconcerned. They both waved to Hudson, who waved back. Meg's socks were pale blue. The past three days she'd been heavily into the pastels: pink, pale yellow, and now this. Quill'd laid it to Andy Bishop's softening influence, but the colors could very well signal rumination. Perhaps even a swing to the contemplative.

"You think Hudson Zabriskie is capable of pushing Dawn Pennifarm into the Zero Room at the Qwik Freeze, hauling the body half a city block to Paramount, and dumping her into the ball mill?" asked John. He had taken the news that Quill was going to break into the paint factory very well. Chase Bank had extended a twenty-thousand-dollar loan. "It doesn't seem quite in character. I'd *much* prefer Helena as a suspect."

"So would Doreen," said Meg. "She thinks that anyone who could run over a flock of defenseless chickens is capable of anything."

The scabs on Quill's ankles had forced Quill to temporarily give up her pantyhose since the assault by the survivors. She forebore any comment relating to poultry and character, but instead commented that they were obviously in a minority of two, given the excitement around them over the star's rumored presence at the beauty contest.

"Are you sure Helena's going to be here?" whispered Meg to John as they walked to the athletic field. The not-too-distant sound of tubas, trumpets, and drums heralded the approach of the Hemlock High School Marching Band. "If she's not, Hudson probably won't stick around. You be careful!"

"Harvey said she definitely was going to show up when I borrowed the cellular thinggummy this morning. We can always ditch the plan if she doesn't, Meg. Look!"

"What?" shouted Meg, over the sound of the band.

Quill gestured to wait a minute. The band started a ragged march at the end of the football field, the crimson and purple uniforms bright flags against the green. Two cheerleaders carried a banner reading WE LOVE HELENA! The drum had been painted to read IT'S A BEAUTIFUL LIFE!! in a semicircle surrounding a fairly well-executed portrait of the actress. The drummer wielded the drumsticks with a youthful enthusiasm that had smeared the paint a bit.

Meg and Quill settled onto a front-row bleacher next to a family of Petersons whose first names Quill couldn't remember. John stood on the field, hands tucked into the back pocket of his chinos. Elmer Henry ascended the two shallow steps to the stage at the north end of the field and raised his hands for silence. The judges, Helena and Hudson among them, sat under an awning to his extreme left.

"You've got the phone?" Quill said. "Although they both look like they're settled in."

Meg patted her purse. "I checked the battery. Everything's fine. What did you tell Harvey we wanted it for?"

"I didn't have to justify it; he assumed we were 'improving field-Inn communications.'"

Meg held up her hand against the sun and scanned the field. "Do you see Myles anywhere?"

"No. He wasn't due back until this evening. Deputy Dave's over there."

"Good. Wave at him."

"Why should I wave at Dave Kiddermeister?"

"Alibi," hissed Meg. "We want everyone to see you here. Then they'll just make an assumption that you were here all along and not burglarizing Paramount."

"Meg! If I find what we're looking for, people will know I burglarized the paint factory. And Helena's house."

"And if you don't?"

"Good point." Quill, not precisely sure how to dress for a daylight burglary, had opted for light cotton trousers (for mobility) and a Lycra bodysuit (it wouldn't get caught on anything if she had to hide in a ball mill). The bodysuit was hot and she wriggled uncomfortably. "You'll ring the plant three short rings if anything happens?"

"Two rings, then I hang up, then I ring again once." She patted Quill's shoulder. "It'll be fine. You've done warehouse-type burglaries before, remember."

Quill had. She and John had broken into the Peterson warehouse to gather evidence for a crime the year before. That effort, to save John from a murder charge, had seemed less— *crooklike* was the word she wanted—than a deliberate break-in in broad daylight.

"Meg," she said.

"Shhh!" hissed the rather large female Peterson to her right.

"*Citizens of Hemlock Falls!*" boomed Elmer Henry, too close to the microphone. "Dang!" he said, and moved back two paces. "Citizens of Hemlock Falls! I welcome you to the first annual Little Miss Hemlock Falls Beauty Pageant!"

A roar of applause swept the football field.

"There's going to be more pageants? The Second Annual? The Third Annual?" muttered Meg. "Swell."

"*Shhh!*" hissed Mrs. Peterson.

"I still think we should have brought the signs," said Quill, worriedly scanning the line-up of little girls on the stage.

"I wanted to bring the signs to help establish an alibi," Meg pointed out. "You said nobody believes in protests anymore. You're right. Besides, we agreed it'd upset the little kids." She viewed the children onstage with misgiving.

Elmer, the microphone adjusted to his satisfaction, said, "Now, I know how anxious you folks are to get started, but first, there's a number of people I have to thank for today."

He turned and beamed on the children behind him, then addressed himself to his speech. The number of people Elmer needed to thank appeared to consist of the entire voting population of Hemlock Falls. The children twisted their hair, picked their noses, and made faces at various relatives offstage. "Hurry it *up*, bozo!" shouted a little girl in pink and white starched ruffles accompanied by a West Highland terrier. "It's hot!" The little girl scowled, adjusted the scraggy bow on her dog's collar, polished her patent-leather shoes with spit and forefinger, and scratched her back. Then, heat and boredom combining to ignition point, she punched the little girl next to her. The child on the opposite side, dressed in a miniature tuxedo, pulled the pink and white one's hair. A short but lively brawl ensued onstage, engaging most of the contestants except for the dog, who watched the proceedings with dignified curiosity.

"Prizes," shouted Elmer into the microphone, sublimely ignoring the melee in process behind him, "will be awarded by that star of stage, screen, and television . . . Miss Helena Houndswood!"

Applause swept the audience once more. The children straightened to abrupt attention. Helena, under the temporary awning set up on one corner of the stage, rose and flashed a brilliant smile. Hudson beamed proudly beside her.

"And now, without further ado . . . our first entry! Miss Merrilee Pasquale and her pet dog Star, singing, 'You Are My Lucky Star.' "

Shouts and wild hand clapping indicated the presence of Merrilee Pasquale's large family in the stands. Elmer held up his hands for silence. "Ladies and gentlemen, I must ask you to hold your applause, please. Hold your applause until after each and every performance. Merrilee?"

Elmer stepped back. The pink and white girl who looked, Quill thought, about eight, skipped to the front of the stage, the terrier's leash clutched in one freckled fist. She stopped in front of the microphone and said with self-conscious sincerity, "This is my dog, Star. An' I'm singing this song because he is my lucky Star. He's the smartest, bestest dog there ever was." Star, who'd taken the opportunity to sit down, scratched energetically for fleas and succeeded in looking temporarily idiotic.

"Sweet," said Mrs. Peterson. "Isn't that sweet?"

"Oh, my God," muttered Meg, sliding down into her seat.

Merrilee waved an imperious hand and bellowed "Hit it!" The music intro to "You Are My Lucky Star" came over the loudspeaker. "Up, Star," said Merrilee, jerking the leash, "C'mon, boy."

Star rolled over, dreamily contemplating the clear June sky.

"C'mon!"

Star waved his paws and thought dog thoughts.

"Up!" Merrilee hauled up on the leash, and perhaps, thought Quill charitably, out of nervousness, elevated the dog into the air. Star, feet dangling, his tongue much pinker than the ruffles on Merrilee's dress, looked momentarily confused.

"Yeeww are my Luck-ee Star," sang Merrilee in a childish treble.

"Gaack," said Star, in response.

"Put the dog down, Merrilee!" shouted a frantic woman whose freckles signified a close, if not maternal, relationship to the child.

"I saaw you from afar . . ." Merrilee stopped, frowned, and said, "Wait, wait, wait, wait. I forgot. Start over."

"Put the dog *down!*"

"I fergot ta dance!" Merrilee abjured her parent, swinging the leash in admonition. Star, airborne, made a movement in mild protest.

The music intro played once more.

"Yeew are my Lucky Star," shrilled Merrilee, dancing. Star, swinging in four/four time, rolled an exasperated eye skyward.

"Merrilee!" hollered Mrs. Pasquale.

Star, whose experience had apparently taught him not to hold his personal safety hostage to parental intervention, corkscrewed out of his collar and regained solid ground. Merrilee tapped on, patent-leather shoes twinkling in the sunlight. Star's ears flattened in a considering way. He elevated his hindquarters and extended his forepaws. Head cocked, muzzle to the ground, he regarded his mistress's shoes with a somewhat baleful eye.

" . . . bee-cawse *yew* are my luckee . . . *Ow!* Leggo!"

Star struck the other shoe with the innate precision of any self-respecting terrier after a large black rodent.

"*Get away from me, you stupid dog!*" shrieked Merrilee. She flung herself on the stage and drummed her heels on the floor. "Aaooow!" Star howled, perhaps in a belated attempt to resume the performance.

"Next entry," said Elmer, stepping over the recumbent Merrilee with all the aplomb of Yeltsin resuming control of the Russian white house, "is Tiffany Peterson in a performance of 'New York, New York.' "

Mrs. Peterson applauded energetically. Hudson, with the other judges, sat on the stage in rapt attention. Quill gave Meg's hand a warning squeeze and slipped unobtrusively off the field.

She drove to the paint factory with the sense she was behind enemy lines, braking carefully at intersections, trying not to accelerate too aggressively. She rolled into the parking lot, her palms wet, and parked behind the Dumpsters at the rear of the building. In the strategy session the night before, John had suggested upper windows as the best bet for gaining entry into the locked building. Paramount wasn't air-conditioned, and in the warm summer air the upper windows would be open for ventilation.

Quill scanned the back of the building. He'd been right. She got back into the car and pulled it under the one closest to the back door. Getting out once she was inside would be no problem.

She climbed on the car roof and got her hands firmly over the sill. She swung back. Her tennis shoes took firm hold on the corrugated wall. She pushed herself up and over the ledge. She dangled half in, head down. Grasping the window frame, she hitched her legs up until she was sitting on the ledge. Then, her right hand tight on the window frame, the left on the ledge, she shifted herself around and dropped her leg, stomach to the wall. She eased herself straight, took a deep breath, and dropped to the floor.

She took a moment to catch her breath. Her knees and ankles hurt. The factory was quiet, the great ball mills shrouded. The scent of linseed oil hung in the air like a heavy drape. She picked her way carefully across the concrete to the round cardboard canisters that held the minerals used in mixing paint. The barrels were stacked on steel shelving that reached to the top of the fourteen-foot ceiling. She scanned the barrels. IRON OXIDE was the third rack up. A wheeled stepladder had been pushed to the side of the shelving. She rolled it across the floor, mounted, and pried the lid off a barrel that looked as though it had been opened before.

Iron oxide, Quill knew, was essentially rust. The mineral she was looking at was black, finely ground, and, when she picked up a handful, felt like the graphite used in pencils, soft and shiny. Quill would have bet her set of oils that she was looking at lead oxide. The same lead oxide that OSHA had labeled a hazardous material. A mineral that caused birth defects, brain damage, and cancers to those who'd been exposed to it for years and years without protective clothing. She dropped a handful into the bread bag Meg had given her, then climbed down the stepladder.

The glycols next. She tucked the bread bag into her jeans pocket and pulled out an empty spice jar. The glycols were stacked in polyurethane vats with spouts on the bottom third, on shelves at right angles to the oxides. Quill filled the jar with a sample.

The last thing, she thought, was that dream about clocks. The budget requests were filed in the accountant's office. Quill searched methodically and found it.

Three days before Helena Houndswood had rolled into town on a Sunday, Hudson Zabriskie had requested funds for five new supervisors. Five supervisors he knew he was going to replace—because he was going to kill all of them.

The phone shrilled as loud as a rifle report. One ring, A pause. Then two. Meg's warning.

The office door opened. Quill whirled, the approved budget request in one hand.

Hudson Zabriskie. With a rifle.

"This," said Quill, "is just like one of those 'B' movies. You won't get away with this."

"I have four times before." He was in the backseat of her car, the deer rifle tucked between his knees, six inches from her head. Quill's hands were slippery on the wheel.

"You were using oil-base ingredients in some of the latex paints. Lead, kerosene. The whole operation exposed the employees to pollutants."

"Made a much better paint," said Hudson. "My own devising, actually. I know paint."

"A lot of the hazardous materials were mislabeled as glycols or iron oxide, both inert matter. It's been years since you've had an OSHA inspection, but you'd get one eventually, Hudson. How did you think you were going to get away with it?"

"Take a left here."

Quill turned and faced him. "Well?"

He jerked the rifle at her. "Keep your eyes on the road. We're still making oil-based. It's not illegal for another six years. If OSHA caught us unaware, we'd just say we made a mistake, that's all. In the labeling room. The QA function was the most brilliant stroke, I have to admit. I simply recalibrated the gauges."

"I don't understand."

"Let's say you have a clock mechanism. What it does is push the hands of the dial into a certain position, right? But what do you design on the face of the clock? If you don't put numbers on the face of the clock, if you put, for example, degrees Fahrenheit, you can turn a clock into a thermometer. I simply redid the gauges in the QA function so they read for, say, iron oxide, instead of lead. Or kerosene. OSHA never checks the gauges onsite. You send them off to NIST to be recalibrated. All you have to do is send the correct gauges and store them in the back room until you need to send them to NIST again. If we get nailed, we apologize, explain that the changeover from latex had been the week before, and we'd screwed up this one time. We'd get a fine. Be properly apologetic for the error. But I wouldn't go to jail. And New York wasn't about to fire me over an OSHA violation. My numbers are too good. And that's what New York cares about, numbers. Would they fire me over screw-ups? Well, never underestimate how much you can blame on the worker, Quill. Stop here."

They were in the granite quarry behind the Qwik Freeze. In the distance Quill could hear the sounds of the Hemlock Falls High School Marching Band playing "Oh, What a Beautiful Morning." She turned off the ignition.

The rifle nudged her skull. "You're going to get caught, Hudson. It's only a matter of time. I can't believe you've gotten away with it for as long as you have."

"Well, I had some cooperation. Sandy. Dawn. Kay. Appropriate bonuses at appropriate times keep a lot of people quiet."

"But Dawn didn't keep quiet, did she? Or wouldn't when she discovered her baby was—"

"Defective," said Hudson. "No. The stupid woman went into a major fit of hysteria. Threatened to blow the whistle. Without her, Sandy and Kay folded, too."

"And what about Connie?"

"Connie?" He raised his eyebrows.

"Did she know what was going on?"

"Well, she must have, mustn't she? But she needed the job. I had Dawn sound her out once about getting paid off. She said she didn't know what Dawn was talking about."

"So she just kept silent."

"She just kept silent." He slid back the rifle's bolt.

Quill turned around to face him. "So you killed them? All of them?"

"Ashes to ashes," said Hudson. "Or rather, paint to paint. Not Sandy and Dot, of course. Doesn't do to repeat yourself. Get out of the car, please."

"You're going to have to kill Helena Houndswood, too, Hudson."

"Helena Houndswood? Why should I?"

"Because Dawn told her what was going on. I found a file in her house, Hudson. She knows about the crimes at the paint factory, and she's already contacted her agent about arranging for the media to blow the whistle."

"You're missing the point, Quill. I haven't committed any crimes. They're violations! Do you understand me? And all that happens is you get fined for a violation. I won't go to jail. I won't serve time. I won't even lose my job. Paramount will pay the fine!"

"Then why did you kill four women? Dawn. Dot. Kay. Sandy."

"Why? Why? No witnesses! Do you know what the media does to people, Quill? Do you have any idea? You take perfectly good human beings, like me"—he gestured with his rifle and Quill, choking with fear, wondered if she'd have the nerve to struggle with him for it—"just trying to do a good job. Trying to adjust to the changes in all these regulations, and all these rules, and all of a sudden what you've done before has been legal, but when you do it now, it's not illegal. But it's going to be illegal; in the future. And where does that leave you? The media comes in, *20/20,* or *60 Minutes* or those guys and Dawn starts bawling about deformed babies and the public crucifies you. *Even when you haven't done anything wrong*! I was within the law. When I started in this business, I was one of the best! I was doing it right. And then the rules changed! Only they don't change now, so that there's no clear-cut line. They change in the future. So what the hell was I supposed to do? Give up my job? Where am I going to find a job in a town this size? At my age, where am I going to find a job in a town any size? So don't tell me I committed crimes. I didn't commit crimes. I committed violations. And you get fined for violations, and eventually New York tells you, 'No more oil-based paint,' and *then* you stop making oil base because *then* it's a crime. And the quality's so bad with latex. So many customer complaints with latex. You know, Quill, more people are satisfied with paint that comes from my factory than anywhere else."

"You told me that," said Quill.

"So then here comes this little bitch," he said bitterly. "This mother, who'd been going along like everybody else, even that Connie turning a blind eye because she knows just like me that we're just committing violations, not crimes, and guess what? All of a sudden I'm going to be nailed up and hung out to dry. Dawn's going to tell the media that I knew. That

I deformed her baby on purpose. And I'd have nothing," said Hudson bitterly. "Nothing. Now get out of the car."

Quill opened her door and slipped out of the driver's seat. Hudson, the rifle steadily held at the back of her neck, slid after her. He nudged her with the rifle barrel. Quill started up the heavily wooded slope to the Qwik Freeze, Hudson breathing heavily behind her. Casting desperately about for the sight of another human being, she saw nothing but trees, shrubs, and tall grass. The Qwik Freeze was built right into the hill. The likelihood of anyone coming on them was slim to none. She said, trying to hide the hopelessness in her voice, "Hudson, you can't get away with this for much longer."

"Sure I can. Where's the evidence? There's no evidence. There's no bodies."

"Dawn had an amniocentesis, Hudson. That leaves enough tissue to make a DNA match. They may never know what happened to Kay. Or to me. But they'll know what happened to Dawn."

"Rickie will get nailed for Dawn and Dot, too," said Hudson as though he hadn't heard her. "I made sure of that. And as for you—well, you're just going to disappear. You're going to go out in a Crimson Blaze of glory. There's *no proof*. None. Nothing links me to this. No one links me to this. Now that I took care of those interfering bitches. Stop here."

The utility door to the Qwik Freeze was barred and padlocked. Hudson braced the rifle on his left hip, the long barrel pointed slightly up, and pulled a slim file from his trousers pocket. "This always takes a minute," he said. "Don't move."

"Somebody will see us," said Quill, stepping toward him. "It's broad daylight."

"I said don't move!" Hudson swung the rifle directly at her.

Quill moved closer, slowly.

"Come on! Come on!" Hudson snapped.

Quill kept her eyes on his, ignoring the rifle barrel.

The middle of the rifle stock caught her shoulder. Quill sprang, shoved Hudson against the door, and grabbed with both hands, hanging on to the barrel, pushing herself against

Hudson's thin chest in determined, frantic desperation so that he couldn't shoot. Crumpled against the metal utility door, Hudson started to cry.

The handle turned. The door opened inward. Hudson shouted, half-fell into the darkness beyond the door, and scrambled to his feet. Quill tightened her grip, the rifle steady in her hands. A familiar figure in gray stepped into the sunlight.

"Myles," said Quill. "It's about bloody time."

CHAPTER 14

"How do I look?" asked Quill.

"Without the rifle? Not half as exciting." Myles's grin broadened. "Just as ready to do battle, I hope."

"Very funny." Quill patted her hair tentatively; Dwight had spent a long time with the curling iron and the mousse, and it felt strange. "You should see what he's done with Connie. She looks magnificent."

"I spoke with her when I came in. She's sitting on the set. Said she's afraid to move."

"I know the feeling."

The two of them were alone in the conference room, which had been co-opted as a Green Room.

"I think I'm nervous."

"You look wonderful. But then, you always look wonderful."

Quill looked at him from under her lashes. "I look awful. You could scrape the makeup off my face with a palette knife. My hair feels like it's been glued. My mother always said the best man to marry is the man who thinks you look terrific when you look your worst."

His face changed. He took her hand. "And what do you think?"

"She was probably right."

"I don't want you to touch me!" shouted Meg, charging into the room. Dwight trotted behind her, dragging his wheeled cart. "This is the way I look when I cook, and this is the way

I feel comfortable when I cook, and I don't want anything different!" She was wearing her usual chef's outfit: black leggings and sweat shirt. A yellow sweat band held her dark hair from her face.

Myles glanced at her feet. "Bright green?" he asked, his eyebrows raised.

"Could go either way," said John as he joined them. "That is, if you're trying to diagnose the sock color."

"You appear to be totally unflapped," said Quill with a touch of envy.

His eyes narrowed in a smile. "Has Helena settled on which parts of the Inn she'll show on television?"

"We've already taped the Shaker suite and the Provençal rooms," said Dwight, who'd been pulling various items from the drawers of his cart. "She's going to run them as leaders. We've set the remotes up near the hiking trails at the falls so Herself can talk about the Eden-like simplicity of the village. We'll go live from the foyer."

Quill took several deep breaths. "I don't think I'd be as nervous if we weren't going to be live. If I am nervous. Maybe I'm scared."

"What's the difference?" asked Myles, his hand warm and comforting in hers.

"Nervous is just . . . you know, nervous. Scared is like, I think I'll throw up if I have to do this."

"You'll be fine," said John. "I have confidence in you, Quill. Any woman who can wrench a rifle from a man who's killed four women and deliver him into the hands of the law isn't going to throw up being interviewed by Helena Houndswood."

Dwight tweaked a curl into place around Quill's cheek. He consulted the clipboard, then surveyed Meg with a thoughtful expression. "I must say you do clean up to advantage, dear."

"It's nowhere near time, is it?" said Quill in a panic. "I thought we were going on the air at ten o'clock. It's only nine-thirty!"

"Herself's a fiend on making sure everything's in place well before airtime," soothed Dwight. "Now. Tell me about your lovely murders. The gentleman in question's been hauled off to the pokey?" He drifted in Meg's direction, a vaguely purpose-ful look in his eye. Meg regarded him dubiously.

"He was arraigned on three counts of murder," said Myles. "We won't be able to prove the fourth."

"Sandy, Dawn, and Dot, and that nice Kay, what was her name? Gondowski?" Dwight took a comb from the breast pocket of his white linen blazer and began fiddling with Meg's hair. She protested. He put a firm hand on her shoulder and said, "Wait, ducky. It'll be painless, I assure you. That Kay. Never found her?"

"Zabriskie's not admitting to anything." Myles released Quill's hand and stretched his long legs out in front of him. "And we can't prove that the second body in the paint is Kay's. There's no DNA match."

"But you'll get him for the others. Right? He's in jail, isn't he?" Dwight shuddered dramatically. "Four murders! A serial killer. You got him on tissue samples, or something?" Dwight moved to the back of Meg's head. At Myles's uncom-municative grunt he wiggled his eyebrows suggestively and pointed to Meg. Meg twisted around to look at Dwight who firmly turned her around to face her sister. Quill, who liked very much what Dwight was doing to Meg's hair, picked up her cue and said, "Yes, Dwight. Myles, that is, Sheriff McHale, was able to confirm Dawn's death because her amniocentesis provided a tissue sample to match the DNA. We didn't have a tissue sample for Kay. But the analysis of the contents of the paint can last week showed two bodies. We just can't confirm it's Kay."

"And that third one, Sandy? She had wonderful cheek-bones . . . I call that a crying shame." From somewhere in the depths of his jacket, he produced a small can of hair spray. Meg glowered, but remained still. Quill nodded encour-agement to Myles.

"One fingerprint, on the trunk of the Willis Chevette, at least links him to it," said Myles. "And we found his hair and skin cell samples in the front seat of the rented Cortina. You know how that goes in court. We'll see. And we've got a minute blood sample from the suit he was wearing the day he allegedly shot Dot Vandermolen. Type AB, which matches hers."

"The way they let these bastards off . . ." Dwight spread matte makeup on Meg's face with quick strokes of his finger. "I ask you."

"Oh, I think we can prove premeditation," said Myles. "Something Ms. Quilliam discovered will make a difference there."

Quill blushed under Dwight's admiring glance. "Do tell, Sheriff," he said.

"The budget request. Zabriskie applied to have the five supervisor positions replaced the Friday before Helena Houndswood came to Hemlock Falls to announce the win."

"So he'd planned to get rid of them ahead of time," said Quill. "There's a lot to be said for the dream tactic in investigations."

"Won't he put up a defense that he was simply planning on firing them?" asked John.

"He could try," said Myles. "Except the payoff money he was giving Dawn and the others to assure silence about the lead oxide was in the form of bonuses for excellent performance. Pretty hard to justify firing your best workers for incompetence. And Connie Weyerhauser is going to testify about the intentional violations and the OSHA scam. So we've got him wrapped up pretty tightly."

"Well, I am just as impressed as all get-out." Dwight held Meg's chin firmly in one hand and began to apply eyeliner. "Did you suspect him from the beginning, Quill?"

"I didn't suspect him at all," said Quill ruefully. "I thought it was Makepeace Whitman."

Dwight turned and raised an astonished eyebrow. "I mean to say! I thought the poor fellow was just devoted to that wonderful environmental cause of his. I was talking about his group's dedication to that marvelous character you have rolling around here . . . the birdy-looking one? The older woman?"

"Doreen," said Quill. "I'm surprised she hasn't come to work yet. She seemed pretty interested in the show."

Meg sent her a significant glance. Quill, on whom the significance was lost, was bewildered.

Dwight fluffed Meg's hair and said chattily, "Doreen, that's it. She just couldn't say enough good things about him. Although I have to say I don't know exactly what the Friends of Fresh Air stand for, but it must be very, very important. He's a lovely, lovely man."

"That lovely, lovely man was dumping lead oxide on Paramount," said Meg tartly, "and submitting two sets of invoices to Paramount. He knew darn well what was going on. He's been arrested."

"I'll tell you," said Dwight, doing wonders with blusher and Meg's cheekbones, "I had a few moments when I really thought Herself might be behind this. Not that seeing her sent up the river on a murder rap would make me cry in my beer. But then, I'm clearly not a star in the amateur sleuth line, like you, Quill."

Quill was wearing an extremely pretty bronze print off-the-shoulder dress. She smoothed the silky material over her knees with a consciously innocent air. "I'll tell you something else, strictly *entre nous*," Dwight continued. "We're not sticking with this Beautiful Living crap forever, you know. No, the boss lady has plans. Think you'll be seeing some surprising things from her in the very near future. Investigative reporting. But *don't* say I told you! There!" He stepped back from Meg, and clapped his hands together with decisive delight.

John let loose a long low whistle. Myles nodded appreciatively.

"Just sit there for one little minute more, ducky. I'll be right back."

"You look terrific," said Quill.

Meg rolled her eyes.

"Now, for the *pièce de résistance*!" Dwight pulled the lowest drawer of his cart open and withdrew a tissue-wrapped package. "Here! I asked for this from downstate ages ago, and it just arrived last night. Try it." "It" was a chef's coat in a swirl of soft, cream-colored jersey. "Such a tacky design, essentially," Dwight fussed. He eased Meg into the coat. "Double breasted! Foul! But I asked for a few alterations and voilà!"

The high collar peaked attractively around Meg's face. The buttons were antiqued gold. The sleeves draped over a tight cuff. Meg moved her arms up and down experimentally. "Hey," she said.

"You look beautiful," said Quill. "Andy should see this. I thought he was going to be here?"

"I asked him not to come," said Meg. "I thought you'd be nervous."

"Me! Why should Andy make me nervous?"

"Well, he sure wouldn't make me nervous," said Meg nervously.

"Then I'll call him."

"Don't call him. If I want to call him, I'll call him."

"Don't you two ever quit?" Helena Houndswood swept into the room, trailed by her producer. She inspected Meg with a coldly critical eye, looked Quill up and down, and nodded sharply. "You'll both do. We're ready. Positions, please."

"Thank you so much, Dwight, darling," said Dwight to the air. "The transformation is simply astonishing."

"Check the cameras in the foyer," Helena said to the producer. "And I want the remotes over the falls and in the kitchen tested." She snapped her fingers at Meg. "You. Into position in the kitchen. And Sarah, you come with me. The rest of you stay out of the way." She swept out again.

Myles smiled. "Break a leg."

"We'll be on the front stairs," said John. "The whole staff. You'll do fine, both of you."

"What's this about Doreen, Meg?" Quill looked around the room, as though expecting the housekeeper to crawl out from under the table. "Gosh, I was sure she'd be here."

"Chop-chop!" said Dwight, snapping his fingers. "Places, ladies!"

"I meant to tell you about this earlier, but you were getting made over." Meg followed Quill into the hall. "She showed up early this morning. Asked for some time off."

"Well, you gave it to her, didn't you? I mean she works like a dog. If she wants to take a day off . . ."

"She didn't say 'a day.' She said some time. And when I asked her how much time, she said she wasn't sure. God and Nature needed her, she said. And then she muttered something about her feathered friends. I know she took those chickens home. You think she's maybe gone to feed them?"

"She took them to Dookie's church. After I explained the theory of sanctuary to her."

"You know what else? All the Friends of Fresh Air are back. They checked in this morning and went right out again."

Quill stopped at the entrance to the foyer. The area was clogged with hot white lights, cameras, and mysterious black boxes. Cables as thick as pythons snaked over every available inch of floor space. "They paid their bills, even Makepeace did, before he was arrested," said Quill absentmindedly. "And they were very quiet guests. Except for Myles arresting Makepeace, they were no trouble at all." She came to attention as what Meg was implying sank in. "Meg! Do you think she went off with them?!"

"Yep."

"She's never actually run off before," said Quill. "I mean, all of her enthusiasms have been local up until now."

"The Friends tour from place to place," Meg reminded her, "seeking out the pure and natural where they find it, and where they don't, saving the planet from man's horny-handed destruction."

"She couldn't leave us!" Quill, dismayed, forgot her nervousness about her first television appearance at the thought of life at the Inn without Doreen. "Meg, how could you let her go? Why didn't you come and get me?"

"She's a grown woman, Quill."

"Places!" shouted the producer.

Quill made a horrible face at Meg, then stepped carefully over the cables to the space cleared in front of the fireplace for the shoot. The cream leather couch had been replaced by three leather chairs. A low coffee table, covered with a damask cloth and set with the Bosses Club prizewinning dishes, stood in front of the chairs. Connie, magnificent in teal and violet, presided over the table. Quill sat next to her. "You match the china!" she whispered delightedly.

"They did a nice job," Connie said. "They're going to give me a place setting for twelve."

Quill picked up a coffee cup. The rose-breasted grosbeak stared at her with a gold-rimmed eye. "Will you keep it?"

"Barb likes it. So I guess I will. Myles arranged for her to watch. See her? She's over there."

Quill turned. The entrance to the dining room was filled with people. Barbara sat in her wheelchair with her father smiling proudly behind her. Kathleen Kiddermeister, Peter Hairston, and the rest of the waiters and waitresses crowded around them. She caught sight of Harvey Bozzel's thinning blond hair. A large space in the cluster of heads indicated the presence of Mayor Henry and Marge Schmidt. Myles had told her the dining room was filled with the chamber members and every citizen of Hemlock Falls that could wangle standing room. Myles and John sat on the stairs, staring down at them. There was no sign of Doreen.

Quill twiddled her thumbs, suddenly nervous again. The minutes before airtime seemed endless. To distract herself, she turned to Connie. "Will you be staying on in Hemlock Falls?"

"Oh, yes. We've set aside the money for Barb, mostly, although we're going to take a few trips." She laughed. "And I've left Paramount, of course. A million dollars pays quite a bit of interest."

"All right." Helena sat in the third leather chair. "Five minutes. Follow my lead, the two of you. Answer the questions just as we rehearsed them. Ready!" The klieg lights snapped on. Quill squinted in the glare. Someone behind the bank of white lights began to count.

"Ten . . . nine . . . eight . . ."

Quill waved at Myles and John. Andy had joined them; from his smile, it looked as though Meg had relented and called him after all.

"Don't see Doreen up there," said Connie in a low voice.

"Meg said she left us, Connie. I just can't believe—"

"Quiet!" snapped Helena.

"Three . . . two . . . one . . . *And!*"

Helena bloomed. She stared into the little red eye of the camera directly in front of her and said in a low, musical voice, complete with upper-class vowels, "Welcome, America, to the beauty in your lives. I'm speaking to you today from a charming hideaway in upstate New York . . ."

Quill, frozen, realized she was in front of eighty million households. She was going to throw up.

" . . . cobblestone, demonstrating the best of taste," Helena said.

"The camera's not on us," Connie whispered reassuringly. "See? They're on the remote." She pointed to Quill's left. A large TV screen showed the remote cameras panning the village. Helena had made good on her promise of golden retrievers and yuppie couples. Five or six blond, well-dressed men and women strolled down Main Street, dogs at their sides.

" . . . the falls themselves create an environment reminiscent of those ducky little villages in the Cotswolds," Helena continued, "and the citizens of this village of elegance and discretion—"

"Whoop!" shouted Connie Weyerhauser suddenly, with a gust of laughter.

"My god!" screamed Helena.

"We have temporarily taken control of this remote station," announced the voice of Mrs. Whitman. She and the twenty or so members of the Friends of Fresh Air filled the remote monitor screen, edge to edge. "Our organization is here to bring an injustice to the attention of the people of the United States!"

"Turn off the goddam remote!" snarled Helena.

"I have to warn those viewers sensitive to violence that the contents of this garbage bag may affront you," said Mrs. Whitman with evangelical fervor.

Helena charged the remote monitor. Connie was laughing so hard that the leather chair vibrated. Quill, bemused, wondered why she hadn't figured it out before; the lack of luggage should have tipped her off. "They're nudists," she said, which, on later reflection, she decided was unnecessary, since eighty million viewers of Helena Houndswood's *It's a Beautiful Life* could see that for themselves. "Thank goodness, though, Connie. I was afraid Doreen had left town, and there she is, right next to that tall guy." She leaned forward, peering at the screen. "If I could see his head, I could tell which of the FOFA members it is. There. He's ducked a little bit. Good Lord! It's Dookie Shuttleworth!"

GAZPACHO

from The Inn at Hemlock Falls

STOCK:

3/4 cup olive oil
1/2 cup freshly squeezed lime juice
2 cups puréed tomato
1/2 cup fresh-cut cilantro, chopped
1/2 cup vodka
salt and pepper to taste

VEGETABLES:

1/2 cup each, chopped very fine:
    seeded cucumber
    celery
    green pepper
    orange pepper
    gold pepper
    sweet red pepper
1 cup each, chopped coarsely:
    Italian plum tomatoes
    Vidalia onion
    1/4 teaspoon fresh hot pepper (use gloves)

Blend stock ingredients in food processor. Chill until very cold. Add vegetables when ready to serve. Serve in chilled silver bowls.

CRIMINAL PURSUITS